BONES OF PARADISE

- A BIG ISLAND MYSTERY -

JANE LASSWELL HOFF

This book is dedicated to the memory of

my husband, Charles Jay Hoff,

and my father, Thomas Ely Lasswell, Sr.,

and

Fred Jr., the WonderDog

- I love you, you mattered to me, and I miss you.

NOTE TO READERS

Hawaiian words used in this book are italicized at their first appearance. Their meanings may be found in the glossary, "Hawaiian Words", at the end of the book. After their first use, Hawaiian words will no longer be italicized.

This is a work of fiction. Names, characters and events are either invented or used fictitiously.

1   THE BONES

THE BONES WERE TRANSLUCENT IVORY and as small and delicate as those you might lift from a fish filet on your dinner plate. They were in a tangled mass that was stuck to a wad of dark fabric, stiff with dirt, which lay in front of me on the autopsy table. As I leaned forward for a better look, my magnifying glasses slid down the bridge of my nose and, for maybe the tenth time, I used the back of my wrist to push them back into place.

The wad of fabric was clenched into a contorted fist by an invasive web of pale, thread-like roots. I lifted a pair of surgical scissors and began to snip at the roots, one by one. With each liberating cut, the cloth relaxed and expanded, releasing the heavy odor of the earth in which it had been buried. When I was finished, the bones didn't fall free; they still clung to their shroud, which I now could see was a pair of men's, navy-plaid, boxer shorts.

The autopsy room was cold, as usual, and the flicker of the fluorescent lights bothered my eyes. I took extra care to steady my chilled fingers as I pinched together the tips of needle nose forceps and gently tugged free each tiny bone. I transferred them to a clean square of hospital-green towel. Some of the bones were easy to grasp but others were oddly shaped and as brittle as curls of dried phyllo. Those were the beginnings of the fetal skull and hips.

JUST A FEW HOURS BEFORE, I'd been sitting quietly at my dining table, having a relaxed breakfast: tea with a little milk and sugar, and half a papaya from a tree in my garden. I was still in my sarong, at ten-thirty, lingering over a puzzle in the Hawaii Tribune Herald. Soft trade winds filtered through the screened doors and played with the edges of the newspaper; I slapped the edges down a few times but finally surrendered to nature and moved the pepper grinder and salt cellar to anchor them. The morning was *Hawaii*-quiet: a helicopter droned in the distance, carrying tourists to view nearby waterfalls, and there was the ubiquitous, island background music of birds singing and cooing. The telephone's unexpected ring jarred my senses and broke the mood.

"Y'up yet?" John's western drawl and deep, smoker's voice were as familiar to me as the question. He always asks me that, no matter what time of day he calls. His joke may not be funny anymore, but I kind of like the intimacy of it. "Doc wants you to look at something. Can you come in today?"

As if I'd say no. I did a fast calculation of how long it would take me to get dressed, grab my gear and drive to the office. "Is eleven thirty okay?"

"Yep," he said, and then he just hung up. Nothing personal; he's just not a telephone guy, our John.

With a new direction for my day, I gathered the breakfast dishes and began to fit them into the dishwasher, all the while wondering what the "Doc", Sam Morris, had in mind. Dr. Morris is the Chief Medical Examiner, the *capo di tutti capi*, of Medical Examiners in the state. MEs do autopsies, of course, but they're really public health officers, in a way. They monitor the dead for signs of accident patterns, new diseases, dangerous new drugs and all sorts of other things. It's a big job and Dr. Morris can't do everything by himself so he's got a

2

team of people who work with him - a team that includes John and me.

I'm a forensic anthropologist, my specialty is human skeletons. When a medical examiner calls me to work it means something out of the ordinary has happened. For starters, on an island like this, you could just "disappear" a corpse into the ocean or drop it down a lava tube and it would probably never be seen again. Not to give anybody ideas. And then there's the stink factor. For a body to have gone unsmelled and unseen for long enough to become a skeleton, and *then* to be discovered, is a rare event. Yet, sometimes years go by before remains are found. I work on cases that are too decomposed for an autopsy - that means their condition can be anywhere in the range of smelly mush, hardened mummy, charred mass or dry, clean bone. There's a lyric from The Wizard of Oz, they're "not only merely dead…really, most sincerely dead."

CUPS AND GLASSES RATTLED as I pushed the dishwasher door shut a little too hard. My mind was already one step ahead of my body. First, I had to get dressed. I mean, really, even in Hawaii I can't wear a sarong to work. And there are some definite dos and don'ts in dressing for the morgue.

Do wear shoes that cover your feet. Flip flops, called slippers or "slippahs" here, simply won't do in a place where God knows what could be on the floor. Body fluids splash and ooze, bugs spring off the table; there's no end to the surprises.

Do dress warmly. The phrase *cold as a tomb* comes to mind. Morgues are kept chilly to inhibit bacterial growth. Of course, there are special lockers and rooms where the corpses are stored, but the temperature of the whole place is usually too cold for my comfort.

Don't be too casual. It's a solemn place for many families and it's important to look professional. Jeans at the office just aren't good enough. It's a question of respect.

Do tie back the hair. I like to wear my hair loose but when I'm up to my elbows in putrid flesh, it's not the time to reach up and brush a stray wisp away from my eyes.

Do wear washable clothes. Even though I often wear protective gowns over my own clothes when I'm working, the smell of decomposition, smoke, dirt, the garbage dump, the pigsty, whatever came along with the human remains, penetrates my clothes and hair. The first thing I do when I get home is strip and start up the washing machine.

I TOOK A SHOWER SO QUICKLY that there was barely time for the water to warm up. Then I pulled my damp, curly red hair into a ponytail. I dressed in a simple, washable, linen skirt and a boat neck, turquoise t-shirt. I wore no jewelry except a pair of turquoise drop-earrings. Turquoise brings out the blue in my eyes and, hey, you gotta look good. I grabbed a cardigan for the cold and some flat shoes.

I keep a satchel packed, ready with the stuff I know I'll need for work. It's an old, giveaway, canvas bag from some past meeting of the American Academy of Forensic Sciences. I hoisted the satchel and my purse onto my left shoulder, and then I slung my laptop bag onto my right shoulder. I picked up my shoes with my left hand and my keys with my right and walked as swiftly as I could through the house, towards the garage. I was feeling ready and organized and a little excited.

At the back door, I dropped my shoes to the floor - people in Hawaii don't wear shoes in the house - and, as they *always* do, my shoes fell upside down and at angles. I did the hokey-pokey, balancing on my left foot to rearrange the shoes with my right toes. After a few ridiculous moments I managed to shoe myself without falling on my *okole* and headed out to the car, locking the door behind me.

4

IT'S ONLY A FIVE MINUTE DRIVE from home to the Hawaii State Medical Examiner's office so, at 11:28 a.m., I cruised into the parking lot shared by it and the *Hilo* Hospital. All the stalls under the few shade trees were taken but I found a place near the office entrance. The hospital, itself, is in pretty good shape but the weathered exterior of the two-storey, cinderblock HSME building has definitely seen better days. It looks sort of haunted. Really. Local kids will tell you it's an abandoned psychiatric hospital. The crazy looking, old, pink paint doesn't help, either. States usually make the non-living a low priority for funding. Nevertheless, the interior of the building has been modernized and retrofitted with x-ray rooms, a ballistics range, and laboratories for analyzing things like drugs, blood, fingerprints and DNA. And, of course, there are the autopsy rooms and body storage areas.

I gathered my things from the car and walked across the blacktop to the employee's entrance. I knew, as I pressed the intercom button, that I was being watched on the security camera over the door. As usual, nobody answered the intercom but I heard the click of the lock being electronically released. Before I could reach for the handle, however, the door was pushed open from the inside.

Lehua was there to greet me. She broke into a smile and bubbled, "Hey! I nevah see you for long time!"

"Lehua!" I said. "Yep. It's me. John called me this morning and told me Dr. Morris has a case for me."

"The one from *Hawi*, I think. They just brought it in a couple hours ago." Lehua looked me over and leaned a little closer. Her voice softened and she slipped back into her usual pidgin, "How you stay?"

"Oh, I'm fine. I've been getting new gutters on the house and stuff like that, but nothing really, you know, exciting."

Lehua does a job at the ME's office that most people have

5

never even heard of - she's a diener. When I first started working in forensics, I had to look that word up. Turns out it's German for corpse servant which, you know, sounds pretty revolting. What Lehua actually does is a little of everything. She really does keep track of the corpses and assist with autopsies but she also cleans up and takes x-rays and coordinates with the folks at the funeral parlors; she does a lot of logging and filing and organizing. She's not the only diener at the ME's office, but sometimes it seems like she's the person who holds the whole place together.

"I go call John," Lehua said.

"No need, he's right behind you," I told her.

John was ambling up the hallway to meet me and came to a stop just behind Lehua, I greeted him over her shoulder with, "Hey, John."

The two of them made a strange pair standing there. Lehua's little, five-foot one inch, Filipina-Hawaiian frame, liberally decorated with tattoos, both tribal and Disney, was shadowed by John's six foot two, middle-aged, *haole* bulk. But, even though they looked so dissimilar, I knew from working with them both that they had a strong bond of affection.

"I was jes' sayin'," Lehua told him, "we no see her for long time. She should come see us even if there's no cases. Huh, John?"

John, his usual quiet self, pulled a half-smile. "Sure she should".

I could never tell when he was being sarcastic. Well, okay, sometimes I could *definitely* tell, but this wasn't one of those times. I can't imagine anyone who would pay a social call at the morgue, not even me.

John looked at me, jerked his head to the side and said, "It's in the lab."

Apparently that was an invitation to follow him because he turned and began walking away, down the corridor. Lehua and I exchanged smiles at his familiar abruptness. After just a few paces, though, John halted and retraced his steps until he stood in front of us again.

He rubbed a hand over the bristle on his chin - a short beard, really - and I noticed, for the first time, a little silver mixed in with the brown. He was silent for a moment while he parsimoniously chose his words and then, finally, he informed me, "I gotta call some folks. They want to be here."

I had no idea what he was talking about. I could have asked for clarification but I've come to respect John's process, so I just waited to see.

He reached past me for the wall-phone, pushed two buttons and spoke three words: "Send 'em down." He returned the receiver to its hook.

As a Death Investigator, John's job is self-descriptive; he investigates deaths. He's also the liaison between the Police Department and our office. Like many Death Investigators, he's a former Homicide Detective. The two jobs have a lot of similarities, but different angles. At a typical death scene the body, itself, belongs to the ME's Office but the crime scene if, in fact, it is a crime scene, belongs to the cops.

In my experience, most Homicide Detectives and Death Investigators are almost supernaturally intuitive and observant; it gives me the creeps sometimes. The trouble with having that kind of sensitivity, though, in a job like theirs, is that it comes with memories - things the rest of us can't, and don't want to, imagine. It takes a toll, and John's personal life is a train wreck. It includes the standard constellation of trouble sleeping, smoking and drinking habits (although I think he might be giving up the smoking), and a trail of ex-wives. John's a good man and a good-looking, big guy and I like him but I sure wouldn't want to live with him.

After he hung up the phone, John stood facing towards me, but without eye contact and not moving or speaking. I was staring straight ahead at his chest or, rather, at the insignia on his chest which was at my eye level. He always wears office-issued, cotton-knit polo shirts, with the official HSME insignia on the breast. And khaki trousers. I have one of those shirts, too, but I rarely wear it. Navy blue. Not my color.

SUDDENLY, THE NEARBY STAIRWELL DOOR BANGED open and three people emerged. I assumed these were the "folks" John had been talking about. Cops: two men and a woman. They must have been waiting upstairs in the conference room. When introductions were made, I was surprised to learn the woman, Detective Mary Mancao, was the lead on the case. There are more and more women on the job these days but it's still unusual to see one in charge. I surreptitiously looked her over. Detective Mancao was quietly and professionally dressed in tan slacks and a soft, button-front, white blouse. Her dark hair was clipped back in a short ponytail. One of the perks of being a detective is you get to wear your own clothes, no uniform. She had a badge clipped to her belt and a no-nonsense black purse hooked over her shoulder and an empty holster at her hip. All guns must be checked at the ME's door - it's one of Dr. Morris's rules.

Detective Mancao's partner, Bobby Kealoha, smiled and shook my hand. "We've met before. I was at that scene near *Kapa'a*, out in the lava fields, when we found that guy from *Honolulu*. It was a couple of years ago."

I vaguely remembered him. He'd aged a little, of course, but he wore it well. He was sharply dressed in a Sig Zane *aloha* shirt, with its beautifully designed Hawaiian pattern, black pants and polished, lace-up shoes. He'd been going to the gym, too.

Nobody introduced the third cop, a youngish guy, maybe Japanese ancestry mixed with something else, slender, friendly looking. I decided to call him Number Three. Well, not out loud, just to myself.

We all walked down the hall together to the room I often use when I'm working on a case. I think of it as *my* room. It's separate from the autopsy arena because sometimes my cases are stinky or messy, or both, and they might contaminate the autopsy room. Likewise, the autopsy room is a busy place with some serious health dangers. It's better to keep separate.

My room isn't very big, maybe twenty by twenty, so it was crowded with the three cops, John, me, and the autopsy table. John stood just inside the door, like a guard, as he always does when I'm there. I have no idea how he behaves when I'm not around.

The room is outfitted with stainless steel counters and assorted pieces of lab equipment: scales, racks of rubber-stoppered glass tubes, boxes of surgical gloves, evidence bags, and piles of green and blue hospital towels. In one counter there's a sink with a long, rubber hose attached to it and a high arching water spout. There are no tap handles, the water's operated by a pedal on the floor, but the sink does have another kind of handle, just like the ones on public toilets, and for the same reason. The sink flushes. There's a light-box on the wall, for viewing x-rays. And in the corner, there's a hanging human skeleton, on wheels. The room's lit with the usual institutional florescent tubes but there are also high wattage surgical lamps hanging from the ceiling, in case better light is crucial.

A plain brown-paper bag, like any generic grocery sack, sat on the stainless steel autopsy table. Someone had used a black felt-tip pen to write the police department case number on the side of the bag. I stood at the foot of the table, with the two detectives to my left and Number Three on my right, in front of John.

"So, what've we got here?" I asked. As I spoke, I reached for a box of surgical gloves on the counter, but John anticipated my move and met me halfway with it. He then offered gloves to the others. I don't know why. I wasn't going to let them handle the evidence any more than they already had.

Before anyone could answer my question, though, I held up my hand in a stop motion. "Wait a sec'. John, what's our case number?" The ME's office has its own case numbers, different from the police department's.

John rolled his eyes. "Hold on," he said. He took one step backwards, into the door frame, and raised his voice a notch, "Lehua! What's the case number in here?"

From the autopsy room, across the hallway, Lehua's voice, muffled by a surgical mask, called back the number. She didn't have to look it up...she's on top of everything.

I wrote the number down on my clipboard and looked up again. "Okay. Sorry. So, now, Detective Mancao, what have we got here?"

Detective Mancao took a small step forward. "Mary," she corrected me.

"Oh, okay. Alright. Mary," I nodded my head and gave a quick smile as I pulled on the gloves. "You can call me Mimi."

"Mimi," she repeated. And she got the pronunciation right.

I was named after my grandmother, Miriam. Mimi, my nickname, is pronounced *Mim'ee*, not *Mee-mee*; an important distinction to make since the latter pronunciation means urine in Hawaiian.

All eyes were on the bag on the table. It was folded twice at its opening and sealed with a strip of blue, evidence tape.

John crossed his arms and leaned back against the doorjamb, seemingly relaxed.

Mary cleared her throat with a little nervous cough. "This is one of those cases," she said, "that gets under your skin."

"Yeah, well, it's obvious *something's* going on. Sometimes one detective will show up to observe, but not three of you." As I spoke, I used a pair of surgical scissors to cut the seal on the evidence bag and then I unfolded and opened the top, but I didn't look inside. I was waiting for Mary's story.

She cleared her throat again and nodded at the bag. "There's a baby in there." She seemed to be at a loss for more words so I just waited while she stepped back and composed herself, straightening to look a little taller, a little more in command. She pulled in a deep breath and continued. "Let me explain better."

I saw Bobby Kealoha's face darken.

"Yesterday," she said, "we got a 911 call. A girl in Hawi had gone to a neighbor's house. The neighbor, a woman, said the girl was shaky and pale, and it took a while but she finally got her to talk. The girl, who is *twelve years old*, had just come home from an abortion. Her stepfather had taken her. The bastard told them at the clinic that her boyfriend had gotten her pregnant."

Bobby shifted from one foot to the other, and then back again. His jaw was clenched and I noticed his fists were, too.

Mary's gaze was fixed on the bag. "When I got there and started to interview the girl, she told me that her mother had pulled her out of school a couple of years ago to stay at home and babysit her younger brothers while the mom was at work. The stepfather didn't work; he stayed at home, too."

Now Bobby and Number Three both began to stir and I heard John making a clicking sound with his fingernails. I knew where this was going.

"She told me her stepdad had been raping her for years and this was the *second* time he'd gotten her pregnant. The first time, when she was ten...." Mary's voice trailed off and it was a moment before she spoke again.

"She miscarried that time," she continued. "She told the stepfather about the miscarriage but he just told her to get rid of it. She saw that it was a boy, so she named him *Keoni.*"

I felt that like a gut punch. My husband's name was

Jonathan, Jay for short. He died a few years ago. Sometimes I called him by his name in Hawaiian, Keoni. I felt tears unexpectedly rim my eyes. The others in the room, if they noticed, probably misunderstood the reason. Mary was still talking and I forced myself to refocus.

"This little girl took the nicest piece of clean cloth she could find in the house, and wrapped the baby in it. Then she had a private little ceremony and buried her child in the yard, next to the back steps, in an abandoned flower bed. That was two and a half years ago and we just dug it up this morning."

All eyes stayed on the bag on the table.

"What happened to the stepfather?" I asked.

The intensity of Bobby's voice spoke broke the spell and we all lifted our eyes towards him. "As soon as he saw the first cruiser show up at the neighbor's house, he split. It was hours before we heard the girl's whole story. By then he was gone. We're pretty sure he's gone to the mainland and, if I have to paddle there myself, I'm going to get that bastard."

Mary turned to me and spoke as if we were alone in the room. Her voice was full of emotion. "You know what killed me? We got Social Services in to take custody of the girl and her little brothers but the girl didn't want to go. She threw her arms around me and held on. And she asked me if I would adopt her."

Our eyes locked in a shared moment of grief. Crap.

John's pager buzzed. I turned my head to watch him as he detached the device from his belt and held it close to his eyes. He squinted a little. For the first time, I realized that his eyes are green. Almost olive. I don't know why I never noticed before.

John returned his pager to his belt and looked up at me. "You need me anymore?"

"Uh, no, I guess not," I replied. Then, as an afterthought, I asked, "Will you still be in the building?"

John was already halfway out the door when he answered back, "I'll let ya know if I leave."

The room felt different when he was gone, like the temperature had dropped or something.

I moved to the right side of the table, next to Number Three. I nodded towards the pile of towels on the counter and asked, "Would you please hand me a couple of those?"

He hopped to, with a quick, "Yes, ma'am!"

He handed me two towels, a green one and a blue one. I spread out the blue one on the table, to the left of the evidence bag.

"Hold the bottom of the bag for me, please," I instructed him.

He pinched two, diagonally-opposite corners of the bag and seemed to put all his concentration into holding them. It seemed an overdone gesture but I realized he might have been trying to impress the others with his diligence. He was clearly junior to them. As he anchored the bag, I tipped the opening towards me until I could see inside. There was just a lone, crumpled wad of dirty, blue-plaid fabric. Mary had said it was the nicest piece of clean fabric the girl could find in her house.

I reached in and gently lifted the bundle out of the bag and placed it on the blue towel. A dusting of dirt softly shed from it. It was a small bundle, not much bigger than if I'd put my two fists together, and very lightweight. I quickly checked inside the bag again to make sure there was nothing left behind.

"Okay," I smiled a thanks at Number Three, "you can let go now."

He stepped back and relaxed slightly.

I collapsed down the brown bag, smoothed it flat and scooted it to the far end of the table. Next, I laid out the green towel, faded from multiple institutional launderings, and

13

placed it to the right of the little cloth bundle holding Keoni's remains.

I released a big sigh, I guess because I knew how much work was ahead of me. "Mary, I'm sorry but this is going to take a long time. I'm going to have to cut away all these roots that've grown through the material before I can even start to look at the bones. It's probably going to be another day, or more, before I can get them analyzed."

"Oh," Mary responded, "but you can see some of the bones now, I mean like right there," she gestured at some tiny, ivory-colored fragments visible in the folds of cloth. "So can you just estimate how old the baby was? Now? Or, you know, do you think you can say who the father was? Somehow?"

Oh, boy. Where was I going to start? "No," I told her. "I really can't tell you who the father was by looking at the bones, but I might be able to get some DNA from them and that might give you an answer. The turnaround time for DNA is about two months now, with all the budget cuts. I'll do what I can."

I paused for a moment, trying to choose my words. "The other thing I need to talk to you all about, before we go any further, is the use of the word *baby*. I'd like to stick to a more scientific term because the word baby has a lot of emotional charge to it, plus it doesn't really apply here."

I slipped into teaching mode. "From conception until about eight weeks into a pregnancy, it's called an embryo. Then, around eight weeks, when all the organs have started to form, we start calling it a fetus, and that's what we keep calling it until birth. After that, it's a neonate or baby. What we have here isn't a baby yet.

"If the girl miscarried, it was probably before three months. A fetus passes through some pretty well-defined stages so I should be able to tell you, within maybe a week, how long she'd been pregnant."

14

"It's going to take a week?" Mary asked.

"No, I mean, I should be able to tell you how many weeks the girl had been pregnant," I explained. "I should have the results for you within a couple of days. Except for the DNA, of course."

Mary didn't seem discouraged by that. She nodded. "I guess we'd better get back to work, then."

There was no use in all three of them hanging around just to watch me cut roots. Mary rummaged in her purse and pulled out a business card that she placed on the table next to the brown paper bag. "Thank you so much for all your help," she said. "Will you please let me know when your report's ready?"

"Of course."

And then they all left. It wasn't really abrupt; it's just that they had other things to do. They said goodbye and a few other small polite things and then they just went on to the next disaster down the line.

And I started cutting roots.

My job is just to analyze the remains, not to go out and investigate crimes. It's not like on television. Honestly, after my analysis is done I don't know what happens next in the case unless I happen to read about it in the newspaper or see it on the TV news. Sometimes, but less often than you'd think, I get called to testify in court. I wanted to know what was going to happen to the stepfather but I knew I probably wasn't going to be kept in the loop. Still, I wondered. Obviously, if the girl was impregnated when she was only ten, then what happened to her was a rape, because a child can't give legal consent for sex. If the DNA showed that the stepfather was also the baby's father, then surely there was a way to prosecute him for rape but I didn't know what more could happen; a miscarriage is not a murder.

2 WALKING OUTSIDE IN HAWAII

THERE WAS NO GOOD WAY to pull up a stool to the autopsy table so I stood for a couple of hours, bent forward over my work. By four o'clock I was cold, despite the sweater I'd brought along, my feet were tired, my back hurt, I was hungry and I needed to pee. I was ready to call it quits at the morgue for the day. I wasn't finished working, though. When I got home, I'd get out my reference books and start searching for some good pictures or medical drawings to help me pinpoint the baby's – damn it, I had to follow my own advice – the *fetus's* developmental age.

I found a worn, green, hospital sheet and gently laid it over the table and then I took a fat, black felt-tip pen off the counter and tore a page from my legal pad and wrote on it, in large, capital letters: DO NOT TOUCH. DO NOT MOVE. I laid the paper on top of the cotton sheet.

I pulled off my gloves and tossed them into the biohazard waste can and then I walked over to the sink and stepped on the pedal to start the water flow. Surgical gloves have a dusting of powder inside of them and I tried to wash it off but I knew that, however much I scrubbed, my hands would still smell like that powder for hours. I gathered my things, turned off the lights, shut the door and went up the hall in search of Lehua.

I found her, sitting at a computer workstation near the entrance door. John and Dr. Morris were standing behind her, looking over her shoulders at the monitor. I walked up, unseen, behind them. I hesitated to interrupt their work until I saw that the picture on the screen was of Lehua's dog, Sweetie, nursing four brand-new puppies.

"Any idea who the father is?" Dr. Morris was asking her.

"I got a very good idea it dat buggah next door," she answered. As she turned to speak to him, she spotted me.

"Oh, hey, you want a puppy?" she asked me. The other two turned to see me.

"Mimi!" Dr. Morris greeted me like we were old friends which, in fact, we were. In the lab, I refer to him as Dr. Morris but, face-to-face, I call him Sam. Sam and his wife, Becky, were by my side when Jay died.

"You *pau*?" Sam asked, using the Hawaiian word for finished. "Sorry I wasn't here earlier. I had to testify in court this morning and it got continued until after lunch." He was still dressed in a button-down shirt, but his tie was gone and his sleeves were rolled up. "Did you find everything you needed?"

"Yeah, sure," I responded, "John always takes good care of me. Although, I thought the *mai tai* he brought me lacked artistic detail."

"I've told you repeatedly," John replied, with a poker face, "that tiny, little paper umbrellas do *not* belong in the workplace."

Sam gave us a look like we were making him wish he had a drink, umbrella or not.

I returned my attention to Lehua's computer screen. "Those puppies are so cute! I can see Sweetie in them, but what does the father look like?"

"He jes' a *poi* dog," Lehua answered, referring to the well-mixed heritage often found in island dogs. "He small like Sweetie, maybe some Chihuahua or something a little bigger, but he got too many toes."

17

"What? What do you mean?"

"They's something wrong with his feet. He got extra toes. I hope the puppies isn't mutants 'cause they got extra toes, too. Those people who own him keep to theirselfs. They live back off the road with one big fence around them. Maybe they got extra toes, too," she laughed. "When that buggah dog came our yard, the lady she come find him. She real upset and she pick him up and keep saying 'Sorry! Sorry!' But when I tried talk wit' her, she jus' walk away. Walter was real mad 'cause Sweetie was in heat, you know, and he knew she was gonna come *hapai*. Walter want go over and, you know, *talk* wit' them but could not. Too tall, is why, that fence. Good thing, too, 'cause he was hot under da collar then and now he kinda like the puppies."

I'd been to Lehua's house before, for her daughter's twelfth birthday. She lives about thirty miles out of town, in an area called *Puna*. The lots there are inexpensive and people can live pretty much any life-style they want. There are people there who are still living in the sixties, wearing tie dye and dwelling in teepees and yurts, and there are retirees with manicured lawns and fancy gates. There are lone wolves growing *pakalolo* and there are folks who just want to retreat from the rest of the world and live off the grid, anonymously. There are also plenty of people like Lehua and her family - people who were born and raised here and like living country-style.

"So," I said, looking at the puppies' precious little faces, "do you think you'll keep them?"

"Maybe, but four's probably too many. We gotta keep 'em for now 'cause Sweetie's still nursing them. You think you might want one?" She knew my dog had died recently.

"I'm probably not ready, but I'll think about it," I answered. I wasn't ready.

I turned back to Sam and John, "I think I'm going to head

18

home now. I'll come back in the morning and keep working. Will you guys both be here?"

John nodded. "I'll be here."

"Yeah," Sam said, "we'll both see you tomorrow."

John walked ahead to push open the door for me and as his hand slid over the panic bar he said, "Drive safe, Mims." With all the roadside carnage he's witnessed in his career, that phrase carries weight.

WALKING OUTSIDE IN HAWAII is a sensual experience. I know so many people who remember the very first moment they stepped foot in the islands, and their stories sound almost identical: *When the plane taxied to the terminal and I made my way up the aisle to the open doorway…the air just hit me. It smelled like flowers; it was warm and humid and soft. I knew, right then, that I was home.*

As I emerged from the ME's office and stepped onto the aging asphalt parking lot, puddled from a rain shower that had passed by while I had been inside, I smelled the greenery nearby and felt the warm afternoon breeze lift wisps of my hair and flirt with the hem of my skirt. It transported me back to the day when I was eighteen and had first arrived to go to the University of Hawaii. I felt that same old delicious pleasure wash over my being.

I went to the passenger side of my car first, to unload all my stuff. I don't usually name my cars but when I bought this one, I knew immediately that it was female. I gave her an island nickname: HoneyGirl. When I opened the door, I felt her exhale the too-warm air that had built up from sitting in the tropical sun. I tossed my gear onto the seat and then I pulled off my sweater and threw it on top of the pile. As I rounded the front of the car, I trailed my finger in the beaded water on her silver hood and whispered, "Hi, HoneyGirl, sorry to have left you for so long."

I headed out of the parking lot and turned right, up *Waianuenue* Avenue. I drove uphill, past a strip of tropical, county watershed land across from some elegant, old "Hilo houses". A couple of more turns and HoneyGirl and I were in my neighborhood, cruising past folks out walking dogs, mowing lawns, and doing all the other afternoon activities of any residential area anywhere. My neighbors and I always wave and smile; it's important to get along when you live together on an island.

I breathed a sigh of contentment as I walked inside my house and kicked off my shoes. I walked from room to room, opening the sliding doors and windows to let in the breeze. I did it slowly and cautiously, though, giving any geckos time to move out of the way. I don't mind the geckos, they eat mosquitoes and termites, and at night geckos chirp, too, with a sound that's sort of like the tongue-noise people make to horses to get them to change gait. Geckos are reminders and, to some, representatives of the shape-shifting *mo'o*, of Polynesian lore; they're a link that infuses our everyday world with the supernatural. I would never hurt one on purpose and it really pains me to hurt one by accident, so that's why I always open windows and doors very carefully.

I changed into shorts and a tank top, and then I stood in front of the bathroom mirror to twist and pin my hair up into a bun – it was slightly lopsided but who was going to see? The glove smell still lingered on my arms and I washed them again, up to the elbows. It didn't help.

I hadn't eaten since breakfast and there were some fat, buttery avocados from my backyard trees, on the kitchen counter. I cut a medium-sized one in half and popped the seed out, and then I poured a large blob of store-bought salsa into the pit-well, grabbed a spoon and shoveled a big scoop of avo into my mouth. I opened a bag of tortilla chips and spilled a few, well, okay, maybe ten or possibly, if I were counting, fifteen, onto the counter top.

My cell phone rang. I fished in my purse for it and checked the caller ID. "Hi, Emma," I answered.

"Hi, Honey. What're you doing?"

Emma was my first friend on the island. She's a real estate agent and she helped Jay and me find our house. Emma's a transplant to the islands, too, but from a far more exotic place than my native Hollywood. Emma was born in East Africa, the daughter of British expats and she still retains a light accent and her lovely colonial manners, now mixed with island casual.

"Eating an avocado. I'm starving. I had a case today and I've been at the ME's all afternoon."

"Oooh, how exciting!" she replied. "I'm just sitting here drinking by myself. I'm not sure that's healthy. Want to join me? You can tell me all about your case."

"Sorry, not tonight. I've got to research some things before I go back to the office in the morning. How about tomorrow afternoon?"

"Oh, *alright.* I'll just have to find somebody else to drink with me tonight." Emma doesn't like to be alone, and she rarely is. People are always coming and going from her house. "See you tomorrow, then. Bring some coleslaw and I'll make dinner."

I disconnected and returned to my avocado. Emma's call reminded me there was about a cup of leftover margaritas in a pitcher in the refrigerator. It seemed like a natural to go with the chips and avocado.

I took my little snack outside to the umbrella-covered table there. I put up my feet on a mesh chair and entertained myself by watching a pair of wild canaries search out a last meal for the day.

IT WAS ABOUT SIX O'CLOCK when I finally went into my office to try to figure out the fetal age of little Keoni. I gathered together a bunch of heavy reference books but there wasn't enough room for all of them on my desk, so I sat on the cool floor and fanned them out around me. I also put my office laptop on the floor, loaded with the digital photos I'd taken of the tiny bones.

Bone cells start as a sort of rubbery fiber work that, as a person ages, will fill in with minerals. It's the minerals that make bones strong and hard, and breakable. When you die, the soft, rubbery bone cells die, too, and just leave behind the bone's shape in minerals. That's why old bones look white - you're only looking at a hardened chunk of calcium phosphate. Entangled in the wad of plaid boxer shorts on the autopsy table had been the delicate and brittle mineral traces left behind from bones that had just begun to form. They hadn't had time to take on the look of bones you'd see in an adult's skeleton.

When fetal bones do begin to take in minerals and harden, in a process called ossification, they don't all do it at the same rate. The first bone to begin ossification is your collar bone, or clavicle; it starts around the fifth or sixth fetal week. However, even though it's the first bone to start, the clavicle is typically the last one to finish; it doesn't complete its growth until you're around thirty years old. Another bone, your thigh bone, or femur, is the next bone to begin ossification, around the seventh fetal week and it typically finishes when you're in your early twenties. So, since each bone is different in its timing, I could use that information to start to narrow down how long Keoni had been developing.

After a couple of hours of research, I felt confident he was somewhere between two and a half months and three months of gestational age when his ten-year-old mother miscarried. I felt no sense of satisfaction; the whole case left me feeling like I had a lead weight in my chest.

As I was finishing up my notes and plopping the heavy books closed, the desktop phone rang. When I rose to answer it, I was surprised at how stiff I'd gotten sitting on the hard floor. I checked but I didn't recognize the caller ID.

"Hello?" I answered.

"Is this Miriam Charles?" the male voice asked.

"This is she."

"Hi, I'm Matt Ortiz, Channel Six News. How are you?"

I froze. What the *hell?*

When I didn't answer his question, he continued, "I'm calling about the fetal remains found in Hawi yesterday. I wonder if you could confirm the mother's identity for me."

How could this be happening? How did he know to call me? I knew Ortiz by his voice; I'd seen him, and heard him, on evening newscasts so, at least, I knew it wasn't a prank call.

My hackles were up. Not only would I *never* identify the girl's name, even if I did know it – which I didn't – but I was pissed off that Ortiz had my phone number. In my line of work, I need to be able to rely on anonymity. Sometimes I'm working on murders and that means there are murderers and their friends and family members who have a vested interest in the outcome of my findings. But more than that, there's an unwritten code about how reporters and law enforcement behave towards each other and he had just crossed the line – no calling at home. I felt like slamming down the phone but Ortiz represented the press and I didn't want to create trouble for the ME's office.

"How did you get my name?" I asked in a very cool, perhaps overly controlled voice. "And why are you calling me at home?"

"Sorry to call you at home. I hope it's not too late," he answered, completely ignoring my question. "I spoke to an officer in *Kona* and was told that they've located the girl's stepfather in Portland, Oregon, and they're going after him. So I was just wondering if you would confirm her identity for me." He seemed to have an inside source and, as is often the case, I wasn't being kept in the loop. But he wasn't getting anything from me.

"I'm sorry, Mr. Ortiz, you'll have to go through proper channels to get your information. Please call the Medical Examiner's Office to ask them your questions. And please do not call me at home. Ever again. It's not professional." *Asshole.* "Good night."

I hung up and called Sam right away. I wanted to be sure that, if Ortiz did call the office, he wouldn't get away with giving the impression I'd authorized anyone to talk to him. When I told Sam what had just happened, he was as shocked as I had been by Ortiz's behavior. I could tell by his tone of voice that he was going to be having a word or two with the manager at Channel Six.

I shut down my computer and turned off the office lamp but I just left my books scattered on the floor; I didn't feel like cleaning up at all. The house was dark, so I ran my hand against the hallway wall to guide myself as I walked to the kitchen. I flipped on the overhead lights and had the familiar sense of being very alone.

I made myself a grilled cheese sandwich, which I ate standing up at the kitchen counter, and then I decided to call it a night. When I brushed my teeth, my hands still smelled like surgical gloves. I put on an old flannel shirt of Jay's and tucked myself into bed.

The evening had turned chilly so I added an extra blanket to the bed. People think that, because Hawaii is in the tropics, it's always warm. I suppose, compared to Chicago or Buffalo, we have it pretty good. On the other hand, mainland homes have furnaces to warm them and windows that close. Here, when it gets down to sixty-two degrees outside, it's sixty-two degrees inside. So, like I said, I put an extra blanket on the bed.

I tried to read for a while but the words on the page began to blur and I dropped the book a couple of times. Finally, I turned out the light, pulled the blankets up to my chin and surrendered to the quiet Hawaiian night.

3 THE WAILUKU RIVER

I AWOKE A LITTLE EARLIER than usual and lay in bed, listening to the last of the coqui frogs and the first of the birds. When I opened my eyes I was greeted with a sky streaked in amazing corals and pinks.

It seemed like a good idea to take advantage of the early start so I got up and made myself an old-fashioned breakfast of bacon and eggs. I could probably be a vegetarian if it weren't for bacon.

Just as I sat down with my breakfast and the newspaper, the rain started. At first, it came in the form of "liquid sunshine", a fine mist that falls while the sun's still shining. Soon, however, the skies darkened and the rain fell heavily on the roof...what local folks call "pounding". We don't measure rain in inches in Hilo, we measure it in feet. It rains nearly ten feet a year. It's a warm, tropical rain, though, and typically starts and stops pretty quickly.

By the time I was ready to leave the house, the skies were blue again but I could hear water still rushing in the stream at the back of my yard. My little stream makes a small contribution to the *Wailuku* River, a river that starts near the top of *Mauna Kea*, where it's fed by clouds and snow melt. The river drops through rapids and waterfalls, almost ten thousand feet, to Hilo Bay. One big waterfall, next to the HMSE and the hospital, is called Rainbow Falls (*Waianuenue* in Hawaiian) because its mist catches the midmorning sun and creates a rainbow.

HONEYGIRL AND I DROVE through the glistening morning sun, down Waianuenue Avenue, towards the office. In the distance, an ambulance, lights on but siren off, was climbing the hill towards me and the Emergency Room entrance of the hospital. As I slowed to turn into the parking lot, I was shocked by a chaotic scene.

Most cops in the state use their own cars for work, usually SUVs or muscle cars. They just mount blue lights on the car top or on the dashboard when they're on duty. In addition to about eight of those babies parked at all angles in the lot, there were also some of the traditional, white Crown Victorias and a few marked, blue and whites. Altogether, that was an awful lot of cops to be hanging around in a parking lot that's normally a pretty quiet place.

I parked at the edge of the hubbub and walked towards the HSME door. A rookie, he looked about seventeen years old to me, peeled off from the cluster of cops near the building. He was holding a walkie-talkie and was doing his best at an *I'm in charge* look.

"What's your business here, ma'am?"

I scanned the group of nearby cops. They'd stopped talking and all seemed to be watching me, listening to hear what I'd say. I recognized a few faces and waited for somebody to step in and relieve the rookie and me from the tension. I didn't want to have to wrestle him to the ground in front of his peers.

The building's door shot open and John stepped out into the sunlight. Cue the Clint Eastwood music. "Mims," he said, and held the door open for me.

"Thanks," I idiotically said to the rookie. Why did I say that? I stepped around him and passed under John's protective arm, into the office.

27

THE ENTRANCE AREA OF THE BUILDING was crowded with large men milling around. Sam and the Chief of Police, Robert Costa, were standing together. On the fringe of the group, I saw Mick Daniels looking very alert and eager. I've known Mick for a pretty long time and I've watched him grow into semi-adulthood. At some point, he transformed into a cop. Although I wouldn't admit it to his face, he's become a good-looking guy in a tall, dark and handsome sort of way.

Suddenly, a few bodies shifted and I finally saw the focus of all the activity. It was Lehua. She was perched on the edge of a roller-footed office chair, holding an ice-filled baggie to the right side of her face, against a swollen eye. Her lip, on the same side, was split and blood was coagulated there. Her elbows and knees were scraped and dirty. And she was in her civilian clothes, not her usual scrubs.

"Wha...?" I started to speak, but John silenced me with a subtle shake of his head. With an equally quiet hand gesture, he signaled to me to stand with him, against the wall, just inside the door.

Sam raised his voice to command level, "Chief Costa...." All other conversations in the room quickly subsided. Besides being the Chief Medical Examiner, Sam is also the County Coroner and, since the time of Robin Hood and Richard the Lionhearted, coroners have out-ranked sheriffs and police chiefs. There are very few times Sam would ever actually exercise that rank but, apparently, this was going to be one of them.

Sam continued to address the Chief, in an authoritative, public voice, "I want one of your people to accompany Lehua over to the ER and stay with her. I want this incident to be thoroughly documented. I'm taking this situation very seriously."

The Chief nodded gravely and opened his mouth to speak

but stopped when Lehua began to shift on her chair. She said meekly, "I okay. I just want go home."

"No," Sam said to her, in a slightly gentler but still assertive voice. "This has to be done by the book. If we catch this guy and it goes to court, I want every *i* dotted and every *t* crossed."

Lehua slumped back in her chair a little and stared miserably at the floor.

"Of course," Chief Costa answered Sam. Then he scanned the room until his gaze settled on Mick, who was standing at stiff attention. "Go get Garrett, outside, and tell him to come in here."

Mick answered with a quick, "Yes, Sir!" and walked swiftly past me towards the door. I gave him a surreptitious, little half-smile as he passed by.

After only a moment, during which we all waited in an awkward silence, Mick reentered the building with another young cop. The Chief's voice was stony as he addressed Garrett, "You take Mrs. Ka`awa, here, and walk her over to the ER. Do not leave her side," he emphasized. "Stay with her until I give orders that you can leave. You understand?"

"Uh, yes, sir," Garrett said, but he didn't move. There was clearly something on his mind. He stood a little taller, as if fortifying himself for the worst, and announced, "Lehua's my cousin. Sir!"

The Chief sighed. He turned to Mick and barked, "Go get somebody outside who's not related to Lehua, in *any* way." Mick did a quick pivot and dived out the door again. It was several minutes before he returned. His short, dark hair was damp and I noticed a slight beading of sweat on his brow. No one was with him.

"Sir!" Mick spoke up. "They are all related to her. Sir!"

The Chief looked incredulous. "*All* of them?"

"All except Anderson, sir, and he's dating her husband's sister's daughter."

It's a small town. Not usually *that* small, but small.

The Chief looked exasperated. "All right, *you* then. You're not related to her, are you?"

I could see Mick's Adam's apple bob as he tried to swallow. I was guessing his mouth was pretty dry. "No, sir!" As an afterthought, he nervously added, "Not in any way, sir!"

The Chief glared at Mick and instructed him, as if we hadn't all heard it before, "Do not leave her side. If anything comes up, you contact me directly. Is that clear?" Mick started to speak but the Chief railroaded right on, "I am authorizing overtime, if it's needed. Keep a record of everything that happens and do not leave her unattended. Period."

"Yes..." Mick's response was cut off by a banging on the door like a battering ram.

We all turned to the security door. The small, square window, one of those safety windows that looks like it has chicken wire embedded in it, was completely darkened. Normally, you could see someone's face through that window. All that was there now was t-shirt. Somebody very, very big was out there. I had a guess who it was...Lehua's husband, Walter.

"Let him in," Sam said. As John moved to open the door, I flattened myself against the wall; I anticipated Walter was going to be moving fast and taking up a lot of space.

Walter exploded into the room and charged toward Lehua. He stopped short when he saw her, though. He didn't kneel by her side or embrace her; he changed his pace and walked very slowly to stand behind her and rest his giant hand on the back of her chair. Lehua leaned her head back until it rested on his hand and arm. Her face relaxed and she let a tear slide down her cheek. She was safe now that Walter had come.

Walter took a moment to compose himself, he inhaled massively, and then he turned to Sam. "What happen?" he asked. Then as an afterthought, he added, "I got my cousins

30

and my bruddah in da truck, outside."

Uh-oh.

Chief Costa spoke up, "Now, Walter," he spoke in a friendly but firm voice, "we don't know everything yet. First thing, we want to make sure Lehua's okay. We're just getting ready to send her over to the ER with Officer Daniels, here."

Oh boy, Mick was going to have his hands full.

The chief continued, "We have a general idea of what happened but we'll have to spend more time working on it. Lehua won't be in any more danger now and I don't want you to put her there again by doing something…" he was searching for the right word, "*inadvisable*, that might complicate things. If we do find the guy who did this…*when* we find the guy who did this…we want to make sure everything's been by the book so that we can nail him at trial. If you and your cousins interfere now, it could make things harder for us to prosecute. You get my drift?"

Walter's a dockworker. He has plenty of family, and plenty of friends at the docks. Things could get dangerous if everybody got involved.

Walter didn't look completely convinced about the Chief's plan of action but I could see that his first priority, at least for the moment, was going to be Lehua. After that, who knew?

Lehua seemed to catch on to the issue at hand, though. She didn't want Walter getting into something that might endanger their family. They have two little boys and a teenaged girl. She was thinking about them, too.

"Walter," she spoke to him very gently, "I no feel so good. You can take me ER now?"

THE OFFICE HAD QUIETED AGAIN. Lehua and Walter, accompanied by Mick, had departed for the ER, on the other side of the parking lot from the ME's office. Sam had told all of his employees to get back to work and he and the Chief had

31

disappeared into Sam's office. It seemed like everything had calmed down and was under control. I still didn't know what had happened to Lehua but I knew John would tell me when he had time. I'd gone to my room, where I was engrossed in carefully placing the fetal bones onto a piece of black velvet, to ready them for photography.

I had laid out the tiny bone fragments in what is called anatomical order, which means I'd positioned them where they'd all have belonged if Keoni were alive and lying on his back in front of me, palms up and toes pointed. There are many reasons to follow this protocol, not the least of which is to make sure there are no duplicate bones. It isn't all that unusual to find more than one set of remains commingled at a recovery site - although I knew that wasn't likely in this case.

Next to the bones, I'd positioned a metric ruler that would show in the photos. My work, like almost all science, is done in the metric system. Anyone viewing the pictures later would have the ruler as a reference to indicate the bones' true size. Next to the ruler I'd put a small sign board, about the size of a paperback book, with the case number and day's date written on it. Normally, placing the ruler and slate in photos of adult bones is no problem at all but, in this instance, they took up about as much of the picture as the tiny array of bones did. I was trying to decide whether to use a lamp to add better light to the photo when Sam entered the room. I was a little surprised to see him instead of John. He pulled the door shut behind himself.

I stopped my work and turned to him. "What happened?" I asked.

He ran his fingers through his salt and pepper hair, only serving to further disarrange it. He looked frazzled and it seemed like the little worry lines on his brow had deepened a bit during the day.

"Mimi, I don't know what to say. This has been an awful

32

day. I feel like I need to get in the water, you know? I don't have time to, but it's been too long since I've been in the water."

"I'm going to *Honoli'i* later. You want to come? Emma's always happy to have company and you could borrow one of the boards."

Hawaiians had, and still have, a need for a balance of land and ocean in their lives, *mauka* and *makai*. When there is stress, many people return to the water to cleanse their spirits.

Sam is *hapa haole*, part Hawaiian and part Caucasian, and he slips back and forth between the two worlds on a regular basis. He and my husband, Jay, met in college on the mainland and formed a brother-like bond. So, Sam's more than my boss and my friend, he's a connection to my husband. As I watch Sam age and progress through life, it reminds me of how Jay would be doing if he were still here. I feel a special closeness to Sam.

"I wish I could go with you," he said, "but, no can. This business with Lehua isn't over yet."

"Sam, what happened?" I asked again.

"Well, as far as I can piece it together, Lehua got here a little late today, so everybody else was already inside the building. She said she had some car trouble or something. Never mind, that's not really the point. She got mugged! She was just walking from her car to the door, in broad daylight, right out here! And she says some guy walked up really fast behind her and tried to choke her. I mean, I just can't believe it. Nobody, except some old security guard way over by the hospital, saw anything. He set off running – poor guy, it's a good thing he didn't have a heart attack. But before the guard could get near her, Lehua - she's such a little thing, you know - she reached back and grabbed the guy by the balls!" Sam's face broke into a wide grin at the thought, and then he sobered again. "I guess that's when he kind of shoved her away and she fell against that light post out there and banged her face up. The guy went limping off into the woods over by the river. By the time the guard got to her, Lehua was down on her hands and knees, cursing a blue streak."

"What was he after? Did he try to take her purse?"

"Well, that's the weird thing because she didn't have a purse with her. She just had her keys in her hand and her driver's license in her pocket. So, it's not clear what he was after. She says she didn't know him at all."

"How come they aren't searching over in the woods for him?" I asked. On the far side of the parking lot is a tangle of forest that borders the Wailuku River.

Sam looked amazed by my question. He asked, very slowly, as though he were talking to someone with a diminished IQ, "Haven't you heard the helicopter this morning?"

In my windowless work area, I couldn't hear many outside noises but, once I thought about it, I realized I *had* been hearing and feeling the vibrations of the large rotor blades; I guess I'd just mistaken them for air conditioning sounds. The penny dropped...everybody in Hilo who lives near the Wailuku River knows what the helicopter means.

"Oh, no...." I moaned.

The Wailuku's smaller waterfalls and pools may look like idyllic spots to wade or swim but local people know the river is treacherous because of its underground, underwater caves. If someone should step in the wrong place in the river, the rushing water's pressure can suck a body down into a cave and hold it there. In Hawaiian, *wai* refers to fresh water and *luku* means destruction or massacre. *Wailuku* is an old name and it may have another meaning, too, but that one fits the river pretty well.

If someone drowns in the Wailuku, the conditions are usually too dangerous for an on-the-ground recovery. From my house, when I hear the constant sound of a hovering

34

helicopter in the near distance, I know there's a search on for somebody missing in the river. It can take days, even weeks, before a body rises to the surface and is spotted and recovered.

Sam shook his head in disbelief. "There was a tour bus at Rainbow Falls and the driver - thank heavens the tourists didn't know what they were seeing – saw the guy try to wade across the river, upstream of the falls. And then he saw him just disappear. The chopper pilot thought he'd spotted the body earlier but he's lost it again. We're standing by for when they fish him out.

"I don't need to remind you, this information needs to stay inside these walls as long as possible. Of course, the press will eventually hear the chopper, so it won't be long before the story gets out. No point in worrying Lehua about any of this yet. I hope it doesn't freak her out."

There was a knock at the door and Sam reached over and twisted the handle. The door opened just a crack. Outside, John pushed it open a few inches more until we could see his face.

"Matt Ortiz, from Channel Six, is outside. He wants to know what the helicopter's looking for."

Sam shrugged his shoulders and rolled his neck to ease the tension in his muscles. "Okay, I'll go," he said to John. He looked weary as he left the room. I didn't know whether he'd yet had a chance to talk to the management of Channel Six about Ortiz but I guessed Sam wasn't in the mood to put up with much more of the reporter's annoying personality.

John lingered behind. "You want to go over to the hospital and get some lunch? We can check on Lehua when we're over there, too."

"Sounds good to me." The hospital cafeteria's food is actually better than you might think. I reached for the green sheet and John helped me gently lower it over the fetal remains. I, again, placed my hand-lettered sign on top of the little mound. We left the lights on and closed the door behind us.

John and I headed up the office hallway towards the exit but, as we neared the door, Sam reentered the building from the parking lot and barked at any staff within earshot, "If that bastard, Ortiz, asks for me again today, tell him to fuck off." He paused and collected himself. "Sorry, ladies and gentlemen. Tell him to *please* fuck off." He collected himself again, "Tell him I'm not available." And he walked into his office and slammed the door.

John and I both had smiles on our faces as we walked out into the midday sunshine. *Schadenfreude.* But my smile quickly faded at the sight of the distinctive orange and yellow County helicopter, hovering low over the river, just a little downhill from the hospital. It was so close that I could feel the concussions in the air from its blades.

I wondered whether the body had stayed where the guy fell, above the waterfall, or had slipped over and made the eighty foot drop into the deep pool at the base of the falls. Legend has it that *Hina*, the mother or wife of the god, *Maui*, once lived in the cave underneath the waterfall, where she was trapped by a giant eel/serpent/monster. Now was there a mugger's body floating in her former home?

JOHN AND I CROSSED THE HOT, asphalt parking lot, passing by the main hospital entrance, to enter through the Emergency Room doors. John raised his ID badge for the woman sitting behind the glass wall at the reception desk. It was a courtesy gesture because she knew him, of course, and they exchanged a little small talk through the tiny holes in the window for a few moments. When she buzzed him through the sliding, frosted glass double doors, I just tagged along behind him, trying to look like I belonged there.

We walked along a totally beige corridor, past small

darkened rooms, each containing a single bed. The rooms all had curtains inside their doorways, hanging from curved tracks on the ceiling. In some rooms, the curtains were pulled; in others, I could see unfortunate souls, looking worried and miserable, or simply asleep. Sometimes a companion sat or stood near the bed. In one room, two young parents bent over a fussy child. At nearly the end of the row of rooms, I saw Walter sitting, sideways, on a chair in the center of the corridor. He was bent forward, with his forearms resting on his knees, looking intently into a room. Probably, I thought, he's too big to fit into Lehua's cubicle while the doctors and nurses are in there, too. Walter was leaning a little to the right, to peer around Mick who was standing at guard, smack in the middle of the doorway.

As we approached him, John asked Walter, "How is she?"

Walter sat up a little and wearily answered, "They getting ready take her more tests. Say maybe she got concussion. She don't want go, but."

I could hear someone talking to Lehua inside the room and I recognized the voice. It's Hilo, for heaven's sake. We've probably only got two degrees of separation here: either you know somebody or you know somebody who knows him.

Sure enough, Katie appeared in the doorway. "Shove over, Mick," she said as she playfully nudged Mick aside. Then she saw me, "Hey, Mimi! What're you doing here?"

"I'm with John," I answered. "You two know each other, right?"

"Yeah, sure," Katie said with a smile. She had on blue scrubs and a white doctor's coat with her name embroidered in red on the breast pocket. Her shoulder length, brown hair was held out of her eyes by some faux tortoise shell barrettes. If you saw her out on the street you'd never guess she's the head of the ER. But, then, you'd never guess what I do, either.

"We just came by to check on Lehua," I explained to her. I

leaned forward to look into Lehua's darkened room but all I could see was curtain and Mick. "I was working over at the ME's office this morning when she got hurt. How's she doing?"

Katie turned to Walter and spoke to him, "Walter, is it okay for me to talk in front of them?"

Walter nodded his head yes. "Sure."

"I think she's fine," Katie told us. "She's just got some minor cuts and scrapes, but she did hit her head and I know Sam's concerned that we make sure she's okay...and, of course, I am, too. So, right now, we're just waiting for someone to come pick her up for a CAT scan - just to be extra cautious."

"No!" came Lehua's voice from inside the room. "I wanna go home, already! The kids is gonna be home soon. Walter, take me home!"

Katie looked back into the darkened room, past Mick. "Well, Lehua, I can't keep you here if you don't want to have treatment but I do want you to know that you're taking a risk, albeit probably a slight one, and I'm advising against it."

Rapidly, Katie's expression changed and she bolted back into the room, pushing past Mick. Her voice rose, "No, you can't get out of bed yet! I'll call for a wheelchair...you took a bump to the head and you...damn it!"

Walter, who had remained seated until that moment, suddenly rose and, taking Mick in his wake, rushed into the room. The curtain billowed behind him. I couldn't see what was going on but John could.

"Lehua fainted," John told me.

"She fainted?"

"Yeah." He watched for another moment. "They got it handled. Looks like she'll be in here a while longer, though. Let's go get some lunch."

38

IN THE CAFETERIA, John ordered the Portuguese bean soup and a ham sandwich. I got the same thing. What? I'm suggestible.

We found places to sit at one end of a long community table, like they have in elementary school lunchrooms. There were three people at the other end of the table but they didn't pay us much attention.

"So," I opened a packet of mustard with my teeth, "what happened this morning?" It was essentially the same question I'd asked Sam earlier but I thought that John, an investigator and former detective, might have more information or, at least, a different slant on things.

"Sam didn't tell you?"

"Yeah, but I figure you'd know more." I was fluffing his ego and he knew it.

"Well," he picked up his spoon and tapped at the surface of the soup in his bowl, "the guy didn't have a car in the lot, we know that much. You've got to have a parking permit for that lot and the guards watch it, so we know there wasn't an outside vehicle." He paused while he sipped a spoonful of soup and then he added a vigorous shaking of black pepper to the bowl and stirred it in. "Maybe he got here by bus or somebody dropped him off, or something, but he didn't seem to have much of a getaway plan. Lehua said the guy looked haole. She said he was skinny and had bad breath. So, I'm thinking he might be one of those tweakers who camps over in the woods between the parking lot and the river. The hospital's complained about them before. In fact, a couple of weeks ago, the county tried to roust 'em all, but they're like roaches; they just keep coming back. When those guys get high they'll go days without sleeping but when they can't keep the rush going any more, that's when they can get violent - nothing usually very well-thought-out, though."

"But, why Lehua?" I asked. "She didn't even have a purse with her."

"Well, that's just one theory, the tweaker idea. It could've been something else. Maybe he thought he could use her to get in the office. We've got all kinds of stuff in the ballistics collection; handguns, shotguns, even an Uzi. Maybe he was after one of those. Course, there are the drugs, too. Hell, we've probably twenty pounds of pakalolo in there right now. And then there's the meth and the coke. It's going to take some time to figure out."

We seemed to have exhausted that topic. I took a few sips of soup while I thought back about the morning.

"Thanks for rescuing me this morning. I thought that kid wasn't going to let me in the building."

"What kid?"

"The rookie."

"Why didn't you just use your badge? That's why we gave it to you."

"I forgot. But I probably would have remembered it if you hadn't shown up so fast."

The state, at Sam's insistence, had issued me a gold badge. It had been because of an airplane crash that had been discovered long after the fact. The NTSB, FBI, HSME, HPD, basically the whole alphabet, had been there and closed off the back country road leading into the site. When I arrived, the posted guard wouldn't let me in because I didn't have any official ID. It took a while before somebody cleared me to enter.

A gold badge means rank, silver's what most cops carry. I get saluted when the rookies see it. That's kind of cool. And an airport gate agent gave me a complimentary coupon for a free drink once. I would have preferred an upgrade to first class, but a free drink's nice.

"You're not technically supposed to have that badge, you

know," John told me.

"Why?"

"The badge isn't supposed to be issued without firearms training."

"Oh," I said. "Oh, hell no. Oh, trust me, that is a bad idea. You do not want me to have a gun. Because I would use it. Like, in the grocery store line when somebody keeps bumping into me with a cart. Blam!" I was getting more animated. "I'm a loose cannon, baby!"

John smiled and said something under his breath. I didn't quite catch it. And just then his cell phone rang.

He squinted at the caller ID and then put the phone to his ear. "Harding," he answered. He listened and, after a few seconds, grunted a half smile. "Thanks, buddy," he said, and pushed the disconnect button.

"And so it goes," he said to me.

"What?" I asked. I seem to say that to him a lot.

"They found a tweaker chick in a pup tent over in the woods. She says her old man went out to get something to eat this morning and never came back. They didn't have any money but she wanted a candy bar and a coke, anyway. Apparently, she's had these cravings before and her hubby wrecked the outdoor vending machine over at the hospital a couple of days ago, trying to break into it. So that source of food's gone. The little missus is just cluelessly pissed that he hasn't come back yet. So, it's looking more and more like Lehua was just in the wrong place at the wrong time, when the guy was looking for cash. I know she didn't have her purse on her but the guy's probably a moron. In a way, this is a good thing – it means it was just a random act of stupidity."

"Did they tell the wife about the drowning?" I asked.

"Don't know."

I'd ordered too much food so I wrapped the sandwich in a couple of napkins and put it in my purse. Knowing myself, though, I'd probably forget about it until it was too dangerous to eat.

We finished up our lunches and bussed our dishes and then we walked back to the ER to check on Lehua again, but she wasn't there. Katie wasn't there, either. A nurse told us Lehua was being admitted, overnight, for observation and Walter and the diligent officer, Mick Daniels, had accompanied her upstairs.

So, John and I left the hospital to walk back to the ME's office. Outside, the drone of the helicopter weighed me down. We crossed the parking lot in silence and I actually welcomed the cool, quiet, sunless interior of the lab. There aren't many places quieter than a morgue.

BY THREE O'CLOCK, I had finished doing all the lab photographs and the work on the Hawi case. I packed up my things and got ready to go home. On the way out of the building, I stopped by Sam's office to say goodbye.

"I'm getting ready to go now," I told him. "I'm finished with the bones. I'll get a report and a bill to you tomorrow or the next day." Then, realizing it was a Friday, I said, "Oh, wait, the weekend. Well, I'll get it to you on Monday, then. All I'm gonna be able to say is that it's a human fetus, probably less than three months gestational age. I'll do more research on that."

"Could you determine sex?"

"No. If you get DNA, you'll know that, but I can't tell off of fetal bones."

"Okay. Thanks, Mimi," Sam said. He looked tired and subdued, too, after all the stress of the day. "See you Monday."

I lugged my stuff out to the parking lot again. The sky had clouded up and the first rain drops were just starting to mist my windshield as I dropped my things on the passenger's seat. I settled into the car and patted HoneyGirl's warm dashboard.

42

I pulled slowly out of the lot and drove through the steadily increasing rain, back to my house.

4 THE HOUSE AT HONOLI'I

I TRUDGED INDOORS and dropped my work stuff off in my office. The rain was cooling the house, so I didn't open any windows. My plan was just to whip up some coleslaw and then head straight out again, to go to Emma's for dinner.

In the kitchen, I got out one of my big mixing bowls. Curls of cold vapor escaped into the air when I opened the refrigerator to search for the coleslaw ingredients. I knew the recipe by heart and it only took a couple of minutes to put it together.

A thought crossed my mind and I reached into my purse for my cell phone. Instead, I found the ham sandwich from lunch. Three hours? Probably okay, if I put it right into the refrigerator. Living on the edge, that's me. I reached into my purse again for my phone. I don't know why I was even bothering to call...I already knew the answer.

"Hi, Honey," Emma answered.

"Hey, what time do you want me to come over tonight?" I asked her.

"Oh, come early, and have a drink first. Come now. It'll just be you and me and a couple of others."

THE HOUSE WHERE EMMA LIVES is in one of the most spectacular locations in Hilo, right next to Honoli'i surfing beach. As I drove down the steep driveway, about ten dogs ran up to meet my car. Well, actually, there were only three but

Barney is the biggest dog I've ever seen so he counts as eight. At one hundred and thirty-five pounds of Rottweiler muscle, with a head the size of a basketball, Barney has the good-natured attitude that comes with bulk. No Chihuahua will ever understand that feeling. I parked and walked around HoneyGirl to pick up the bowl of coleslaw from the car floor on the passenger's side. The dogs danced around me, stepping on my feet.

The front door to Emma's spacious two-storey house was, as usual, wide open. There were two small baggies of water, each with a penny in it, stapled over the doorway; I think it's some folk remedy to stop flies from coming inside, or something. It's a straight shot through the house, from the front door to the back door, so I could see Emma and Katie, with their backs to me, sitting under an umbrella-shaded picnic table on the broad, cement, backyard *lanai*. I was surprised to see Katie there so early. She's usually at the hospital until late in the day.

Emma half turned and shouted out, "Hi, Honey! Pour yourself a drink, there's wine or vodka-cranberry, and come join Katie and me outside."

I wedged the coleslaw bowl into an impossibly crowded refrigerator and then I poured myself a glass of red wine from an open bottle on the counter top. As I carried my glass outside to the picnic table I asked them, "Where's Kelly?"

"In the water," they replied in unison. Kelly was, of course, out in the late afternoon surf lineup. It's complicated but Kelly, who is now Katie's boyfriend, was once Emma's boyfriend.

I walked around to the far side of the table and set my glass down before I tried a side mount of the picnic bench. When I looked up at Katie, I blurted out, "What the hell happened to your face?" I probably could have thought of a more polite way to ask that question but there was a large bandage running across her nose and she had two slightly black eyes.

"Walter," she answered. "Didn't you see us? You were there. It was when I was talking to you and John in the ER. I saw Lehua trying to get out of bed so I ran into her room because I was worried that she might faint. Which she did. Thank God, I caught her before she hit the floor. She's so small it was an easy catch. So, I was lifting her back onto the bed when Walter came crashing into the room. He ran into Mick and knocked him into me and then all three of us went down. I was on the bottom of the pile. I think something on Mick's belt banged my nose. It's not broken or anything…" she touched the bandage on the bridge of her nose.

"Oh, my God, so Walter *and* Mick both went down on you!" Tasteless, I know, but an easy shot. Emma and I laughed but Katie looked only minimally amused.

"What's this about my girlfriend and *two* other men?" asked Kelly as he rounded the outside of the house with his surfboard under his arm. His body was still wet from the ocean.

"I need more to drink," Katie declared and she rose from the table and walked back to the kitchen. As she reached the doorway, we all felt and heard a low rumble, something like an earthquake. I looked at Emma with a question on my face.

"Mick," she answered me.

Oh yeah, Mick and his muscle, cop car. Barney leapt to his massive feet and loped off to greet his master. All these relationships are so intertwined. Mick grew up with Emma's sons and, even though they're away at college on the mainland now, Mick stayed behind and went to the Police Academy and now he rents a room in Emma's house. It's a small town – on a small island, in a small state.

Soon Mick, looking much more relaxed than when I'd last seen him at the hospital, emerged onto the lanai. Barney was at his heels, a big slobbery smile on his face, looking about as

46

pleased as a dog can look. Katie followed behind them both, carrying a replenished glass of wine. It was *Pau hana* time.

5 THE PALACE IN HILO

OVER THE WEEKEND, I spent hours at my desk, finishing up the report on Keoni's remains. Writing reports is usually tedious, and that one was no exception, but the weather was chilly so I didn't mind staying indoors. The National Weather Service issued a Winter Storm Warning saying that the upper slopes of Mauna Kea and *Mauna Loa* were having significant amounts of snow, sleet and black ice; the road up to the observatories was closed. Winds swept the snow-cooled air down into town and temperatures plummeted into the lower seventies in the days and the upper fifties at night. People in town wore sweaters and long pants and socks. We're a bunch of hothouse flowers.

All day, both days, I heard the helicopter flying over the river until dark. My mind kept wondering about the tweaker's wife. She was a meth addict living in a pup tent in the woods behind the hospital and that was, surely, not the life she'd dreamed of as a little girl. Now her husband had drowned and she was alone in that cold tent. At what point do you get it that you've hit bottom?

I also thought about Keoni's young mother. How was it possible for a ten-year-old to drop out of school without anybody noticing or doing anything? Okay, maybe I was selling the system short; maybe somebody had noticed but why hadn't *somebody* helped? What was going to happen to her? And her younger brothers? Damn.

Usually the cases I work on involve people who've been dead for a long time. When they're found, at first nobody knows their stories. But most people die the way they lived. People found stuffed in abandoned freezers often have had lives filled with pain and chaos. I don't really want to hear about their stories, not because I don't care but because I *do* care – and I don't want to hold that pain in my memory. I do my best at my part in getting justice for them but I'm not emotionally equipped to do much more. I would have rested a lot easier over the weekend if I hadn't been having thoughts popping into my head about the children or the tweaker's wife. I need to stay detached. The cases have to be just puzzles to me; I like solving puzzles. I need to just do my reports and then let the cases pass on through the system. Otherwise, I could end up like John.

At last, on Sunday afternoon I adjusted the printer settings to best quality and made a final copy of my report and bill and tucked them both into a fresh manila envelope for presentation to Sam the next morning. I also emailed Detective Mancao and told her my report was done. And, then, on an impulse, I decided to go to a Sunday matinee at the Palace, one of my favorite places in Hilo.

The Palace Theatre is a ninety-year-old, restored beauty. There's no air conditioning but in the lobby there's always a basket of paper hand fans that you can borrow for the night. The side doors, to alleys, are left open during movies and concerts so the cooling breeze can blow through the theatre. What that means is that movies shot in as different places as New York or the Sahara Desert are accompanied by the sounds of rain falling and coqui frogs chirping. Like so many other things in Hilo, it's a mix of funky and eccentric and charming.

It was just getting dark when the movie got out and I drove home.

The house was chilly and quiet and I was glad I'd left a light on for my return. I so miss coming home to Jay and Fred, the WonderDog.

Later that night, the temperature dropped a couple of degrees lower than it had even on the nights before.

6 GOING TO BED WITHOUT DIENER

STRONG, WARM SUNLIGHT FLOODED, yes flooded, into my bedroom on Monday morning and the birds were ecstatic about it. I laughed when I caught my reflection in the mirror. I had on a bright floral print sarong to which I had added a flannel pajama top, my hair was sleep-tousled in a tangle of curls and there was ink on my face that had transferred from the magazine page I'd fallen asleep on the night before. I wiped my face on my sleeve and padded up the hallway to the kitchen.

Glancing out of the big picture window over the sink, I noticed that the tree branches and palm fronds were dead still. The trade winds had cut out and there was a haze in the air. Vog. Vog's like smog except it's caused by a volcano instead of factories and cars. Usually the trade winds blow vog away from Hilo and over to Kona or out to sea but, for a few windless, warm days a year, the trades stop and vog settles over town. I put the kettle on and went to get the newspaper. When I opened the front door, I could taste the metal and smell the sulphur in the air. It's just one of those island things; if you're going to live next to an active volcano, this is going to happen. I grew up in L.A. - I've seen worse.

I walked barefooted, down the path to the street. With no wind to rustle the leaves, it seemed extra quiet outside. Then I realized it was extra, extra quiet. I didn't hear the helicopter any more. I pulled the newspaper out of the delivery box and unfolded it. There was a large, half-page, colored picture of Rainbow Falls under a headline that read: **RESCUE DIVERS RECOVER BODY FROM RIVER.** Nice alliteration. I stopped, in midstep, and continued to read:

> **At 5:35 p.m., Sunday evening, County Fire and Rescue personnel sighted the body of a missing person near the area where he was last seen on Friday. A spokesperson for the HPD confirms that a helicopter search has been ongoing since a local tour bus driver reported seeing a man disappear in the Wailuku River, near Rainbow Falls. Rescue divers entered the river and recovered the body that was then transported to the Hilo Hospital Emergency Room. The victim was pronounced dead at 6:58 p.m. The Medical Examiner has initiated an inquest. An autopsy is scheduled to determine the exact cause of death. The victim's name is being withheld pending notification of next of kin. Individuals with information about the incident should call the Hawaii Police Department, Hilo Division.**

I returned to the house and sat at the long dining table, my feet resting on a small footstool that Jay had made for me. I leisurely sipped a mug of coffee and read the rest of the paper. I wasn't in any hurry to deliver my report to Sam, anymore, because I knew he'd be tied up doing the autopsy on the drowned guy.

I showered and dressed in a coral-colored shift to which I added a shell necklace and some gold hoop earrings and a couple of gold bangles. One time I read a Coco Channel quote that said something like, you should put on all the accessories that you think look good and then take one off. So I took off one bangle. If Coco's spinning in her grave, it's not because of me.

WHEN I PULLED INTO the parking area outside the ME's office around ten o'clock, the lot was back to its old self. I left HoneyGirl's windows cracked a little (I knew because of the voggy weather that it wouldn't rain, for a little while anyway) and I strolled towards the office, unencumbered by my usual bags and equipment. All I needed to do was turn in my report. Afterwards, I was thinking, I'd go shopping for some of those little solar lights to put next to the front path of my house. It was a lovely, quiet morning.

When I pressed the intercom button I was surprised that Lehua came to greet me at the door.

"What're you doing here?" I asked her. "I mean, I'm glad you're up and around, but are you feeling okay? I thought you'd be staying home for a while."

"Oh, no," she replied, shaking her head emphatically. "When Walter say he going stay home take care me, I got better quick. He make such a mess when he stay home!"

"Well, I'm glad you're back; I was worried about you." I could see the scuffs on her palms from dropping onto her hands and knees on the asphalt. And there was still a bump and dark bruise on her right cheek and temple. "You okay now? No headache, or anything?"

"Yeah, I fine. Just shook up, you know?" She lowered her eyes a little.

"Well, yeah. Of course." I started to make a crack about her grabbing the guy by the balls but then I remembered that he was dead. Not so funny, after all. I laid my hand on her left shoulder and gave it a gentle squeeze, the universal sign for *I can't think of what to say but I want to let you know I care.* After a moment, Lehua recovered her smile and covered my hand on her shoulder with her own.

"You looking for Dr. Morris? He back in the autopsy room. The drown guy there and I had go identify him. It give me chicken skin to see him."

"Do they know who he is yet?"

"No."

"I'm sorry. I didn't realize you'd have to deal with that. That's creepy. So, it was the same guy, huh? The guy who assaulted you?"

"Yeah, it was him, definitely. His skin was all white and waterlog. It was bad. Now they going bring over the wife for make an positive ID."

"Ick."

"Yeah. We gotta watch her so if she faint, you know. That can happen sometime." It seemed Lehua had already forgotten that she had fainted only a few days before. "Dr. Morris say somebody else can show her; I no have to."

"Oh, definitely. There's no reason why you should have to be around for that. I'm so sorry all of this happened to you, Lehua." I gave her a quick half-hug. Then I ruffled the papers in my hand as some sort of lame visual aid and said, "I'm just going to put my report on Dr. Morris's desk."

"Yeah, okay." Lehua nodded her head and turned to walk towards her desk. She looked a little stiff; probably her knees still hurt from hitting the ground.

I crossed the corridor and entered Sam's empty office. The lights were on and there was a cup of cold coffee on his desk. I plopped my report on top of a pile of other paperwork and then I did a quick pivot to leave the room and go to find him. My eyes only hesitated for a moment on one of the pictures on the wall. It was an old photo of Sam and Jay, standing together, laughing.

SAM WAS IN THE AUTOPSY ROOM with another one of the dieners, Ozzie. They were both dressed in blue scrubs over which they wore paper aprons, booties and caps. They also had on Plexiglas faceshields that looked like welders' masks, meant to protect them from the splatter and fine spray that happens when Sam saws into the craniums and cracks open the chests of the cadavers. And, of course, they both had on gloves - always gloves.

I stood just inside the doorway, not wanting to enter the room unnecessarily. Even from twenty feet away, I could see details on the body. The drowned guy's skin was water-bloated and bloodlessly pale. No muscles were operating any more to hold his eyelids shut or open - they were somewhere in between – and he had the dead, filmy eyes of a man held under water for days. His jaw was slack and the tip of his tongue rested on top of his lower teeth. He had the typical body hair pattern of a Caucasian male, some on his chest and arms and legs and around his genitals. The autopsy table has to be the least private place there is.

Sam had made deep incisions in the cadaver's chest, in the shape of a Y, with the two prongs of the Y at the shoulders and then a straight line from the center breast down to the groin. He and Ozzie were engaged in pulling the ribs open, like cupboard doors. I could see a slight layer of exposed belly fat. Human belly fat is a surprising color, the sharp yellow-orange of cheddar cheese. The purple-brown organs were visible, too. There was the metallic smell of blood in the air, mixed with the putrid smell of the decomposing bowels.

"Sam," I called to him.

Sam looked up and paused in his work when he saw me. "Oh, hi, Mimi. Did you bring your report?"

"Yeah, I left it on your desk and..." my sentence was interrupted by a hand on my shoulder. I turned to see John standing behind me.

"Doc, I've got some strange news," he announced to Sam.

I moved forward, just a step, to let John into the room but he stayed where he was, framed in the doorway.

"Lord, what now?" Sam asked.

John looked like he was a little bit going to enjoy delivering his story. His speech slowed to an even more pronounced drawl than usual as he began, "I just got a call about the wife. The one who was going to come in and ID that guy, on the table there? Well, when they went to fetch her from her tent, she was in the middle of a knock-down-drag-out fight with some fellow. They had to separate them and that young cop, the one who went to the hospital with Lehua the other day, Daniels, he had to chase the guy through the woods a little bit. When they got everybody settled down, comes to turn out that the fellow she's arguing with is her husband." John paused for effect. "He went out to get her a coke and a candy bar on Thursday and he's just gettin' back this morning. She was fighting with him because he forgot the coke, or drank it already, he's not sure. So, her husband's not missing. And this guy, here, on the table, is somebody else."

"Wait, so you're telling me that this guy, here," Sam's hand paused at the edge of the open rib cage, "who Lehua just identified as the guy who assaulted her, is not the husband of the woman in the woods? How did that happen? How did the cops get the idea, in the first place, that he was her husband?"

"You'll have to ask them," John answered. "I guess she's the one who told them her husband was gone and he must have fit the same general description. I'm supposing she's probably not a real reliable witness, being a crackhead and all."

Sam slowly shook his head in wondering disappointment at the human condition. He sighed. And then he shook it off.

"Come over and take a look at this arm," he beckoned us. Sam picked up the corpse's left arm for better viewing. John advanced to the table and I followed, a pace or two behind.

The man's pale, bloated skin was deeply blotched above the elbow with the blurred blue-black marks of tattoos. "These look like prison tattoos to me," Sam muttered.

"And there's no tan," I observed. Somebody without a tan is

unusual in Hawaii.

"That says prison, too," John remarked.

"Well, his fingerprints ought to show up on AFIS then," Sam said to John. "Go ask Lehua if they've been put into the system yet."

I could see the greasy, black smudges of fingerprinting ink on the corpse's hands.

The FBI runs AFIS, the Automated Fingerprint Identification System. Besides storing the fingerprints of criminals, if you've ever applied for a job that requires a background check with fingerprints, AFIS probably has your prints, too. More than a hundred million Americans are in the system. In less than half an hour, AFIS can produce the name, criminal history, picture and physical description of someone in the system. If this guy had been in prison, then his fingerprints would quickly identify him.

"On it," John responded to Sam. As he turned to walk out of the room he added, "Mims, come with me?"

I looked at Sam and shrugged my eyebrows and my shoulders and said, "Be right back, I guess..." and then I turned and followed John.

WHEN I CAUGHT UP TO HIM, John was already at Lehua's work station, using her computer. I could see he was working on the AFIS website.

"She didn't enter them yet," he commented to me. "I'll do it."

"Okay." I waited for a moment. "Why'd you want me to come with you?" I asked him.

"It didn't have anything to do with this," he answered, still typing. "Something came in over the weekend. I didn't call you at home because I'm pretty sure it's not modern, but you'd better take a look at it, anyway. While you're here. Just let me finish up this entry."

John's a one-handed, single-finger typist - yet another reason why the wheels of justice grind slowly. While I stood waiting, the entrance intercom buzzed and John and I both looked over at the security camera monitor to see who was at the door. Without hesitation, John bent forward to press the small, gray intercom button on the desktop speaker. "Come on in, David," he said as he buzzed the door unlocked.

David Chung's another consultant, like me, who works for the ME's office. He's a dentist. In the lab we take x-rays of a deceased person's dentition and then David compares those to the person's old dental x-rays, if they exist and we can get ahold of them.

David also analyzes the teeth for traumatic damage that might tie into the circumstances of death - trauma such as getting punched in the face or going head first through a windshield. There are so many, very important things that can be learned from the teeth, that Forensic Odontology is another subsection, like Forensic Anthropology, of the American Academy of Forensic Sciences.

The Odontology section has always struck me as one of the more unusual groups at our annual meetings. Every year they have a Bite Mark Breakfast at which they show slides of bite marks on victims or on evidence at crime scenes…while they eat breakfast. I went once and I'll probably not go again. I'd prefer not to think about people biting each other, especially while I'm eating.

I analyze the teeth, too, but I'm looking for different signs: age, health, the person's ancestry and any personal habits that would show on them, like smoking. Even though they're not bones, teeth are still a part of the skeleton; in fact, they're the *only* part of the skeleton that's exposed during life

David smiled when he entered the room and saw John and me waiting for him. "Hi, you guys! I didn't expect to see you here, Mimi. Are you working on this drowning thing, too?"

"Nope," I told him, "I'm turning in a report on something else. No teeth."

David gave me a quizzical look.

"Fetal remains," I explained. "No teeth."

His face fell. A fetus. That's just grim news. I could see he wanted to ask questions. But he didn't. "Hey. Well. Sam called me this morning and asked me to come by today for this drowning guy. See if I can help ID him." He paused for a second and then added, "I heard there's been a lot of excitement around here lately. How's Lehua doing?"

I answered. "She's okay, I guess. I was kind of surprised, but she came to work today. She's had a crappy morning, though. The police asked her to identify the guy who assaulted her on Friday. You know it's the drowned guy, right?"

"Yeah. Sam told me. Tough for Lehua, huh?"

"I think she was a little rattled to have to see *that* body, especially all bloated like that."

"Where is she?" David asked.

"Oh," I said, looking around the area, "I don't know. She was here a little while ago. I saw her when I came in."

"Maybe she took a break," John offered.

I would have taken a break. In fact, I would have stayed at home, if it had been me.

John returned to entering the data on the computer but he spoke over his shoulder to David, "Dr. Morris is doing the autopsy right now so it might be a while before you can do your exam. I was just going to show Mimi something that came in over the weekend. You want to see it, too?"

"Sure." David looked at me, raising his eyebrows and nodding yes.

John finished up at the computer, with a final emphatic tap at the keyboard to enter the data, and then he rose from the desk and led us down the hall to my little work room. I felt dwarfed walking with the two of them. I'm five feet four but

John and David are both over six feet tall. I think David's probably a little taller than John but he's got a looser, less military bearing.

JOHN FLIPPED ON THE LIGHTS and held the door open for David and me. Little Keoni was gone, probably just stored as evidence in the cold, walk-in locker with all the other bodies. I wondered if, someday, he would get a proper burial somewhere. I gave my head a little shake and tried to return my attention to the room. That's the way it is at work. The new cases just keep coming in and the old ones leave, never to be seen again by me.

In the middle of the autopsy table there was a human cranium, the bone bleached ivory white. It rested on top of a ragged, aged, plastic sack that, itself, was sitting on top of a brown-paper evidence bag.

"Looks old," David murmured.

I slipped on some gloves and carefully lifted someone's former head from the table. I turned it over so that the teeth and palate were visible to us all.

It takes two parts to make a skull: a cranium - the upper face plus the part that holds the brain - and a mandible, or lower jaw. When a body decomposes, without tissues to any longer hold it in place, the mandible separates from the cranium. What was sitting on the table in front of us was not a skull, just a cranium without a mandible.

"I think it's archaeological," John said. "Plus, it was found in a cave."

"I think so, too," I said.

David nodded his agreement; all it took was one look at the teeth for the three of us to recognize the cranium's antiquity. The molars, the teeth in the back of your mouth that you use to grind food to a pulp, were flat on their chewing surfaces, not bumpy. You almost never see that in modern people.

60

Ancient people who used stone grinders to process their food, like the Hawaiians who ground *taro* into poi, just naturally had more grit incorporated into their diets and, so, the occlusal surfaces of their molars wore flat as the people aged.

"What makes it officially archaeological?" David asked. "I mean, how old does it have to be? What's the cutoff line?"

"Usually, fifty years," I told him. "But there are a whole bunch of laws that have to be followed if the bones are Native Hawaiian or, on the mainland, Native American. That's when NAGPRA kicks in."

"What's NAGPRA? Wait, let me guess. Um, North American Government...."

I gently set the cranium back onto the table. "Native American Graves Protection and Repatriation Act," I recited slowly. "It was originally created to stop looters from "collecting" bones and artifacts from Indian graves on the mainland. Even museums were supposed to return their collections to the tribes."

"How could they make them give back museum pieces?"

"If you put a bible in the coffin with your grandmother and then somebody dug her up and put her bones in a museum and sold the bible to a collector, wouldn't you want those things back, to be reburied?"

"My family's Buddhist," he reminded me, "but I get the point."

"Sorry, I wasn't thinking. Well, anyway, NAGPRA's been a real can of worms in Hawaii."

"Why's that?"

"Well, first off, Hawaiians aren't native Americans, are they? I mean, obviously, Hawaii's nowhere near the Americas, physically or culturally. But, then, there's an even bigger problem because there *aren't* any tribes in Hawaii to return the bones or artifacts to."

"Oh, yeah," David muttered. "I hadn't thought of that."

"Yep," I sighed, "a big, fat can of worms."

"Glad I'm just doing the teeth."

I turned to John, "You said it was found in a cave?"

I was puzzled. It's true that caves were sometimes used as burial places for Hawaiians. But I had a problem with what was on the table in front of me. Bone color tells a story. For instance, bone that has been exposed to the sun turns dry and white over time; we call it sun bleached. Bone that has been in contact with soil, takes on the color of the soil and we call it soil stained. But bones that have been sitting in the interior of a lava cave, shouldn't be sun bleached or soil stained. The cranium sitting on the autopsy table in front of us was both. So...something was fishy.

"Yeah, and when it was found, it was sitting on top of that plastic grocery sack, too. I think that's a clue," John deadpanned.

"Okay," I announced, "I'm officially saying the age of this cranium appears to be archaeological. It's typical of an ancient Hawaiian. You can carbon date it, if you want, but we all know those teeth belong to someone who lived way more than fifty years ago." My statement put the Medical Examiner's office out of the loop; the cranium would be turned over to another branch of government.

"And, just FYI, it's a female," I told John. "Probably in her late twenties or her thirties."

David was bent over the table, glasses off, peering at the cranium. "How can you tell it's a female?"

"Oh, there's a bunch of things there. Like the size of the mastoid processes."

"Why those?"

"Well, you know. Men have broader shoulders and thicker necks than women. Do this," I said to him, "put your finger just behind the base of your ear. Do you feel that blunt mound of bone?"

David raised his hand and felt behind his left earlobe. "Yeah, I know where the mastoid processes are."

With my hand touching my own left mastoid process, I turned my head to the right and tensed the muscles of my neck. "Now, turn your head to the right, like this. Do you see this muscle on me?" I traced the outline of a muscle, about the thickness of a cigar, which stretched diagonally from my mastoid process down to the small knob formed by my medial clavicle (the center end of my left collar bone) at the front base of my neck.

"You can trace the muscle on yourself," I said to him. "So, the sternocleidomastoid…."

"The SCM, I remember it from Gross Anatomy. Thank God for acronyms."

"Yeah, the SCM. It's one of the muscles that makes a man's neck thicker than a woman's. As you know, when bone's alive it builds up to anchor your muscles. So, since men have thicker SCMs, their mastoid processes are bigger, too. Bigger and blunter. And those," I nodded my head to the mastoid processes of the cranium on the table, "are small and delicate, like a woman's."

"Cool."

I looked up and saw John casually rubbing behind his ear. At any other time, it wouldn't have been a noticeable gesture at all.

David picked up the cranium. "How about her age? You estimating that from dentition?"

"Partly." Now we were back into David's field again. "How old do *you* think she was?"

"Oh. Okay. Well, she's got all her wisdom teeth, so she's probably at least eighteen." He turned the cranium to catch the light better. "If her other molars came in at normal times, the first ones around six years old and the second ones around twelve then, based on the wear accumulated on those teeth over the years, we can kind of estimate how many more years it would have taken to get the degree of occlusal wear on those wisdom teeth. So," he gently placed the cranium back onto the tabletop, "I agree with you - she's probably in her late twenties."

"I should've paid more attention to those damned trains travelling towards each other, going different speeds, back when I took algebra in high school," John muttered.

David and I smiled science-dork smiles at each other.

"Okay, folks," John said, "that's all I need to know."

"Wait!" David cried, "I want to know how it got sun bleached and soil stained in a cave."

John shrugged, "Some guy probably found it eroding out of the ground. Probably been exposed like that for a while and that's how it got sun bleached and soil stained. Guy didn't want to touch it so he found a flyaway plastic bag and used it to pick up the skull and carry it to a nearby cave. To do the Hawaiian burial thing."

"Yeah, it sounds like it could've happened that way," David mused.

I noticed they were both assuming the person who handled the skull was a guy. "Well, gentlemen," I pronounced, "my work here is done. I'm going shopping. Anything else you need, John?"

"Nope."

John flipped off the lights as the three of us filed out of the room. I could see Sam, across the corridor, still at work in the autopsy suite. When he saw us in the hallway, he called out, "David! Hi. I won't be much longer. Hey, John, will you see if Lehua's done with that AFIS check yet?"

"Sure," John called back. From where we were standing, I could see as well as John could that Lehua wasn't at her workstation. John was just covering for her; she'd had a rough morning.

The three of us drifted up the hall and, as we neared Lehua's computer, I saw that the screensaver with the picture of the new puppies was on.

"Oh, David, you've got to see these." We both leaned towards the screen to get a better look. "Sweetie just had four new puppies. Aren't they cute? Lehua says the father has extra toes and the puppies do, too."

"That's a genetic trait, isn't it?" David asked. It was a rhetorical question so I didn't answer.

His voice softened and he said, "My old dog, Susie, just died and I think my other dog, Pinkie, might like a companion. Do you think Lehua might let me have one of them?"

"Oh, I'm sorry about Susie. But I'm pretty sure Lehua would love for you to take a puppy. Or, even, two." I could see John waiting for me at the exit, holding the heavy door open for me.

"Eleven forty-five," John announced to us. With the door open, we all could hear the familiar warning sirens going off around town. At eleven forty-five a.m., on the first Monday of every month, all the islands' tsunami warning sirens are tested. It's both reassuring and disturbing.

David was still entranced by the puppies. I patted his shoulder and said, "See you later, David."

"Yeah, good seeing you, too." His gaze never moved from the screen.

I walked to the door and tilted my head up to enjoy the morning sun. As I brushed past John's outstretched arm and passed outside into the warm breeze, he sent me off with his usual, "Drive safe, Mims."

HONEYGIRL WAS WAITING FOR ME just where I'd left her. She's usually good that way but sometimes, I swear, when I've been gone too long, she moves. It can't be me, right? Like I'd forget where I parked? A plumeria blossom, cream colored

65

but lightly edged in pink, had floated from a nearby tree to land on the windshield and I lifted the flower from the glass to tuck it behind my ear. The left ear means you're taken and the right ear means you're available. I tucked the blossom into the elastic band holding my ponytail.

"Okay, let's go shopping," I said when I'd settled myself in the car. I checked my rearview mirror and turned my head to look over my shoulder as I reversed slowly out of my parking space but I heard a sharp crack under the tires.

"What?" I exclaimed. As I continued backwards, I could see that I had run over a small, black box on the ground. It looked like a cell phone. It was a cell phone. There was no one nearby so I put HoneyGirl in park, released my seatbelt and opened the door to investigate. It was Lehua's cell phone and I could tell that because it had a cover on it that said LEHUA in rhinestones.

"*Fuck*," I whispered to myself.

I picked up the smashed phone and climbed back into HoneyGirl. I didn't fasten my seatbelt; I just put her into forward and reparked. I rested my forehead on the warm steering wheel for a moment. "Fuck."

I walked back to the office door and buzzed the intercom.

John's voice responded immediately, "Mims."

"I need to come back inside," I said. I felt a little shaky for some reason.

The door buzzed and John pushed it open for me. I walked in but I didn't speak, I just held out the phone in front of me, for him to see.

"What happened?" John asked.

"I ran over it in the parking lot." I looked around the office in vain, "Where *is* Lehua? I saw her when I came in this morning but I haven't seen her since. I think, maybe, she was upset from having to ID that guy. Do you think it's possible she didn't feel good again and went over to the hospital by

66

herself?"

"I don't know, but I'm going to find out right now." John walked briskly down the hall until he was standing outside the autopsy room and I heard him ask, "Has anybody in here seen Lehua?"

I could hear an indistinct reply and then Sam emerged quickly from the room. He looked like he'd finished the autopsy; he'd taken off all his protective gear except for his blue cotton scrubs. Now I could make out his voice as he walked rapidly past me, towards the workstation.

"When was the last time anybody saw her? Why didn't somebody say anything to me earlier?"

John didn't respond to Sam's questions but fell into step behind him.

"I saw her when I got here, around ten o'clock," I volunteered. "She seemed a little upset about that drowning guy but, you know. She's a pretty tough cookie. She didn't seem upset enough to leave without telling anybody. I wonder if she didn't feel good and went over to the hospital on her own."

"John," Sam ordered, "get on that."

"Her keys and things are still here," John observed as he reached for the desk phone. His hand paused on the receiver and he said, "Aw, screw it, I'm just going to walk over, it'll be faster."

John moved towards the exit door but halted temporarily when Sam asked him, "Is her car outside?"

John pushed open the door and looked into the lot, "Yeah, it's right there, where she always parks. But, Mimi, where did you run over her cell phone? Were you parked by her?"

"You *what*? Why did you run over her cell phone?" Sam asked me.

"Hang on," I said to Sam, "I'll tell you in a second."

I walked over to stand by John, in the doorway, and I

pointed to a spot a couple of aisles away from Lehua's car. "No," I told him, "I was parked where I am now, over there. Her phone was under my car."

Sam looked solemnly at John and said, "Get over to the hospital. If she's not there, check with the security guards and ask if they've seen her out in the parking lot."

"Right," John answered. He walked swiftly away. The door closed behind him with a solid *thunk*.

"Mimi," Sam said to me, "would you go check the lady's locker room? Not that she'd probably have been in there for this long, unless you're right and she doesn't feel good. If she is in there, though, I don't want to go barging in."

"Sure, Sam." I was glad to have something to do, something to contribute. I was starting to feel a little panicked, partly because Sam and John seemed to be so upset.

"Oh," I said, "and I ran over her cell phone when I was backing out of my parking place. Her phone was under my car."

Sam didn't respond. He seemed lost in thought.

IT DIDN'T TAKE ME LONG to check the locker room and the restrooms. No Lehua. When I got back to the workstation, Ozzie was seated alone at the counter. "Hey, Ozzie," I said, "where's Dr. Morris?"

"In his office." He swiveled in his chair to face me. "What's going on? Where's Lehua?"

"Don't know," I answered. "When was the last time you saw her?"

"I wasn't paying attention. Maybe before ten. I was with Dr. Morris in the autopsy room all morning." The phone rang and he answered it. He listened, without responding for a moment, and then he put down the receiver, looking confused. Ozzie walked towards Sam's office and I followed. He knocked twice on the half-open door as he entered the room, more for form's sake than for permission.

"Doc, John just called. He says Lehua hasn't been over to the hospital and the guards haven't seen her, either. He's on his way back over."

"Okay." Sam's face was grim. "You got any ideas where she is?" Sam asked him.

"No, sir, I don't," Ozzie answered. "But I'm gonna go look around a little."

"Right," Sam answered.

When Ozzie left the room, I moved forward to sit in one of the chairs at Sam's desk. Sam took off his glasses and pinched the bridge of his nose, something he does when he's tired. "What the hell's going on?" he asked.

"Are you going to call Walter? Maybe he's heard from her." I knew that suggestion was an iffy one. Walter might overreact.

"Yeah, I suppose that should be my next step," Sam answered, as he slipped his glasses back into place, "but I hate to bother him if she's just looking for a little privacy."

I sensed John had entered the room so I wasn't surprised when he slipped into the chair next to mine. "Hey, Doc, Walter just called me. He's trying to get in touch with Lehua but she's not answering her cell phone," he cut his eyes towards me and said under his breath, "and we know why *that* is." He continued, "A neighbor just called him at work and said she thinks somebody's broken into their house. The front door's standing open. Walter's heading home. I didn't tell him about Lehua - just that her phone got broken. I thought you'd better talk to him."

"What the *hell* is going on?" Sam repeated. He dropped both elbows onto his desk and ruffled his hair with his hands. "Call Chief Costa for me, will you John? And tell him what's happening. Tell him we probably need him to come by here again. And ask him to send somebody out to Lehua's to check

69

on her house."

"On it," John answered, and he was gone.

"Aw, crap, I've got a meeting," Sam groaned. "Mimi, before you leave, would you tell John to page me if anything comes up? I've got to get changed and I'm already running late."

"Sure, Sam." I backed out of his office, closing the door behind me, and wandered across the hall. John was sitting in Lehua's chair, talking on the phone. I scribbled a note on a pad of paper: *Sam's got a meeting. Page him if something happens. I'm leaving.* I slid the note in front of John. He just nodded his head and kept talking.

I slipped out the door and walked back to HoneyGirl. I didn't feel like shopping any more.

BACK AT MY HOUSE, I changed into shorts and a t-shirt and then I made myself a tuna sandwich and decided to lie down on the couch for a while to read, I just wanted to let my mind relax and wander far away. I must've fallen asleep, though, because when the phone rang, it surprised me. I lumbered up and slipped a little on the hardwood floor before I got to the phone.

"Hi, Baby, what're you doing?" Emma asked.

"Oh, I guess I was taking a nap, but it wasn't on purpose. What time is it?"

"Time to come over and have some tea, but you have to hurry because it'll be cocktail time soon. What're you doing for dinner?"

"Uh, nothing, I guess." I didn't want to say anything about Lehua yet. There could be a simple explanation for everything.

"Well, come and stay for dinner, too. Mick will be here, and Katie and Kelly."

"Okay." I hoped I didn't sound like I felt, half-hearted. "I'll be there in about twenty minutes. You want me to bring anything?"

"Just yourself," she answered, cheerily. "See you soon. Bye."

7 FLOATERS

EMMA'S HOUSE is on the right bank of the Honoli'i river.
I think. I mean, how do you decide which bank is right and
which is left? Anyway, it's on the town side, nestled about two
hundred yards from where the broad, slow moving river
meets the ocean. If the weather's nice, and it usually is, we sit
outside at an old wooden picnic table and watch the palms
sway and the river flow by. When I arrived, nobody else was
there except Emma and the dogs.

"Do you want honey in your tea?" Emma asked me, as I
walked through the open front door.

"Yeah, and how about adding some whiskey, too." I plopped
down on a stool at the kitchen counter.

"Help yourself."

"Just kidding. Probably. When does Mick get home? I'm
hoping he's up to date on something that happened at work
today."

"He shouldn't be long; he just called to say he's on his way.
What happened at work?"

I tried to change the subject. "The surf looks kind of big
today. It was crowded on the road coming down here."

"It's been like that for two days," Emma answered. She
handed me a mug of tea, "Come on, let's go sit outside. What
happened at work?"

We walked, accompanied by the dogs, out onto the large
patio.

She was going to hear about it soon, anyway. "Do you remember Lehua?" I asked her. "She's the one who got mugged in the parking lot, last Friday, by that guy who drowned in the river."

Emma nodded yes.

"Well, Lehua was at work when I got there around ten o'clock this morning and then, as melodramatic as it sounds, nobody's seen her since. And I ran over her cell phone in the parking lot when I was leaving. It was under my car but it wasn't even close to her car."

"Oh, my God."

"That's not all. It looks like her house got broken into today, too. I left work a few hours ago and I haven't heard anything more so I'm hoping maybe Mick knows something. I don't have a good feeling about this."

"Oh, now I want to call him," Emma said, looking speculatively at her cell phone on the table. Suddenly, all three dogs leapt to their feet and raced through the house and out into the driveway. Emma didn't miss a beat, "But, I guess I won't have to, because here he is."

I realized that we, the dogs, Emma and I, had felt the vibrations in the air before we ever heard the growl of Mick's engine approaching the house.

Emma rose from the table and walked towards the house to greet Mick. "Drink your tea up, honey," she said to me, "it's cocktail time. It's a terrible thing to get off schedule. What do you want, wine or vodka-cranberry?"

I looked at my still warm cup of tea. "Um, wine, I guess."

After a couple of minutes, I heard Mick enter the house and the *shrick* sound as he ripped open the Velcro tabs on his bulletproof vest. He exchanged a few words with Emma and then I heard her say to him, "Mimi's outside; she's been waiting for you. Here, take this glass of wine out to her but don't start talking until I get there. I want to hear *everything*."

MICK APPEARED IN THE DOORWAY with an extra-large glass of red wine for me and a beer for himself. Barney was with him and he had his big-dog smile on. The other dogs danced behind them. "What's she talking about?" he asked as he sat down across the table from me.

From the kitchen window, we both heard Emma cry, "I said don't start talking until I get there! I'm just getting us some *pupus.*"

Mick took a swig of beer and I took a few last sips of tea. Emma soon appeared with a glass of red wine for herself and a bowl of wasabi-flavored macadamia nuts that she set on the table.

"Okay, now you can start," she pronounced.

"Start what?" Mick asked me.

"Do you know anything about a burglary down in Puna today? It was at Lehua and Walter Ka'awa's. You know, you took her to the ER last week."

"Yeah, sure, I remember them, but I didn't hear anything about a burglary. I was up at the hospital most of the day."

Oh, yeah. John had said that Mick had to chase down the tweaker husband in the hospital woods. That brought a smile to my face, which I tried to hide. I told Mick what had happened at work with Lehua.

"Can you go call somebody and find out about it?" Emma asked him.

"Yeah," he replied, "I'm going to take a quick shower, too."

Emma threw her hands up in mock exasperation. "Well, hurry up; we're on pins and needles here!"

EMMA AND I SPENT the time until Mick rejoined us, talking about small things like shoes and the ducks in the river. When he came back, Mick was barefooted and dressed in jeans and a black t-shirt and he was carrying a fresh beer.

He swung one leg over the picnic bench and straddled it. Now that he was wearing a t-shirt, I noticed that he was starting to bulk up. You know, like a man and not a kid any more. Katie said the nurses at the hospital swooned whenever he came into the ER. She actually said "swooned".

Mick took a long pull at his beer and then said, "I made some calls and I'm getting a call back in a few minutes but, for now, here's what I know. The Chief, himself, ordered a couple of cars to be sent down to Walter and Lehua's. The first car got there not too long after Walter got home; it was this guy named Carlton Puhi. I kind of know him; he seems like a good guy. That's who I just talked to.

"Walter told him the front door was wide open when he got home. Then the neighbor came over and said the door had been open like that for at least an hour and a half and that's why she'd called Walter. The house has an alarm but it hadn't been triggered and it didn't look like there was any forced entry. Walter said he couldn't find anything missing except their dog, Sweetie, and her puppies. He was really upset about that. Puhi said it looked like somebody had disabled the alarm, by entering the code, but Walter said only the family knows the code and the kids were in school and Lehua was at work."

"Didn't anybody tell him about Lehua?" I asked.

"Nope," Mick replied, "I don't even think Puhi knew about her then. So, a second car gets there, a guy named Silva. Walter thought maybe the dog had gotten upset by intruders and had moved the puppies, by herself. So, he got a leash and a box to put the puppies in, if he found them, and started searching in the nearby woods, looking for them. Silva and Puhi let him go – it gave him something to do."

"Oh, no," I moaned. "A break-in's just all they need, on top of everything else. I can't believe this is happening."

Mick's cell phone sounded and he snapped it to his ear.

75

"Daniels," he said.

Emma and I shamelessly eavesdropped, but Mick's half of the conversation gave annoyingly little information. The whole transcript would have looked something like: "Yeah...but where? Okay, I know that one. That can't...so when did that happen? Shit. Yeah, she's here. Thanks, man."

Emma and I looked at each other and rolled our eyes. That conversation would have been *so* different if we'd been having it.

Mick snapped his cell phone shut but held up his hand to motion us to wait. He took a couple of swallows of beer and said, "I'll tell you about that call in a second, but let me finish what happened at the house first." He paused to recollect where he'd been in the story, and then softly slapped his hand on the table top.

"So, they're standing there, trying to wrap their heads around what had happened to the house and the dogs and everything, when Walter got a call from Dr. Morris. I guess the Doc finally decided to tell Walter that nobody had seen Lehua for a while and the office was getting worried and wondering if Walter knew where she was. Well, Walter just sort of lost it then, and started freaking out. Then his sister, who lives close by, drives up. She's bringing his three kids, plus hers, home from school. Walter just sort of wrapped everybody into a group hug and told his sister and the kids that Lehua was missing, along with the dogs. Then everybody started crying and the sister got on the phone and started calling other relatives to come over. Puhi started to worry things were going to get out of control.

"Right about then, Silva gets a call from the Chief who tells him he's ordered a search for Lehua at the hospital, in the woods, and somebody should bring Walter back into Hilo. So Silva talks the sister into taking all the kids to her house. He's driving Walter back into town now. The kids wanted to stay and look for the dogs but Walter didn't think it was safe and, of course, Silva didn't want them wandering around the house, either. Puhi stayed behind to secure the area and wait for Crime Scene."

Mick pushed up from the table and headed back to the kitchen, saying, over his shoulder, "I gotta get another beer."

I ate a couple of wasabi mac nuts, which I don't really even like.

WHILE WE WAITED FOR MICK, Emma slipped some bobby pins between her lips and held them to one side of her mouth, like spindly, black metal cigarettes. They danced to her words as she began to simultaneously speak and pin her dark, curly hair into a bun. "The guy who mugged Lehua drowned, right? He couldn't be involved in any of this, right?" Once her hair was secured, a few tendrils quickly escaped and sprang into a frame around her face and neck.

"Yeah," I told her. "Right. They made Lehua look at his body this morning, to say whether he was the guy who mugged her. I saw her just after that. She said he was the guy and I could tell she was upset by seeing him. Floaters are really gross."

"Floaters, honey? Really?"

"Well, yeah, that's what we call corpses that've been in the water for a while."

"Honey."

"I know, but that's what they're called. Anyway, wait 'til you hear this. When they went to get the guy's wife from the woods so she could ID him, it turned out that her husband was sitting right there in the tent! Well, not sitting; they were having a big argument because it had taken him, like, three days to go get her a candy bar. Mick was there. I heard he had to subdue the guy a little."

Emma and I both silently laughed at that picture. Well,

maybe not completely silently.

"So," I told her, "everybody has to start all over again trying to figure out who the dead guy is. Because it's obviously not tent-guy."

There was a rare moment of silence between us, and then I added, "When I saw Lehua at work, it was just after she'd seen the body and that seems to be the last time anybody saw her."

"What an unholy mess," Emma murmured.

Mick rejoined us at the table. The humidity was already creating beads of sweat on the freshly opened bottle in his hand. "That second call," he told us, "was another guy I know and he said what Silva had already told me, that they're going to start a search for Lehua. Unfortunately, there aren't any security cameras in the hospital parking lot. But," he said to me, "since you found her cell phone, they're asking if you'd go back to the ME's office."

"Now?" I asked with surprise.

"Yeah, that's what they said."

"Uck," I closed my eyes and tipped my head back. "Good thing I didn't drink too much wine yet. I don't know how much more I can tell them, though. This is just too weird."

"Maybe Mick should drive you, Honey," Emma said.

"Naw, I'll probably just go on home after," I told her. Besides, Mick was on his third beer, at least.

"Well, let me send you off with some crackers and cheese, anyway. We don't want you to starve," she offered.

With a sinking feeling, on my part at least, HoneyGirl and I headed back to the hospital.

I PULLED INTO YET ANOTHER HECTIC scene in the parking lot. This time, in addition to the randomly parked cop cars, there were Fire Department vehicles and a pickup truck with crated dogs in the back. Lehua's car was still in the same parking place as earlier, but someone had put up crime scene tape around it. That disturbed me in a way nothing else had until then.

The evening clouds were underlit by the sun, as it dropped behind the volcanoes. Birds were settling into their overnight perches and an early Hawaiian bat was swooping low to snatch unlucky bugs from the air. It would be very dark within an hour.

Nobody challenged me as I walked to the door to press the buzzer. A uniformed cop, someone I didn't recognize, opened the door from the inside for me. Sam and Chief Costa were standing in the lobby again, along with a man and woman dressed in jeans and cowboy boots. Funny, how different the place looked in the evening. Quieter, lonelier, even with all the people there.

"Ah, Chief Costa," Sam said, "do you know Miriam Charles, our Forensic Anthropologist?"

The Chief looked tired. "Yes," he gave me the slightest of smiles, "we know each other. Mimi, would you mind talking to Sergeant Oshiro and going over what happened to Lehua's cell phone? He's just stepped outside but he should be right back." It wasn't exactly a command but he didn't seem to expect an answer from me, either.

"And," Sam said, "these are the dog handlers, uh, Piggy and Duffy Spencer."

We didn't reach out to shake hands but I nodded towards them both and greeted them, "Peggy and Duffy. Hello."

"Piggy," the woman responded.

"Piggy," I repeated.

Sam cleared his throat. "Would you all excuse us for a moment? I need to talk to Mimi." Without waiting for their consent, Sam put his hand between my shoulder blades and guided me into his office, where he firmly shut the door behind us and leaned back against it.

"I can't believe they brought those damned dogs," he told

79

me. "The handlers are friends of the Chief's wife so I guess he's under a little pressure from her to try them out. You know how I feel about them, though."

I *did* know how he felt about them. I felt the same way. You know, on TV programs I've seen dogs make some extraordinary finds but I, personally, have never worked with a dog that could find its own food dish. After I spent one insanely hot July afternoon in Mississippi, digging up a broken sewer line because of a dog named Duchess, I kind of lost interest in working with them anymore. But, what the hell, I didn't think they could hurt anything, either.

"And, *Piggy*?" Sam laughed. "Should we call her Miss Piggy or Ms.?" He gave a brief, tired smile and he distractedly ran his fingers through his hair. Then, in a more somber voice he said, "Walter's here. He wants to start searching for Lehua right now - and I would, too, if I were him. But we have to wait until the dogs've had a chance. The handlers need some article of Lehua's clothing to give the dogs her scent but her locker's padlocked so John's gone to rummage around to try to find something we can break in with. It all seems to be taking too long. Poor guy, I can't imagine what Walter's going through. Did you know that somebody broke into their house today, too?"

"Yeah, I heard."

"That's just crazy." Sam closed his eyes for a couple of seconds. Finally, he rallied, stood straight again, and opened the door.

I was guessing Sam felt responsible, somehow, for whatever had happened to Lehua and I was glad he could decompress with me, even for just a moment.

I FOLLOWED SAM BACK to the reception area, next to Lehua's work station. The Chief was gone but the dog handlers were still there. Sam excused himself again and went outside to join the others, leaving me there with Piggy and Duffy. The minutes were dragging by and I was feeling tense.

I glanced towards the work station and nervously tried to make small talk. "Too bad there's nothing of Lehua's here that the dogs could use."

The work station wasn't much more than an open alcove with counter top on three sides and overhead cabinets. Under the counter was a tangle of electrical and computer wires from various, generic pieces of office equipment. My eyes searched for a sweater or some other personal article that Lehua might have left behind but I saw nothing. Piggy and Duffy's eyes scanned the area, too.

Piggy noticed the computer's screen saver and moved closer to look. "Oh, how adorable!" she exclaimed. My heart really wasn't into making small talk about the puppies but Piggy didn't know Lehua. In this case, she was the one who had the gift of detachment. I know how that works.

"Yeah," I answered her, "Lehua's dog just had them. The picture's new." My stomach was feeling achy. "See the extra toes? Funny isn't it?" I noticed my voice was flat and didn't sound like I found it funny at all.

Duffy moved closer, to see the puppies, too. "Lundehund," he commented.

I had no clue what he meant, and I didn't care either.

"Oh, right!" Piggy answered him. "That's one of the new AKC breeds this year." Then to me she said, "They call them Puffin Dogs because they were bred to hunt puffin birds. Did you ever see one of those?"

"A puffin? Yes. Well, not in person - in pictures. They're pretty big aren't they? Don't they live in New Zealand or somewhere like that?"

"Oh, no," she corrected me. "They live up around the Arctic Circle. They nest on really steep cliffs and, see, that's the thing about the Lundehunds," she pointed at the screen, "they have

81

six toes, instead of the normal four for dogs, and their paws are really flexible, almost like hands. People bred them like that, to hunt puffins, because they can actually climb up the cliffs to get at the birds." She couldn't seem to take her eyes off of Lehua's computer screen.

"When puffins became a protected species, people stopped breeding Lundehunds and they almost went extinct. Back in the 1960s, there were only six of them left in the whole world; all the ones alive today were bred from those six. There still aren't very many of them, I'd guess less than two thousand."

The woman knew her dogs. I wished she'd shut up, though.

"I've heard they're hard to own because they bark a lot," she mused. "And they're hard to housebreak. And you can't leave them in the house, anyway, because they can get into *everything* - they can actually climb up into the cabinets!"

Finally Duffy spoke, "Just because those puppies have six toes doesn't make them Lundehunds. They look like some kind of mongrel mix to me."

That brought a small smile to my face. "Lehua thinks the father's a mutant," I told them. I sure hoped Lehua was okay.

Behind me, I heard footsteps in the hall and turned to see John. I felt relieved by his presence; he always seemed so calm and in control. He had on latex gloves and was carrying a bolt cutter in one hand and, in the other, a pair of women's socks.

"I got her locker open," he said to Duffy. He held out the pair of socks, "Will these do?"

Duffy and Piggy said, yes, they would do and then everything began to move very rapidly. Out in the parking lot, the dogs were quickly uncrated and the search was launched. I stood on the sidelines, just watching. Soon, I found myself standing alone in the deep twilight, feeling useless. Then I remembered the Chief's request and so I began to look around for Sergeant Oshiro.

I FOUND OSHIRO STANDING under a light post, swatting at the moths that were circling his head.

As I walked up to him I announced, "Hi, I'm Miriam Charles."

"Yeah. I figured. John described you."

"Really? What did he say?"

Oshiro shrugged. "Caucasian. Female. Blue Shirt."

Blue? For heaven's sake. My shirt was seafoam green, if I'd ever seen it.

"Well, that's me," I said. "How can I help you?"

"Just tell me what you saw here today. What happened. You know."

As I showed him where I'd been parked and told him about running over Lehua's cell phone, we strolled over to the site where it had happened. The overhead parking lot lights were on and we both could see one, loose rhinestone embedded in the asphalt. Oshiro took a flash picture of it and then he stooped to collect it in a small, plastic, evidence bag.

I told the sergeant about the conversation I'd had with Lehua when I'd arrived that morning, and that I hadn't seen her again after that. I told him I'd been with John and David for a little less than two hours and that the tsunami warning was going off when I was leaving. No one had mentioned to the Sergeant yet that David had been in the office so Oshiro realized he needed to contact him, too. I checked my cell phone and gave him David's number.

It was dark and a little overcast when we finished talking. I could hear the dogs and people in the woods, and I could see flashlights. It didn't seem like a very good time for them to search the woods but it seemed like an intolerable idea to wait. I was worried the searchers might miss something in the dark. If the dogs were any good, though, they'd be working more on smell than sight. Then I heard the helicopter approaching, overhead. Of course. I felt a wash of relief as I saw its strong search light beam on and begin to illuminate the woods and the river.

I had told Sergeant Oshiro everything I could think of and the helicopter's noise had made conversation too difficult to continue, anyway. He handed me his card and made hand gestures to tell me to call him if I had any additional ideas – or at least I think that's what he meant. I nodded yes to him and raised my hand in a goodbye gesture.

I took shelter in HoneyGirl for about five minutes, just in case something else occurred to me. But what came to my mind was *Caucasian. Female. Blue Shirt.* Seriously? A friend of mine, a professional writer, a *wordsmith*, for heaven's sake, carries around a little notebook and scribbles in it all the time. He won't show anybody what it says. But, one time, he told me he'd gone back to see what he'd written about me the first time he'd met me: *Funny. Nice.* Aw, come on. I mean, those aren't bad things. But what about vivacious, striking, colorful, perceptive, generous, light-hearted, incredibly bright, hard-working, resilient, witty, sophisticated yet down to earth? *Nice*, huh? Well, it beats Caucasian, female, blue shirt.

I went home, took a shower, had a glass of wine and went to bed, too early. I didn't sleep well and all night long, it seemed, I heard the helicopter.

8 FIBBIES

WHEN I AWOKE, it was after dawn but the sky was gray and it was raining. I couldn't hear the helicopter, but that didn't necessarily mean anything more than that its light was no longer needed for the search. I grabbed an umbrella and sneaked outside to get the newspaper, hoping nobody saw me in my oversized sleeping shirt. It was my "sick shirt" - the one so old and worn that it had holes in it, the one so soft and familiar and comforting that I saved it for when I was sick or upset.

The newspaper didn't have any information about Lehua or the search for her. Any discovery would have been too late to make the papers, anyway. I settled at my dining table, some freshly cut pineapple and a cup of sweet, cream laden coffee in front of me, and tried to do the cryptogram in the paper but I couldn't concentrate. For a while, I watched a gecko cruise slowly across the wall. I thought about shooing him outside but I knew he'd be too fast for me. It was Kitchen Gecko. We have a relationship. I'd rather he'd live outside but I suspect he considers me an intruder in his house – a nuisance. We know each other and startle each other sometimes but the house has become a shared space.

I wanted to call the office, but I didn't want to interrupt Sam or John. I felt restless and frustrated. *Not this time.* We each have our part in the loop and I'm not the only one who does a job and passes it on. People's lives or, more correctly, their deaths become numbers and reports and, then, archives. But Lehua wasn't a case. Lehua is part of my real life. I wanted, no I *needed*, to know where she was. I needed to know she was safe. I needed to know the children still had a mother. But I knew, deep down, what my greatest need was. If Walter lost Lehua, if Lehua died…. It's almost like PTSD - every time a friend, or even someone in a movie, loses a spouse, it stirs up a profound sadness in me. Memories of Jay's death come flooding back. I do care about Lehua, of course I do, but I had a second level of fear working behind the obvious concern for her safety. If I saw Walter lose his wife, my own heart would be on the edge of breaking again.

I decided to call Sam's wife, Becky. "Hey. It's Mimi. How're you doing?" I knew my voice didn't sound very cheery.

"Well, I'm tired," she replied. "Sam was up and down all night; he kept getting paged. He finally gave up around three o'clock and went back to work. He said he might as well be getting no sleep at work as at home. But, then, I still couldn't sleep anyway because the noise from that helicopter was just driving me crazy. Mimi, this is just awful."

"I know, I feel…" I heard the cutouts of sound that signal a call interrupt.

"Oh, hold on, that's Sam now," Becky told me. "I'll call you back."

"Sure," I responded, and we quickly hung up.

I SEARCHED AROUND for something mindless to do while I waited for Becky to call back. There was some ironing that I'd been trying to ignore. I turned on the TV in the living room and set up the ironing board in front of it. At least I had a sense of purpose, no matter how trivial.

While the iron was heating, I made a quick trip down the hall to my bedroom and bath. I stripped off my sick shirt and popped a toothbrush into my mouth while I grabbed some

86

jeans and a t-shirt and bra. Of course, I couldn't put the shirt on because of the toothbrush in my mouth, but I could still sort of hang the bra over my shoulders and do a one-handed pull-up of my jeans.

And then, as these things happen, the phone in my office rang. I dropped the toothbrush onto the counter, spit a mouthful of foam into the sink and ran for the phone.

"Hello?"

"Hi, it's Becky."

The doorbell rang. Crap. "Hang on Becky, I just have to get the front door."

"I can call back," she offered.

"No, no; I want to talk to you, just hang on a minute." I pulled a towel from the guest bathroom and wrapped it around myself, sarong-style, to cover the unhooked bra and unzipped jeans and dashed, phone in hand, to the front door. I rounded the ironing board like a champ and skidded up to the front door. Larry, the postman, was shading his eyes and looking through the tall window next to the door.

The TV, which I'd forgotten about, had come on to a channel with an infomercial playing at full blast for male performance enhancement.

"Larry! Hi!" I panted as I pulled open the door.

Larry gave me his usual tolerant smile. "Hi, Mimi, I've got a package for you. You need to sign for it." He held out a little tray thingy with a form on it for me to sign.

I could feel my towel/sarong starting to lose its grip. I grabbed it with my left hand and clutched it to my chest.

"Um, would you mind holding this phone?" I asked Larry.

"Sure," he suppressed a smile, as he relieved me of the phone.

I created a completely illegible squiggle on the form and we traded phone for signature pad again.

"Do you just want me to leave the box here, on the porch,

for now?" he asked, seeing that my hands were somewhat occupied.

"Yeah, that would be great. Thanks, Larry."

"No problem. And, uh, Mimi?"

"Yeah?"

"You've got some foam or something right here," he pointed to the left corner of his mouth.

Oh, God. I managed to mumble, "Thanks, Larry. See you."

I softly closed the front door. The iron had given up and turned itself off. The TV was still blaring about erections lasting more than four hours. I muted it. I walked down the hall with the towel clutched around me, back to my bedroom, when I realized the phone was still in my hand.

"Oh, God, Becky! I forgot! Sorry."

She was laughing. "I heard the whole thing!"

"Yeah," I answered, "but you didn't *see* it. I was half dressed, with unzipped jeans on and a towel wrapped around my top, and it was slipping off so I had to hold it with one hand, and my hair's a big mess and there was toothpaste foam on my mouth!"

"Mimi, sooner or later, Larry's going to get the wrong idea about you," she continued to laugh.

I plopped down on the edge of the bed. "Bless his heart. He's always so nice and helpful but he must think I'm crazy by now. He always seems to come when I'm doing something ridiculous."

"Why, what were you doing?" she asked.

"Ironing."

I could kind of tell she was shaking her head. "Well, thank heavens there are still things to laugh about," she said. Then her voice shifted and became more serious, "I just called to tell you, because I knew you'd want to hear, that Sam says they still haven't found any signs of Lehua. The dogs are exhausted and they're taking them away now."

I felt my spirits drop. Stupid dogs.

"The helicopter's going to start looking in the river for her. It's not looking good. Walter's gone back home to be with the kids. Poor guy."

"Are they looking other places besides the river?"

"Oh, sure," Becky answered. "All the cops on the island are on alert and the airports are watching for her, too. I mean, not that anybody thinks she'd leave Walter and the kids. They're saying it's just a precaution – whatever that means. Sam's so upset and tired. I know he didn't get any sleep last night but he's got to stay at work now because some guys from the FBI are coming over from Honolulu to interview him about that drowning case."

I just felt weary to my bones.

"What're you doing today?" she asked me.

"I don't know. I wish there was something I could do to help out, but I don't know what. Why does the FBI want to talk to Sam about that drowned guy, anyway?"

"Oh, haven't you heard? His fingerprints showed he'd been in prison. In Arizona, I think. Somewhere like that. He just got out about a month ago. He was Swedish or Finnish or something - and the brother of some banker over there who went missing about a year ago along with about a gazillion dollars."

"Whoa."

"Yeah. Nobody really knows what happened to the banker, but Interpol had asked the FBI to keep an eye on the drowned guy while he was in prison, just to see whether his brother might try to make contact. They quit watching when he got released."

"Oops," I said.

"Yeah, oops. Well, *now* they're paying attention, so Sam's got to spend the afternoon with them."

"But why would some Swedish guy mug Lehua?" I asked.

"Don't know."

"Do you know why he was in prison?"

"No, Sam didn't tell me. I've got a lot of questions for him when he comes home but, if I know him, he's probably just going to have a drink and some cheese and crackers and go straight to sleep."

"Poor guy, can't blame him," I said. "Well, let me know if you hear anything more about Lehua, okay?"

Becky promised she would call with any updates and then we hung up.

I TRIED TO COLLECT MYSELF. I brushed my hair, rinsed my mouth, finished getting dressed, and then stepped out onto the front porch to retrieve the package that Larry had left.

In the near distance, I could hear the helicopter again, searching the river. And in the slightly farther distance, I could see a Hawaiian Airlines plane dropping low over the bay on its way in to the Hilo International Airport. Most flights come from one of the other islands and, as far as I know, there really aren't any international flights in or out of our little open-air airport.

I picked up the box and went back inside. It had nothing special in it, just some replacement lids for my kitchen storage jars. I don't know why that would require a signature. Maybe Larry just says that for his own amusement.

My phone rang again and this time the caller ID said it was the office.

"Y'up yet?"

"John, it's noon."

"Doc wants to know if you can come back in. The Fibbies asked to interview everybody who was here yesterday morning. Since you and David and I were together, they'd like to see us all at once. David's on his way. Can you come, too?"

Without much enthusiasm, I said, "Yeah, sure." The only reason I wanted to talk to the Fibbies, slang for FBI agents, was because it might help Lehua somehow. "I'll be there in half an hour."

And then I heard the dial tone. Would it kill him to say goodbye?

I searched the refrigerator for something fast to eat and then I dressed rather quickly. I pinned my hair up, on top of my head, and slipped on a sleeveless, Hawaiian print dress. I grabbed a white cotton sweater for the air conditioning. I wore only gold hoop earrings and one bracelet. Then I added two more. Coco Channel would just have to deal with it.

I WAS THE LAST ONE to arrive at the meeting. The conference room, on the second floor of the building, is a very simple, rectangular room with beige walls, old-fashioned metal Venetian blinds and gray industrial carpeting. A long conference table, surfaced with some type of fake, woodgrain finish, dominates the space. The chairs match the black metal legs of the table and they offer uncomfortable, vinyl-padded seats – the kind that stick to the back of your legs. There's a whiteboard, as opposed to a blackboard, on one wall. The decor is magnificently crowned with florescent lighting recessed into an acoustic ceiling. Expense has been spared.

Sam was sitting at the head of the table, on the far end of the room and the two FBI agents were seated to his right. The one closest to Sam was clearly the senior of the two; he was older and had an alpha male look to him. John was to Sam's left, and then David; I sat down next to David.

Introductions had apparently already been made because Sam only said, "Mimi, this is Agent Wagner." The senior agent nodded his head to me. Then Sam looked at the junior agent and said, "And, I'm sorry, I'm afraid I'm going to mangle your name, maybe you should say it."

The younger man gave me a thin, humorless smile. "Thomas Brinkerhoffenstein."

"Yes," Sam continued, "and this is Miriam Charles, our Forensic Anthropologist."

"Good afternoon," I said. The FBI unsettles me.

"Agent Wagner," Sam announced, "I'm just going to turn this meeting over to you, now."

The chair in which Agent Wagner sat was not a reclining one but he was leaning back in it about as much as he could. At Sam's words, he grabbed the table's edge and pulled himself more upright. He paused to scan all of our faces. His steel gray hair was naturally streaked with some silver highlights and his haircut style looked like he hadn't changed it since the sixties. To my astonishment, he was chewing gum. That didn't seem very FBI to me but maybe he had a medical reason for it, like acid reflux or something. I saw his tongue shove the gum over into his left cheek and then he began to speak.

"We have been sent here to interview you all for two reasons." I noticed a southern accent, not twangy but from the Deep South. "One, we are acting on behalf of Interpol in the hopes that information you have may shed light on the whereabouts of a man, the brother of the recent drowning victim y'all are working on. And, two, we are seeking information about the abduction, itself."

Abduction? Did he mean Lehua? I could tell from the others' reactions that this was news to them, too. Before any of us could respond to what he'd said, though, Agent Wagner continued, "I'm going to go ahead and turn the rest of this meeting over to Tom, here." He nodded to Brinkerhoffenstein and then sort of fell back into his semi-reclining pose again. Agent Wagner looked like he had one foot edging over the line of retirement; I guessed he was probably grooming Brinkerhoffenstein to take over the job when he finally put his wingtips out to pasture – or wherever old wingtips go.

All heads turned to the younger agent. He cleared his throat and officiously shuffled some papers, then tapped their bottom edges on the tabletop to straighten them. When he spoke, he didn't make eye contact with any of us, but seemed to address the papers.

"At the moment, and most urgently," he said, "I am looking for information about two days: last Friday when Ms. Ka`awa was assaulted, and yesterday, when Ms. Ka`awa disappeared."

"Wait a minute," Sam interrupted. "Agent Wagner said 'abducted'. Are you talking about Lehua? Do you have reason to think she was kidnapped? Why are we searching the river for her if you think she's been kidnapped?"

"I'm sorry," Agent Brinkerhoffenstein replied stiffly, "I can't reveal information in an ongoing investigation."

I could see a vein pop on Sam's left temple, and his face began to color, but his voice stayed steady. "If you want our cooperation, then you'd damned well better reconsider that position. We're all law enforcement here and Lehua is one of us. As far as I know, we could all be in danger." Sam turned to Agent Wagner, "What is this bullshit? Are you going along with this?"

Agent Brinkerhoffenstein looked at David and me and said, "*They're* not law enforcement."

I saw the vein pop on Sam's right temple. "This meeting is over," he announced as he began to rise from his chair.

"Jeez, Tom," Agent Wagner said to his protégé, "take it down a notch. We want their cooperation. And Mrs. Charles and Mr. Chung, as consultants to this office, should be accorded the same level of respect as Dr. Morris." I noticed he only called Sam by the title, doctor.

Sam was burning mad; I knew that look. He was standing at the table's end, leaning forward so that his fists rested on the tabletop, like a knuckle-walking, silverback gorilla, ready to charge. He had locked eyes with Brinkerhoffenstein and was staring him down. Without breaking his gaze, Sam said, "Why don't you take back over, Agent Wagner?"

There was a tense silence and, finally, Agent Wagner gave a resigned sigh and said, "It looks like that might be the best way to proceed."

At those words, I saw Sam relax, just a notch. He slowly shifted his eyes to Agent Wagner, who held his gaze and gave a single nod of his head. Sam dropped back into his chair. In a dead-serious voice Sam said, "You can start by telling us why you think Lehua has been kidnapped."

Agent Wagner wearily leaned forward in his chair again. He raised his hand to his mouth and placed his chewing gum into a scrap of paper, torn from the edge of one of the many papers in front of him; he folded the paper multiple times until it was a minute package. Agent Wagner was, apparently, not the kind of guy who hurried.

"Well, first off," he told us, "you might have noticed Tom used the word *abducted*, not *kidnapped*. Kidnapping implies someone is being held under some kind of condition, like ransom. Abduction just means taken. And, yes, unfortunately we're talking about Mrs. Ka'awa. Her husband, Walter, found a note this morning when he got up; it was tucked inside the screen door of his house. It was, apparently, written by his wife. The first thing she said was that Mr. Ka'awa should not tell anybody about getting the note - advice which, fortunately, he ignored. She also said she's fine; she doesn't know where she is but she knows why she was taken and she'll be released soon, within a couple of weeks. She asked her husband to please not look for her. Mr. Ka'awa confirmed that it was her handwriting."

"A couple of *weeks?*" David exclaimed.

"Yes," Agent Wagner replied, "that's what the note said. And there was no mention of ransom, or any other conditions, for her release." He paused, and then added, "And, by the way, the Bureau has suggested that the County helicopter be retasked since we've found no evidence to suggest that Mrs. Ka`awa is in the woods or the river."

"So, what's your plan?" John asked. His voice surprised me. I realized, at that moment, that John had stayed quiet and nearly motionless throughout all the agitation.

Wagner blew a little puff of air from his lips, "Well, for now, we're trying to collect and review all the evidence. I, personally, am favoring the possibility that the abduction is somehow tied to your drowning victim. It's just a lot of coincidences that a guy we already had our eyes on, came here to Hilo, accosted Mrs. Ka`awa, then turned up dead, while she went missing."

He did have a point about the coincidences but I couldn't imagine how they all could fit together. It also seemed like a big piece of the puzzle was missing so I spoke up, "Would you please explain – Dr. Morris probably already knows some of this – what the Interpol connection is?"

"Actually, I *don't* know very much about that," Sam groused. He shifted in his chair and directed a scowl at Wagner.

Agent Wagner leaned back again. He really didn't look so good. Maybe he had acid reflux *and* his back hurt, or maybe he was constipated; there were so many possibilities. Hemorrhoids?

He addressed his answer to Sam, rather than to me, "Well, as you probably already know, INTERPOL stands for International Criminal Police Organization." He pronounced police in the rural southern way, with an emphasis on the first syllable. "Their headquarters are in France and what they do is, they coordinate police searches between countries. In the beginning, Interpol just did that for Europe, but now hundreds of countries have joined in, including the United

95

States. Interpol doesn't make arrests - it doesn't even have a police force or jails; all it does is coordinate. Okay?"

I nodded understanding even though Wagner was still speaking only to Sam. Sam was stone-faced. Didn't scare me, because I know Sam, but it seemed to be unnerving Wagner.

"So," the agent leaned forward and tapped a light pattern on the table top with his right index finger, "about four years ago, your drowned guy, Mr. Eskil Bentson, was on the mainland where he got himself arrested for auto theft. The guy is, was, from Norway and he was in the U.S. on some kind of legitimate visa. Then the genius stole a bait car."

Still getting no response from Sam, Agent Wagner turned his eyes to me and continued, "You know what a bait car is?"

I found his tone somewhat condescending, even though I really didn't know what a bait car was.

"Bait cars are decoys the police leave out on the streets, just hoping somebody will be stupid enough to steal them. They have locator-transmitters planted in them. Bentson was known to be part of a ring that was stealing cars and driving them over the border into Mexico - so it's not too surprising that he took the opportunity to boost a real nice car when he found it, just sitting there."

Wagner continued his intermittent table tapping. It didn't seem to be a nervous tic, it was more like some kind of internal Morse code. "Well, this particular car he stole, he didn't go to Mexico with it like he usually would have done. It was a real nice, customized convertible that had been confiscated in a drug bust. Bentson seemed to be having himself a little *staycation*, just cruising around town in it, picking up hookers and letting the wind blow through his hair. The cops were following him the whole time, hoping he'd lead them back to his ring, but he never did. They finally decided not to wait any more and they busted him for just being so damned stupid and annoying. Pinhead refused to cooperate or give up any of his people. He got sentenced to four years for car theft and that landed him in one of those private prisons. Tallahatchie, Mississippi - not a country club.

"Now, here's an interesting fact, and one that I think may be relevant to us. In Tallahatchie, Bentson's cellmate was a fella named Nelson *Kuali'i*. He's originally from here, on the Big Island. We're guessing Kuali'i might have something to do with why Bentson showed up in Hilo after he got out of prison. But, for now, it's only that - a guess. When that new prison for Hawaiians got built, the one in Arizona, Kuali'i got transferred there but Bentson stayed behind at Tallahatchie. So far as we know, that was the last time the two of them had any contact."

This time, I knew what he was talking about. A few years back, Hawaii tried to save money by closing down state prisons and sending the inmates to private facilities on the mainland, run by Corrections Corporation of America. It was *not* a popular policy. The prisoners from Hawaii had a lot of trouble integrating with the mainland prisoners and ended up starting a gang called the United Samoan Organization. The USO membership soon spread from prison to prison and then, unfortunately, back to Hawaii. To try to deal with the problem, Saguaro Correctional Center in Arizona was opened to exclusively house prisoners from Hawaii. All of Hawaii's mainland prisoners were transferred there from other CCA prisons around the country, including Tallahatchie County Correctional Facility in Tutwiler, Mississippi.

SO THE DROWNED GUY, Bentson, had been cellmates with a Hawaiian guy. When Kuali'i was transferred away to Arizona, Bentson stayed behind in Mississippi.

Wagner continued, "Kuali'i is still at Saguaro; he's got another three-to-five to go. The Bureau's sent an Arizona agent to do an interview. We haven't heard back from him yet, though."

Or *her*, I thought, relatively sure I was the only one at the table doing that mental edit.

"Eskil Bentson, he stayed at Tallahatchie until an early release about a month ago. Day he got out, they deported his sorry ass back to Norway." He squirmed a bit in his chair. "We don't know how he got back into the U.S. again, but these things do happen."

Wagner stood up. I didn't think he had finished speaking but he wordlessly turned to fiddle with the window blinds. And then he just stayed there, with his back to us all, staring out the window. His hand moved to his pocket and then up to his face and I saw his jaws working and realized he was chewing gum again. Nicotine gum, maybe? I saw Sam and John shoot glances at each other. Wagner hadn't really explained the Interpol connection yet and I was just about to break the silence and ask him about it again when he turned back to us and resumed his story.

"The reason Interpol got involved isn't because of Eskil Bentson at all, though; it's because of his brother, Anders. That guy's a whole 'nother story. Anders Bentson was a banker in Norway, an 'upstanding member of the community', as the cliché goes. But then, one Monday about a year ago, he just didn't show up for work. He and his wife were missing - just gone. Their house was all torn apart. At first, the police in Norway thought they were dealing with an *abduction* and they wasted some time investigating it that way. Pretty fast, though, they realized that a shitload of money from his bank was gone, too." Wagner quickly glanced at me and dropped his eyes. "Sorry," he murmured.

Wagner thought I was too delicate to hear the word *shitload*? I thought about trying to blush, for John and Sam's amusement, but I knew I couldn't pull it off.

Wagner sat back down at the table, on the forward edge of

his chair, and said, "As soon as they realized something fishy was going on, Norway asked Interpol to put out a watch for Anders and Anna Bentson. Apparently, it didn't take more than a couple of days until notice came in from Switzerland that Anna had been seen on a surveillance camera at a bank in Zurich. After that, both Anders and Anna Bentson went completely off the map and nobody's seen them since. That's why Interpol asked us to monitor Eskil Bentson's prison communications. You know, just in case Anders tried to make contact with his brother." Wagner shrugged his shoulders and raised his eyebrows a little in a 'why not?' gesture to indicate what an easy task that was.

"We started that watch about eleven months ago and saw nothing. We thought we were off the hook when Eskil got released and deported back to Norway. Next thing we know, here he is again. In Hawaii. Dead."

"Alright," Sam seemed slightly less irritated. "So, what do you want from us?"

Agent Wagner slumped back in his chair again and said, "Well, like Tom was saying, we just need to go over everything you all can remember that might have anything to do with Mrs. Ka'awa's disappearance. I mean, Bentson's identity is confirmed, right? And his cause of death is explained. But we still have some big questions left about what he was doing here, in Hawaii, and why he assaulted Mrs. Ka'awa, and whether he has any connection to her abduction. And, also, of course, whether there's any possible connection to Anders Bentson and the missing bank money.

"We've checked but found no evidence that Bentson ever visited the hospital. It almost looks like he was targeting Mrs. Ka'awa for some reason. We've also checked with taxi and bus drivers and nobody remembers transporting him to this area. The police are going to interview his former cellmate's family to see whether any of them is aware of Bentson's presence here in the islands."

"Well, let's just get on with it, then," Sam groused. "We've got other work to do."

The rest of the interview brought up no new information for me. All anybody really knew was that sometime between about ten o'clock, when I arrived at the office and spoke to her, and eleven forty-five, when the tsunami sirens were blaring and I ran over her cell phone, Lehua was abducted. *If* she was abducted. There appeared to have been no witnesses to anything unusual in the parking lot and, because her phone had been out of sight, under my car, no one had noticed it.

JOHN AND SAM STAYED BEHIND with the agents but David and I left. We walked together out of the building into the midafternoon sunlight. David's blue Volvo was parked just a few stalls away from HoneyGirl.

"I just don't get it," David pondered. "The note sounds like she's okay, but *a couple of weeks?* What the hell is that about? Do you think that's just some kind of creepy delaying tactic so nobody looks for her?"

"I don't know," I replied, helplessly. "I kind of wonder if I could've made a difference if I'd just stayed with her for longer that morning, talking or something. This just sucks. And I feel really bad for Walter and the kids; nobody's even mentioning them."

"Do you know if they ever found their dogs?" David asked.

"No," I rubbed my eyes, "I don't know anything. Do you think it would be interfering or out of place for us to call Walter, or go visit him?"

"Jeez, I don't know. My wife wanted to send flowers but I thought that seemed too much like Lehua was dead. They've got a big family circle, so I'm sure they're being fed."

We both smiled at that. They were probably being

100

inundated with food. I imagined the kids were being smothered by aunties and uncles and *tutus* and cousins, and that Lehua's fear, that Walter would be staying at home and making a mess, was now coming true.

A very light mist whispered over us from a small, dark cloud coming in off the ocean. We could have stayed there talking if we'd had anything more to say, but we didn't, so we both went on our unsettled ways.

9 PREGNANT BANANAS

IT WAS MIDAFTERNOON and it wasn't sprinkling at my house so I telephoned my neighbor, Stephanie, to ask whether she wanted to go for a walk. I needed to work off some of the stress from the day.

Stephanie lives on a cul-de-sac, about half a block from my house. When we walk together, we do about two miles, moderately fast. Half of our course is up pretty steep hills, so that means the other half is down pretty steep hills. Our walks are probably more aerobic than other people's because we talk the whole time.

I put on exercise shorts and a tank top. My shorts didn't have a pocket so I slipped my cell phone into my bra. A stray thought about radio waves and cancer flew through my brain, but it didn't take up roost. I locked the front door and jogged down the driveway.

In the near distance, I could see Stephanie walking down the hill to meet me. She had a relaxed smile on her face. Walking usually raises my spirits, too, so I hoped maybe the endorphins would cancel out the radio wave issue.

As soon as we were in earshot, Stephanie spoke up, "How are things at work? Do you have an update on Lehua? I've been hearing bits and pieces on the radio but they seem to be doing a lot of speculating."

"Yeah, that seems to be their way. I've been down at the office this afternoon, getting interviewed by two FBI guys, which was not that much fun. As far as I can tell, nobody seems to have much of a clue about anything."

"The FBI? Why were they here? What happened?"

"Well, they're thinking that maybe this thing with Lehua ties into a crime that happened in Europe. It's complicated. Mostly, all they wanted from me was to hear everything I could remember, all over again. But they did tell us something really crazy. They got a sort-of ransom note."

"What! But that means they know she's alive!"

"Yeah, it should mean that. I hope it does. I shouldn't have called it a ransom note, though. In fact, it's specifically *not* a ransom note. The FBI guy was very particular about his terms. Lehua handwrote it, herself, and in it she said she's fine and please not to look for her - which is so *not* going to happen - and that she'll be back in a couple of weeks. *Weeks.* There were no demands made at all."

"Like she's having an affair or something and just wants to be left alone for a while?" Stephanie asked.

"I didn't really get that sense off of it and I don't think anybody else is thinking that way, either. I was imagining more that she really is being held by somebody who just gave her a pen and paper and told her what to write. David...you know him, David Chung?"

"Yeah."

"David's worried that whoever took her might be trying to buy time. It really terrifies me that somebody might hurt her."

"How can something like this be happening *here?*" Stephanie shook her head in disbelief. "So, what's the FBI going to do?"

"I have no idea. They've really come here for some European, Interpol-related thing, and I'm worried that's what they're most focused on, instead of Lehua."

"What's the European thing? Can you talk about it?" Stephanie asked.

"Yeah, I guess I can, mostly because I don't know much of anything that hasn't probably been in all the newspapers in Europe already." I explained the whole car thief with a banker-brother story to her.

"Our meeting with the FBI was kind of tense because Sam and one of the agents were butting heads. In Sam's defense, the guy was kind of a jerk. You know how they say young rattle snakes are the most dangerous because they haven't learned how to judge what's appropriate prey yet? It was sort of one of those situations. The guy was just green and cocky and he pissed Sam off.

"But, basically, Interpol had asked the FBI to keep an eye on the drowned guy while he was in prison because they wanted to see whether his missing banker-brother might try to contact him. Oh yeah, I forgot to tell you, when Bentson was in prison, his cellmate was a guy from here, Big Island."

"Oh. That's probably significant, isn't it?"

I shrugged my shoulders.

"So, how did Eskil get back into the U.S.?" she asked.

"Nobody seems to have an answer for that one. So much for Homeland Security, though."

We crested a hill and turned onto a more heavily used road.

"Is that all," Stephanie asked, "just the two FBI agents? There should be more people out looking for Lehua. She can't be far away; we're on an island for heaven's sake."

"Yeah, it seems like it's just the two FBI agents. And the police. But, you know, I still don't get why anybody would have taken her in the first place. All I can think of is it's something to do with work. Or maybe she saw something out where she lives...like a pakalolo farm that needs a few weeks before it's ready to harvest. Her house got broken into, too."

"The newspaper said nothing was missing."

"Well, that's not exactly true," I told her. "Their dog, Sweetie, and her puppies are gone."

104

"Are you kidding? Like, somebody stole them?"

"No. Believe me, they're cute but they're definitely not show-dogs or anything. There could have been other stuff missing, too, but Walter didn't notice. He's under a lot of stress."

"I can imagine," Stephanie sympathized.

"The FBI guy thinks Eskil had something to do with Lehua's disappearance. I can't imagine how, though. It's crazy."

We turned off the main road, onto a small lane, and walked past beautifully landscaped houses with small waterfalls cascading over bare lava rock in their yards. There was a stand of wild, white ginger at the end of the lane and we both stopped to take a deep breath of the fragrance. Then we turned around in the cul-de-sac and started to retrace our route.

For the rest of our walk, even though we changed topics, I felt myself gathering determination. I was set on keeping my nose firmly stuck into the cause of Lehua's disappearance – I wasn't willing to consider any alternative.

THE SUN WAS SO LOW, when I walked up my driveway, that its rays were dancing in golden spots high in the tree tops. I stood for a while, appreciating the view of my backyard. There's no problem getting things to grow here; quite the opposite. If you aren't careful, vegetation will just take right over. I looked to the top of one of the Queen palms. Up high, maybe thirty feet off the ground, in the thickness of the fronds and date clusters at its crown, an autograph tree had taken up a home and grown to about three feet tall, and from the side of that, a fern had taken hold. Plants growing on plants growing on plants.

I noticed a few fallen avocados on the ground and walked over to retrieve them. One had already been pecked at by birds so I picked it up and tossed it over the fence and into the jungle. I gathered three good ones, though, to take inside. They were starting to ripen faster than I could eat them.

Next to the avocado trees was a stand of bananas. One tree had a bunch of apple bananas ripening on it. In the same group there was another tree, taller than all the others and, about a week earlier, the gardener had pronounced it pregnant. When I expressed surprise, he'd said, "Can't you see it? Look how thick it's getting at the top; it's pregnant now." Who knew?

The birds were noisily settling into their nighttime roosts. As I turned to walk to my own roost, I felt a blast of energy. The birds flew out of the trees. The ground moved beneath me and I heard a rumble. I swayed to keep my balance but I dropped one of the avocados. It took my brain a moment to register that an earthquake had just rocked me. The unnerving thing about earthquakes is I never know whether they're preludes to bigger ones to come, or not. I hesitated to go inside the house. Finally, I decided to just wait outside for a moment. I retrieved my well-warmed cell phone from my bra and sat down on the grass to text my friend, Rob. He'd just moved to Hilo, from Los Angeles.

Did you feel the earthquake?

We have quakes, daily, but most are so small nobody feels them. Our earthquakes aren't the same as the west coast ones, generated by tectonic plate movements. Ours happen because large fields of old lava just slump; they're compressing down. There can be some residual shaking but, mostly, they feel like one big thump. An earthquake can generate a tsunami, too, especially if a lava field calves into the ocean. We haven't had a significant tsunami in more than fifty years but one rule about living here is, if you feel an earthquake while you're near the ocean, you should get to higher ground right away.

Within two minutes, I got an answer to my text:

Sure did. 4.4 epicenter Honomu

That was fast, he must've had some sort of app on his phone. I hadn't realized the information would be available so quickly. *Honomu* is only about ten miles up the coast from Hilo, so no wonder I'd felt the quake. I texted back:

That's what earthquakes feel like here –
one big bump.

His reply shot right back. *I was like OMG!*

Do you want to have dinner tomorrow
night? You choose the place.

And, so, life was back to normal that fast. I decided not to worry about aftershocks. I answered yes to Rob's text, picked up the avocados, and went back inside the house.

I MUNCHED ON some salted nuts while I mentally reviewed what I'd had eaten so far that day. I concluded that I needed to eat better. I used to be such a good cook when Jay was alive.

I opened the refrigerator to peruse the offerings. Friday's ham sandwich was still there. Not worth the risk. I tossed it into the trash.

I was feeling restless so I grabbed some more nuts and turned on the TV. Outside in the dusk, it started to rain, lightly at first but soon harder and harder until it was making so much noise on the steel roof that, no matter how much I turned up the TV's volume, I couldn't hear the dialogue. I tried putting on captions but they were so badly spelled that I couldn't follow the story. Finally, I just gave up and decided to go snuggle into bed and read a good mystery. It had been a long day. Again.

10 POHOIKI

WEDNESDAY MORNING DAWNED, barely, through heavy gray skies and a steady rain. Gusts of wind throughout the night had rocked the trees and several times I had heard the deep, concussing thuds of large palm fronds dropping to the ground.

I shuffled, still in my pajamas, up the hall towards the kitchen. I glanced into the back yard to see if there were any downed avocados to pick up before the birds got to them. To my dismay, I saw that my pregnant banana tree had toppled over. It was about three times my weight and there was no way I could right it by myself. I decided to think about it later. First, I needed breakfast and the newspaper.

I checked the street to confirm that none of my neighbors was watching and then I scurried out the door, grabbing a faded black umbrella and popping it open. With one hand, I wheeled the large garbage can in a slightly drunken path down towards the street and the newspaper box. I was half-way there when something cool and wet plopped onto my head and then moved rapidly down my back, under my pajama top. It was not a raindrop.

I gave an involuntary squeak and dropped the umbrella, grabbing at my top. Something fell at my feet; it looked like a tiny twig but it was twitching violently. I bent to look more closely and that's when a gecko leapt from somewhere on my body to the ground and rushed away. It was missing its tail, which it had apparently jettisoned in its escape attempt, and I realized that was what was twitching on the ground. Icky, icky, ick. Ick. Ick. Note to self: next time, check the umbrella better.

By then I was rain-soaked but I inanely raised the umbrella over my head, anyway, and continued to the foot of the driveway. I left the garbage can there and grabbed the newspaper out of its sheltered box and hurried back to the house. The day was not looking fabulous so far.

A quick scan of the newspaper revealed no update about Lehua. I squished my way to the laundry room where I peeled off my sodden PJs and dropped them with a splat onto the floor, and then I went to take a nice warm shower.

I had gotten up a little early with a specific goal in mind – eating better. Wednesday is a Farmer's Market day in Hilo. Booths at the vibrant marketplace are full of exotic tropical fruits and vegetables, alongside stalls of brilliant flowers and local handicrafts. So, even though it was still pouring rain, I decided to roll up the cuffs on my jeans, wear some rubber slippers, and head to town. Just because it was raining at my house, didn't mean it was raining at the market.

AS I DROVE PAST THE ME'S OFFICE and the hospital, I slowed down to check out the parking lot. It looked like it usually did - no crime scene tape, no search dogs, no cops milling around.

I continued down the hill, past Carvalho Baseball Park, Hilo High School and the public library. I noticed that the massive slab of rock in front of the library, the one that *Kamehameha, the Great* is said to have lifted to prove his right to kingship, was covered with offerings of flowers and *tī* bundles, all getting soaked by the rain.

At the bay front, I turned right for a few blocks and then slowed to search for parking. The closer I got to the marketplace, the harder it rained. I drove into the municipal

110

parking lot across from the Farmer's Market but the only empty stalls were under coconut trees. Number one tip for maintaining a car in Hawaii: do not park under coconut trees. Or, and for the same reason, do not stand under them.

I reentered the stream of traffic on Kamehameha Avenue. A ragtag group of guys was splashing through a soggy soccer game in the field next to the road. I was starting to rethink the whole marketing idea and had just turned mauka, up *Pauahi* Street, poking along, when my cell phone rang. I fished my Bluetooth out of the cup holder in the central console, flipped it open and hooked it over my ear.

"Hello," I answered.

Nothing.

"Hello," I repeated. I wondered if I had the ear thingy connected right. "Oh, for heaven's sake, *hello.*"

"Mimi?"

It was John. My heart froze. He hadn't asked if I was up yet. Oh, God, please let Lehua be okay. I could hear other voices in the background.

"John?"

"Hey, I've been looking for you. Can you come to the office?"

"Yeah. I'm downtown. Do you need me right away?"

"Soon as you can. They've found a body out by *Pohoiki*, back in the woods there, and they're waiting for us."

"A body? It isn't...."

"It's not Lehua."

"Oh, thank God." I felt my heart racing from adrenaline and worked to calm myself. "Okay. I've got to go home and get some things. I should be there in probably around, like, thirty minutes."

"Right," he said, and hung up. I guessed that meant we'd be driving together since he was waiting for me.

POHOIKI IS A SURFING SPOT in an area just south of the eastern-most tip of the island. It's inside a park called Isaac *Hale* Beach Park, named after the first Hawaiian soldier killed in the Korean War. It's not much of a tourist destination because the currents there are too rough for easy swimming and there really isn't much of a beach, but locals know it's a good surf break, plus it's the only boat-launch ramp in the whole Puna district. It's in a sparsely populated area and I was not especially surprised to hear that someone had discovered a body there.

Dense green jungle grows right up to the edge of the very short, steep beach at Pohoiki. Loose, black stones on the beach have been rounded by thousands of years of wave action; in time, they'll get pulverized into black sand. On this island we have white sand beaches created from coral, and black and green sand beaches created from lava. But Pohoiki is too new to have formed sand yet. Each new wave washes the softball-sized stones up the shore with a whooshing sound, and then the same wave recedes with a louder, clattering noise of the stones falling back towards the ocean. It is not comfortable at all to have your feet in the way of the rushing wave of stones. One of the most amazing things about Pohoiki, though, is that volcanic activity heats the ocean water at the boat ramp to bathwater temperatures. Really, warm saltwater waves are some sort of beautiful dream to me.

I drove back home quickly and collected my things. On the way out the door, I grabbed an apple and a bottle of water. Sometimes at a recovery site somebody brings us lunch, but I wasn't counting on it.

JOHN WAS LEANING AGAINST PUA, the office's old converted ambulance. He had on hiking boots, worn jeans and his usual navy-blue HSME polo shirt. *Pua* was idling and ready to roll, carrying all the shovels and buckets and assorted equipment that we usually need in the field. I climbed up into the passenger seat while John settled himself on the driver's side. It was going to take about an hour to get to the site - we probably could have gotten there faster, because there are still functioning lights and sirens on Pua, but we were not responding to a life or death situation…well, not in that sense. Pua carries a heavy load and is an extra-wide vehicle, and John is a slow, cautious driver.

"Any news about Lehua?" I asked, as I clicked my seatbelt into place.

"No, not about her, but there's a little bit about the dead guy."

I waited for more. Finally, I prompted, "What is it?"

"There's no record of him re-entering the U.S. after his deportation but apparently there is a *third* brother and Passport Control shows that he flew into Hawaii about a week ago."

"What? Oh, wait, let me guess," I said, "he and Eskil look a lot alike."

"They were brothers."

"So Eskil probably used his brother's passport to get back into the U. S. What's this third brother's name?"

"Lars."

"Any more Bentsons around that might pop out of the woodwork?"

John shifted his eyes over to me and gave a little smile, "You never know, but the Fibbies say it's just the three of them."

"Well, has anybody been in contact with Lars? I mean, *did* he really come over here last week, or did Eskil use his passport?"

"Lars's passport was used to enter the U.S. three times in the last year. The first time, about six months ago, it looks like he just did a quick turnaround in New York; he was only in the country for four days. The next time, there are credit card records showing he actually did come to Kona. Eskil was still in prison back then. Right now, though, Lars is in Norway and he's having some problems explaining why his passport shows him coming into Hawaii a week ago and never leaving again. He says it must have been stolen."

"Yeah, right. But it's a pretty big coincidence that Lars was here just a couple of months before Eskil showed up, huh?"

"Yep, Norway's a long way off."

The police band radio came alive in the truck's cabin. I've never been able to understand it. Maybe I can make out one or two words, but mostly it sounds like someone purposefully speaking gibberish.

John picked up the microphone and said, "She's with me. We're about forty minutes out."

There was another spate of static and gibberish and then John reseated the microphone.

"What was that?" I asked him.

"You couldn't understand, could ya?" John smiled at me; I amuse him. "That was the crew down at Pohoiki. They just wanted to know when you're going to get there. They've ordered you some tripe stew for lunch and they want to make sure it's hot when you get there." He was kidding. I hoped. Tripe stew's a local favorite, just not one of mine.

I decided not to take the bait. "Any other developments?" I asked him.

"I'm going to let Brinkerding tell you about those."

"I don't want to talk to that guy; I don't think I like him. I want you to tell me."

John was silent.

"John?"

"You didn't say please. What's happened to your manners?"

"Oh, bloody hell. *Please.*"

114

John shifted in his seat and reached outside to adjust the sideview mirror. "Since you asked so nicely," he said, "I will tell you." He tapped the mirror again to get it just right. "The Bentsons are from Oslo and the family has an old estate there. Anders, the banker, being the eldest of the three brothers, inherited it when his parents died; he and his wife, Anna, lived there. When they disappeared last year, since they didn't have any children and since Eskil was in the can, the youngest son, "Passport Lars", moved in and kind of took over their lifestyle, including their two, new Volvos in the garage, the income from some rental cabins on the property, the country club membership, even the family dog. Old Lars seems to have been living a pretty good life with his two brothers out of the picture."

"They left their dog behind? What kind of people do that?" I realized I was assuming they actually had left on purpose, absconding with a shitload of money.

"Lars seems to be taking good care of the dog," John reminded me. "He even took it with him on that trip to New York."

"Wow. That's expensive. Why would he do that for such a short trip? Didn't you say it was just for four days? Did he bring the dog with him to Hawaii, too?"

"Doubt it," he answered. "You know that's a hard thing to do."

"So," I pondered, "since Lars is so comfy in the family home, he probably wasn't very happy to see Eskil when he got deported back there after prison. Maybe Lars just handed over his passport and encouraged Eskil to leave again and start over somewhere far, far away. Maybe after Lars had vacationed here he suggested it to his brother and it didn't have anything to do with Eskil's Hawaiian cellmate, after all."

"Could be." John shifted in his seat and I could tell, from the experience of many trips taken together, that he had

115

exhausted his chattiness for the time being. More talk would just make him uneasy. So I made myself as comfortable as Pua's bench seat would allow and, except for a few small comments between us, the rest of the trip passed in silence.

AS WE NEARED POHOIKI, we entered Mango Alley, a narrow road - really just a single lane – bordered on both sides by old, stately mango trees. Their upper branches have grown together over the road so that it looks like you're driving through a green tunnel. When the mangoes are ripe, you can just stop, open your car door, and grab the fallen, fresh fruit from the road. But the mangoes weren't ripe yet. As we drove along, we were sheltered from the rain by the leaf canopy, with only occasional big plops of water hitting the roof of the cab and the windshield.

Since there isn't room for two-way traffic in Mango Alley, it's an established courtesy, an aloha thing, for cars to find spots to pull to the edge of the road, as far as possible, so that others can pass. But *everyone* was pulling over for us – probably it was the unnerving sight of the HSME's ambulance going towards the beach. News travels fast here; some of the drivers may have already known why we were there.

The road ends at a T intersection, with a very small coastal lane to the left and a small parking area and boat ramp, to the right. The black, lava rock coast and the crashing waves of the ocean are just a short distance past the intersection and a half moon bay stretches out, off to the right, where an artificial breakwater of massive boulders and concrete forms shelters the boat ramp.

I could see a cop in an orange rain slicker with reflective stripes on it, turning away traffic from the parking area and boat ramp. The cop recognized Pua, and John, and waved us forward; we pulled into the parking area and stopped, at an idle. I counted six police cars in the lot. Someone knocked on my window and I turned in my seat to see a familiar face, Eddie Paiva.

Eddie's a detective; he's been gradually working his way up the command chain over the years and has just made captain of the Criminal Investigation Unit. Maybe that's why he's getting a little gray at the temples. His medium height frame is still trim and fit looking, though. As I rolled down my window, Eddie lifted his large umbrella to shelter us both from the rain. The outside air smelled of salt spray and wet rocks.

"Hey, Eddie. What've you got going here today?"

"We got a present for you, over there, across the bay. We set up some tarps, you see 'em? They're way over there, on the other side." He turned his head and stared in the direction he was talking about, across the half moon bay, as though that might help me see. The windshield was sheeted with water and everything was blurry; I couldn't see much of anything past Pua's hood.

I held my tongue. I would have preferred to survey the area myself before anybody walked around there much. I imagined all the feet that might have trampled on possible evidence while putting up the tarps. I just had to trust that Eddie had seen to it that the scene was thoroughly checked before the tarps were pitched.

"Okay. I'll walk over there and take a look," I told him. "And then I'll come back and get whatever supplies I need." I turned to John, "Does that work for you?"

"You're the boss."

Well, sort of. At a recovery site like this. Nice of him to say.

"Okay, Eddie, I'll be right with you." I released my seat belt and rolled up the window as I watched Eddie walk a short distance away to say something to the cop directing traffic. John inched the ambulance over to a parking space and turned off the loud, diesel engine. The windows immediately

117

began to fog up from our bodies' heat. I pulled on my rubber boots and zipped up my rain jacket, pulling the hood up, and then I tugged at the heavy door handle.

"I'll follow you in a minute," John told me.

We both climbed out of the ambulance and I saw John head for the men's rooms. The steadily falling rain was warm and, even though there was a cool onshore breeze, my jacket blocked it and I knew I would start to feel clammy soon.

I STARTED OFF BY MYSELF, walking to the right of the boat ramp, past a small, red house that perches right there, wildly close to the water. I'd been on the trail plenty of times before and knew my way well but I still had to watch my footing on the wet, loose rocks.

Soon, Eddie caught up to me. We walked a moment in silence and then he said, "A guy taking a piss found him."

"Again? What is it with guys?" It's an unbelievably common way for bodies to be found: by men ducking into the bushes off the highway for a quick pee, men wandering away from picnics for a whiz in the woods, men taking a few steps off the path to take a leak. Men, urinating in and on nature.

"I'll bet he uses the porta-*lua* next time," I said.

"Yeah," Eddie chuckled. He was just being polite. It wasn't that funny. He changed the topic, "Hey, how's everybody at your office holding up? About Lehua and all?"

"Stressed. But, you know, besides her family, I think Dr. Morris may be taking it the hardest. He always feels like he's responsible for everything that happens there. You got any news? John and I were talking on the ride down here and he told me a few new things about the drowned guy's family."

"You mean about the third brother and the passport and all?"

"Yep. You have any other news?"

"Nah, I've had my attention down here all morning. I went

118

out to Walter and Lehua's on Monday when the break-in was reported but I've been involved in other cases since. Well, I shouldn't really call what happened at their house a break-in; that place is alarmed up like Fort Knox. I think they had a burglary once before and Walter's just about put a moat around the house. Whoever got in, punched in the alarm code. I'm guessing it was probably Lehua."

I could hear voices and see the two, bright blue tarps about a hundred feet ahead in the undergrowth. I was startled by what Eddie had just said, about the idea that Lehua had punched in the code, and I wanted to ask more but I needed to stay focused on the task at hand. So I postponed my questions until we had a break later in the day.

"Is that Cyd?" I asked him.

"You know her?"

"Yeah, I do."

I can't remember any more how I first met Cyd but it was a while back, when she was stuck in a boring job, trying to make ends meet. Only recently did she land her dream job, as a crime scene photographer. This was going to be the first time we'd work together.

As Eddie and I left the path and neared the closest tarp, I saw four male cops sitting under it on folding, tripod seats. There were boxes of gear and a couple of coolers scattered around. What Eddie had called a tarp was actually a large, vinyl, picnic tent, maybe twenty by ten, with its own aluminum frame and poles. The rain was sheeting down the vinyl and creating a curtain of water around the perimeter.

At the sight of their captain, the cops quickly got to their feet. They were all dressed in their black, short sleeved, uniform shirts with their matching black cargo pants tucked into polished, black, lace-up boots. Lots of black. They also all had on black HPD baseball caps and orange rain jackets.

Cyd was about thirty feet away, so absorbed with snapping

pictures that she didn't even notice my arrival.

I pulled my jacket hood forward and ducked my head as I passed under the mini-waterfall at the edge of the canopy. The cops knew who I was, they'd been waiting for me to arrive, so Eddie just went counterclockwise around the group to introduce them to me. I grabbed a notepad and pencil from my pocket and quickly jotted down their names and a one word description of each one, as a memory aid. And just in case any of them saw my notes, because those guys seem to notice *everything*, I kept the descriptions neutral:

1. *Craig Medina – glasses*
2. *Carlton Cunningham – blonde*
3. *Brandon Atagi – smile*
4. *Mitch Kaupu – wow!* (I wrote *tall,* even though Brandon was a little taller.)

I tried not to stare at Mitch. But. Just. Wow. His features and golden brown skin looked mostly Hawaiian although I guessed that, like Sam, he had some haole ancestry, too. He had thick, slightly curly black hair, deep brown eyes and a strong jaw with a Hawaiian, rounded-square chin – more George Clooney than Cary Grant. Full, almost sensual lips were smiling at me, with just a little tilt to the smile, revealing even, white teeth. The lips were smiling at me and I was aware that time was ticking by. I felt a rush of embarrassment. I want one of those, I thought. I want a man again. Well, not just any man. I want a good man. Jay was going to be a hard act to follow. I dropped my eyes to my tablet and felt my mouth close. Lord, had my mouth been hanging open?

Finally, at the sound of all of our voices, Cyd looked up and called me by name. She gave a little wave and came to join us. I was still struggling to focus my attention on work.

120

"As you can see," Eddie said to me, "We have two tarps up. This one's for us and our equipment and the other one's sheltering the body. The guy's tent is over there."

I scanned the area briefly. The body, which was about twenty feet away, looked like a mostly skeletonized human, still clothed. It was lying on its back, as though the person had just stretched out there for a nap and gone permanently to sleep. Except, it looked like the legs were bent at the knees so that the shins and feet were tucked a little bit under the thighs, and to the left. Sort of a classic, drop to the knees and then fall backwards, pose. Another twenty feet, or so, beyond the body there was a small, nylon, two-person pup tent, in camouflage colors. An assortment of garbage bags, filled with recyclable bottles and beer cans, and other throwaway items, including a single bicycle tire, littered the area around the tent.

John appeared from the trail behind us and wordlessly joined the group. He didn't need an introduction.

"The guy's tent," Eddie continued, "is crammed with stuff, even a battery-powered TV. I don't know how he could fit inside of it, himself. Craig and Carlton are going to inventory it and Brandon and Mitch will be available to help you out, however you need."

"At first glance," I said, "you know, knock on wood, it looks to me like this is going to be a fairly straightforward recovery. Everything appears to be on the surface and pretty much intact. Have you swept with a metal detector yet?"

"No."

"Okay, just let me do a quick surface survey and then I'd like somebody to do a sweep with the detector while I'm getting my things together. You don't have to go too far out right now, just about a ten foot perimeter around the body. Who'll be doing it?"

Eddie looked a little abashed. "Our detector guy isn't here."

"That's okay," John broke in. "We've got a detector in the truck. I'll do it."

"Alright," I said, "I'm just going to do a little walk around this immediate area while John gets the equipment. And you guys," I addressed Carlton and Craig, "can go ahead and get started with your tent inventory. Just, you know, try to keep the foot traffic to a minimum."

Eddie nodded at them and said, "Get to work."

Craig and Carlton shifted gears and immediately began to gather their equipment. They looked glad to finally have something to do.

I turned to Cyd, "What have you photographed so far?"

"I've just been taking pictures of the general area and the tent, from a distance," she told me. "I stayed away from the body."

Good instincts.

"Okay, then," I said. "John, would you grab my canvas bag from the truck when you go back? And, Cyd, would you mind waiting here?"

"No problem," Cyd replied, and she settled herself on one of the vacated tripod chairs.

Eddie sent Brandon and Mitch along with John to help carry things and then, looking around as though he were missing something, he said, "I'm going to go back to the parking lot, too, for a minute. If you need anything, just send Craig or Carlton."

AND, SUDDENLY, I WAS ON MY OWN. The first, organizing moments of the day set the tone for the rest of the project and, so far, the atmosphere felt cordial and easy. The supervising police officer, in this case Eddie, makes all the difference in the way an investigation goes. When I was starting out, a few times I had trouble with older, tough guy detectives and it had taken a while to gain their respect.

Sometimes it was a question of just having to wait them out or, with others, having to out-macho them - never gagging or barfing or acting repelled by what we were dealing with. I also stored up an arsenal of jokes. Even if they were trying to ignore me, once they'd joined in laughing at something I'd said, everything eased up. I hope all that macho bullshit is a thing of the past.

I noticed, with relief, that the rain was beginning to lighten. I kept my hood up but unzipped the jacket's front.

Typical of tropical forests, the tree canopy overhead blocked most of the direct sunlight from reaching the ground so the vegetation on the forest floor was sparse and consisted mostly of rotting, fallen branches sitting on a spongy carpet of wet leaves. There were isolated patches where the light penetrated, though, and vines and thick mounds of philodendrons grew in those spots. A small hillock of those plants was blocking the sight line between the footpath and the body and tent, explaining why a discovery hadn't been made sooner. Although, you'd think somebody would have smelled it.

I approached the body, being very careful where I stepped, and knelt down next to it. I felt cool dampness soak into the jeans fabric at my knees. I was on the body's left. To avoid confusion, in anatomy and medicine, left and right always refer to the body's, not the observer's, left and right.

The skull was partially exposed and mostly clean, although patches of dark brown, decomposing tissue adhered to a few areas. On the shady forest floor, the bone hadn't sun bleached. The cranium was face up, but was tipped slightly to the left. The mandible had separated from it and righted itself. A few of the upper, or maxillary, front teeth had fallen out of their sockets (more properly called alveoli) and they were lying where they had fallen. None of the teeth showed any dental work, as far as I could see, although there were some large

123

cavities visible. And under the cranium, there was a muddy mass of dark hair and sloughed scalp tissue with very small, beetle-like insects crawling busily through it.

The smell was the typical, putridly sick, sweet smell of death. It's similar to the taste in your mouth after you've vomited until there's nothing left to vomit - that kind of acrid, nasty sweetness. The smell would surely have been much worse a few days earlier, at the height of maggot activity.

The soaked clothing had slowed down decomposition a little bit on the parts of the body that were covered, but the areas of the long bones that were exposed to the air were nearly skeletonized. Joints, at the elbows, knees, wrists and ankles were still held intact by the tough tissue of the tendons.

The clothes on the body were men's clothes – a dark brown t-shirt with the logo of a brand of motor oil on the front, no belt, a pair of black and green, plaid boardshorts and some inexpensive, black rubber slippers. A worn piece of macramé with three small white shells incorporated in its weave was still in place around the distal right radius and ulna – the wrist area.

The body appeared to be intact, even the small bones of the toes and fingers, along with their nails, were present. Rats wouldn't be interested yet. They usually wait until bones are dry - at least a year - because they gnaw on them to get at their calcium.

Of course, a woman can wear men's clothes, and vice versa, but one quick look at the skull gave me plenty of indicators that Eddie's assumption was right - the remains looked male. I'd take the bones back to the lab and measure them and run analyses on them to make sure of it but my eye is as trained to see the traits of age, race and sex on bare bones as most people's eyes are to judge those characteristics on a living person. I mean, sure, there are times for all of us when we see

124

somebody on the street and think to ourselves, *Is that a man or a woman?* Likewise, there are times when it's hard to read the signs on a skeleton. Usually, though, sex and race are pretty obvious. Age is tougher, just like it is with living humans, because some people just age better than others.

I scanned the corpse for any obvious signs of trauma such as bullet holes, stab marks or blood stains on the clothing. Nothing stood out to me.

"CYD," I CALLED OUT, "would you come over here?"

"Sure." She quickly rose to her feet. Her short, blond hair was covered by a green baseball cap. She had on a clear, plastic poncho draped over a gray t-shirt, khaki pants and a khaki vest with a lot of zippered pockets for all her bits and pieces of photography equipment.

As she neared me I said, "Can you just stand there and take some pictures of the body, from a few feet away, to show its general position and condition? We can take more detailed photos later, after the metal detector gets here."

"Yeah, sure."

"Is this your first body?"

"No, I did a stabbing last week. But this is my first skeleton. It's not as bad as I thought it would be. I mean, it's kind of smelly, but it's not awful."

"Yeah, this one's not too bad. They can be way worse."

"Oh, my God, Mimi!" She broke into a big smile, "I can't believe we're working together!"

"Crazy, huh? Look at us. Who'd ever guess this is what we do?"

I spotted John and Eddie, followed by Brandon and Mitch, returning from the parking lot. Cyd and I lowered our voices to near whispers.

"Did you see Carlton?" she asked me, "He's adorable!"

"Yeah. You and your blondes. But what about Mitch?"

125

Cyd gave a soft moan. "That is one fine looking man. You've gotta know women faint just so he'll catch them. Hell, I think I feel a dizzy spell coming on right now."

We both shook our heads in wonderment and laughed softly together but then straightened our faces and our attitudes as the returning men drew nearer.

Brandon and Mitch stopped at the canopy to drop off the equipment they'd carried back but John and Eddie walked over to stand next to Cyd and me. John was holding the metal detector at his side, with the attached earphones wrapped around the base of his neck.

"Where do you want me to start?" he asked.

"Uh, hang on a sec," I softly said to him. Then I raised my voice a bit, "Brandon and Mitch, I have something I'd like you to do, please."

They walked over to join us.

"I know you already did a ground search of the area before John and I got here but I'd like you two to split up and just walk around again. The skeleton seems to be complete so you don't need to be looking for bones or teeth but I want you to poke around in the bushes and *pukas*. Birds and insects can carry away all sorts of stuff from a body. It's usually light-weight, of course, so look for pieces of cloth and hair, shot gun wadding, that sort of thing. Wear gloves and be careful where you put your hands. I don't want you to get bitten by a centipede." Blessedly, Hawaii doesn't have snakes.

They both looked a little amused by their task but they set off, good naturedly, to comply.

I returned my attention to John. "Sorry, I just wanted to get them started on that. I think if you start with the detector about ten feet out and sort of walk in tighter and tighter circles until you get back to the body, that should do for now. I can already see some brads and a metal zipper on his pants but check for metal everywhere, especially around his chest

126

and head and hands. Are the tent poles going to bother you?"

"Naw. I'll work around 'em."

John knew what to look for - things like rings, bullets, broken knife tips and coins. We both knew he'd also find junk. Even off the beaten track, humans have scattered a surprising amount of litter over the earth's surface.

While John worked, I stepped back to stand with Eddie and Cyd. John could hear the beeps of the metal detector through his earphones but, obviously, we couldn't. He stooped a few times to brush away leaves or soil only to discover rusted screws and old bottle caps. Not until he began to pass the detector over the body did he begin to talk to us.

"It sounds like both pants pockets have something in them," he said as he continued to slowly sweep the flat, Frisbee-shaped detector back and forth. "And I think there's something over here, too, under the left side of the head." Finally, he lowered the detector to the ground and dropped the earphones back onto his neck and said, "That seems to be it."

"Could that thing by the head be a bullet?" Eddie asked.

"Maybe," I answered him, "but I don't think so. I haven't seen any trauma to the skull yet. But, you never know. It could also be an earring, or something."

"Oh." Eddie seemed a little disappointed.

"Do you guys want to use the detector for anything?"

"No, I think we're good," he answered.

"Well, don't put it away," I told John. "We should do the area underneath him after we move the body."

I FOLLOWED JOHN as he temporarily stowed the metal detector and earphones under the equipment canopy. The rain had stopped.

"You bring gloves?" I asked him.

He didn't answer but he opened a metal footlocker that

127

Brandon and Mitch had carried in and extracted a box of size small gloves for me. Of course, he'd remembered.

I had developed a plan for handling the corpse. I turned to look back at the body. "I think what I want to do here," I said to John, "is just to slide a piece of board or something, underneath the body and then pick up the whole thing and take it back to the lab. That'll be easier than trying to process it here. What do you think?"

"It's your call."

"Well, I know that, but I guess I want to know if you think it will work, logistically. Like, do we have equipment with us that would work for that?"

"Yeah. We could slide him onto a stretcher first and then put that onto a gurney. We've got a canvas pole-stretcher in Pua. There's no gurney here but I'll call back to the office and get them to send the van down here with one." He was referring to the smaller HSME van that was used to transfer bodies from the scenes of death to the morgue. We don't usually transport bodies in Pua.

"Okay," I said, "that'll work. Even if they leave soon, we'll have over an hour to get the body onto the stretcher."

"I doubt they'll get here that fast," he advised me, as he took out his cell phone. "I'll call them while I go get the stretcher." He raised the phone to his ear as he walked off towards the parking lot, again.

Brandon had appeared out of the overgrowth and had been waiting quietly while John and I talked. I could see he was gingerly holding something in his gloved hand.

"What've you got?" I asked him.

"I'm not sure." He held his hand out for me to see. "It's a nest I found in those vines over there. I think there might be some hair in it. It's kind of matted down, though, and it doesn't look exactly like human hair. Maybe it's pig hair or something." Mitch came to watch and Eddie walked closer, to

128

join us, and craned forward to see, too.

"Looks like pubic hair to me," I said. Brandon recoiled a bit. I was just jerking his chain. I mean, really, if he'd thought about it, the body was still clothed so it wasn't very likely a bird had gotten to the pubic hair.

"Just kidding," I told him. "But it's actually kind of close to that. I think it may be from a beard. Why don't you go put it in an evidence bag? And ask Cyd to take a picture of the place where you found it, okay?"

He nodded yes to me and walked over to talk to Cyd. He was carrying the nest at a greater distance from himself than he had been before.

I REALIZED I WAS still holding the box of latex gloves that John had handed me.

"What time is it?" I asked Eddie.

He glanced at his watch. "Thirteen-fifteen. You hungry? We got some bento boxes, but," he paused, "John said something about you wanting tripe stew instead." He had a big fat grin on his face.

"No," I said in an exaggeratedly sweet voice. "Thank you so much for thinking of me, but I believe I'd prefer the bento box."

"Right. I'll send Mitch. What kind of drink you want? We've got cans of soda or POG."

"Oh, no contest. POG, please." Passion fruit, orange, guava juice – POG.

On the mainland, working at isolated sites like this, the lunchtime fare is usually sandwiches and sodas. Hawaii's the only place I've ever gotten a bento box. I'm sure that , traditionally, they came in Japanese bamboo or lacquer boxes but now they come in plastic "clamshells". Modern day bentos in Hawaii usually contain a selection of fish and meats, including the ubiquitous spam, pickled vegetables and

129

seaweed and, of course, rice. They come complete with small packets of soy sauce and chopsticks, rolled in a paper napkin. It's not exactly health food but it's a step up from baloney sandwiches.

We'd gotten a late start and I felt like the day was slipping away from me so, while Mitch went to fetch the bentos, I said out loud to myself and to Eddie, "Back to work".

I plucked eight gloves from the box - four I stuffed, as reserves, into my jeans' pocket and then I double gloved my hands. I also slipped a small trowel from the equipment locker into my rear pocket. My jacket got tossed on top of my canvas satchel.

Eddie followed me over to the body where, once again, I knelt next to it. Really, it was amazing that no dogs or wild pigs had disturbed it.

I reached for the cranium and very gently tipped it to its right, so that it was facing skyward, and then I carefully lifted the mass of hair and scalp that had been resting underneath it. Earwigs scattered from the mass, some crawling over my gloves. I shook them off. Maggots began to roil and churn in the damp, fluid-soaked soil. When I saw a small glint of metal, I let the mass drop back into place. The metal was probably what John had picked up on the detector.

"Eddie, would you please look in my canvas bag and bring me the little, white plastic ruler and an erasable marker?"

He found them right away and brought them to me.

"Now," I continued to speak to him, "put the case number and date in that clear space on the ruler and then set it down here, next to the skull."

I wanted to have the ruler in the photographs but I didn't want to touch the marker or the ruler with my own hands at the moment; they were kind of slimy from lifting the scalp.

Eddie complied with my request with his usual competence. Normally I would have asked Brandon or Mitch to do such a minor task but they were both busy, doing other things.

Cyd rejoined us from photographing Brandon's nest and I addressed her, "I need you to squat down here next to me and, when I lift the head and hair gunk again, I'd like for you to take a picture of what's underneath. I see some metal and I want to get a photo of it *in situ* before I pick it up. Make sure you get that ruler with the case number in the photo, too, okay?"

"Yeah," she said, as she studied the scene. "I think I need to try with, and without, the flash. It's kind of dark under this canopy."

"I'll get some evidence bags," Eddie volunteered.

"Thanks. Would you also grab some of those little orange flagsticks over there, too?" We keep little orange flags, the kind that people use to mark seedlings in their gardens, as markers for the position of evidence at sites. It would be nice to have the little plastic-tent markers that I've seen used on the mainland but, you know, budget restrictions.

Cyd knelt next to me, camera at the ready, and I leaned forward and lifted the mass of hair and scalp again. "Oh, yeah, I see it," she said.

I gave her time to take three or four shots. "Done?" I asked.

"Mmmhmm."

"Well, stay right there. I'm going to lift whatever it is out of the soil and I want you to document it."

I took the trowel from my pocket and, about two inches away from where I could see the glint of metal, I carefully angled the blade under the object and slightly raised about a quarter of a cupful of earth underneath it. I paused there and Cyd took a couple of pictures. Eddie was back and he handed me a flag that I slipped into the ground where the metal had been. Next, I lifted the trowel and its contents about four inches above the ground and Cyd took a few more shots.

131

Eddie handed me a brown paper evidence bag and I placed it flat on the ground, resting the trowel and its scoop of earth on top of it. The soil fell loose pretty easily, exposing a simple, gold hoop-earring. It was still clasped but the ear it had fit into was no longer around. I put the plastic ruler next to the earring and Cyd took a few more close-up photos.

I tipped the earring and a little soil into a tiny, sealable plastic bag, and dropped that into the larger, brown paper bag. Cyd and I stood and I pulled my gloves off, inside out, and carried them over to a biohazard bag under the equipment tarp. That's it; I'd been there a couple of hours and all I'd done was to recover an earring. Not like TV at all.

"PAIVO," EDDIE'S VOICE WAS MUFFLED by a bite of rice and katsu chicken. The rest of us quietened our lunchtime talk while Eddie listened to his phone for a long while, without speaking. "I'll call you from the road," he finally responded to the caller and then snapped his phone shut.

"Gotta go," he said to us all. "Mitch, you take over here. I don't think I'll be back soon, if at all, today."

He began quickly gathering his things. Over his shoulder, he said, "Mimi, see you later. Are you going to be in the lab tomorrow? I'll come by and see how you're doing, if you are."

"Yeah, I expect so; I should be spending most of the day there."

Eddie resealed his bento box with a rubber band, to take with him, while he continued talking. "John, good seeing you. Mitch, stay in touch with me. I've got a thing to see to in Orchidland. Sorry to have to leave so fast."

I couldn't say he left at a trot but he was certainly walking very fast. I wondered what was going on in Orchidland but, once again, none of my business. Probably.

We were all quiet for a moment, left in the wake of Eddie's departure. Then conversation started back up again as we finished our lunches. Coupled with the humidity, it was starting to feel uncomfortably warm. I noticed that Craig and Carlton, who had been working in the guy's tent, were perspiring heavily.

Carlton was seated, cross-legged, on a flattened, plastic trash bag on the ground. "Man, that tent's hot," he said to Mitch. "Do you think the captain would mind if we take our uniform shirts off?"

"It's fine with me," I volunteered. "There's nobody around and it's probably going to get even warmer." Hey, *carpe diem*.

"I don't see why not," Mitch decided. He took the initiative and unbuttoned his own shirt; the others followed suit. They all had on their standard, black t-shirts underneath. Tight, black t-shirts. I could see Cyd bite her lip and give me a little thumbs-up. Yeah, life is good. Well, for some of us – maybe not for the guy on the ground.

WHILE WE WERE FINISHING UP our lunch, Craig told me he and Carlton had found a wallet with money and ID, in the tent. "But the Captain told us not to tell you what it said. He told us you don't want to be prejudiced before you start doing your work in the lab."

"That's right," I said, slightly surprised. "Thanks." It's great for me to be able to verify my findings against a known ID – *after* I've finished my report. But, if I hear ahead of time who it might be, that information could, unconsciously at least, influence the pathways of my thinking. "I am *not* saying this officially," I told him, "and I could change my assessment later, but it appears to be a white male."

Craig and Carlton exchanged glances.

"What?" I asked them.

"Are you sure about that?" Carlton asked me.

"No. I just told you, I could change my mind about it once I do more work in the lab. I probably won't, though. I'm pretty

133

sure it's a white male."

"It's just that Craig and I were thinking the wallet wouldn't still have money in it if it wasn't really his. You know, if he stole it or something."

"Oh, just give it to me," I said, with resignation. I had a feeling I could resolve this pretty fast.

Craig jumped up and jogged over to the tent, returning quickly to hand me the wallet. He had put on gloves and he held the wallet open for me so I could see the driver license picture and information. The picture was of a distinctly Asian man, named Devin Kitagawa.

"Nope, it's not him."

Craig and Carlton squirmed a little. I could see that they doubted me but were being too respectful to say so.

"Craig," I said, "tell me what the height is on that license."

Craig read it carefully and then said, "It says five feet five inches."

"And what's the age?"

"Twenty-three."

"Okay," I said to the two of them, "men usually over-report their heights on driver licenses. And women under-report their weights. But, for academic purposes, let's go ahead and assume he was truthful this time. So he was just a little taller than I am."

I reached into my canvas bag and retrieved a cloth tape measure. I stood up and measured the distance between the bottom of my left patella, my knee cap, and the front of my ankle.

"This bone," I told them, "my shin bone, is called a tibia. Fourteen inches. Write that down."

Carlton used a paper napkin to scribble on.

Craig was still standing in front of me. I reached forward and tugged on his pant leg until he stepped closer. I felt around for the bottom of his patella and, when I found it, I put the tab end of the tape measure there. Then I dropped the tape down the front of his leg until I reached the same spot on his ankle, more or less - since he had on boots - that I had used to measure my own tibia's length.

"Seventeen inches," I reported. "Craig, how tall are you?"

"Just about six feet."

"Okay, five feet eleven," I said with a smile. I saw him blush a little.

"Write that down, too, Carlton. Now, both of you come with me over here to the body."

Cyd, Mitch and Brandon walked over with us, too. John stayed put.

"This bone, right here," I said, pointing to the corpse's exposed left tibia, "is the same bone I've just measured on Craig and on myself. Craig, since you've got gloves on, would you mind measuring it?" I handed him the tape measure and showed him where to place it.

"This is just for the purpose of explaining to you guys what my logic is. Of course, I'll do a much more exact measurement later on. Okay, so," I asked Craig "what does it measure?"

"Sixteen and a half inches."

"Common sense should tell you that taller people are usually going to have longer legs than shorter people, right? So, doesn't it make sense that this guy, who has a tibia close in length to yours, Craig, is going to be closer to your six-foot height than to mine?"

"Yes, ma'am."

"Alright, so what I'm saying is, this body here doesn't seem to me to match the height on the driver license you found in the tent. Besides, the age and race are wrong. Kitagawa's a young man – this person was at least middle aged. If I were you, I'd check your computers to find out what Devin Kitagawa is doing these days and how his wallet got here."

135

"The Captain was going to check the records when he left," Carlton told me. "He said he'd call when he got the information."

"Alright, then. I've got to get back to work figuring out who this guy really is," I said. "And if you two find any more wallets over there, don't tell me."

"HERE'S THE PLAN," I told Mitch and Brandon. "First, I want you to take this canopy down so the poles don't get in the way. Then, we're going to try to transfer the body from where it is now, onto a stretcher. Once the gurney gets here, I'll need you guys to help lift the stretcher onto it. The remains won't weigh as much as a fresh corpse, but it will still be pretty heavy, and we sure as hell don't want to drop it. When we get the body out of here, I'll go to work checking the ground underneath it. After you move the canopy, I want you to get some evidence bags ready - write the case number and date on them. I'm going to bag the hands and feet separately, so you can get some bags ready for that, too. Label them 'right hand', 'left hand', 'right foot', and 'left foot'." I thought for a minute and then added, "And label another small bag, 'teeth'. Everybody double gloves, got it?"

"Yes, ma'am," they both responded.

I turned to Cyd, "Just take a lot of pictures. Try to get all the phases of the transfer. If you need us to halt for a minute, or to move so you can get a better shot, say so, okay?"

She nodded assent.

I returned to the body and carefully examined the hands and arms again for signs of trauma, such as defense wounds. I wanted to make sure I wasn't disturbing any evidence by moving the body.

When people are being attacked, it's common for them to defend their face and chest by putting their hands up. Women tend to put their right hand, palm out, in front of their face and their left hand, also palm out, in front of their throat and heart. Men tend to react differently. They typically put their left hand, palm out, in front of their face but pull back their right arm a little, ready for a counter punch or a grab for the other person's weapon. So defense wounds are more common on women's right arms and men's left arms. The markings can sometimes be very subtle, just tiny hairline fractures.

I didn't see any obvious signs of defense, or any other wounds on the hands or arms so, with Mitch and Brandon's help, I placed the bones from each hand and foot in separate bags. I also separately bagged the cranium and its mass of hair and decomposing scalp, the mandible, and the loose teeth. I put all the bags into a cardboard box, which I stuffed with wadded paper as cushioning. It's important that the bones and teeth don't knock around during transport because they could crack or abrade against each other. When I'm back at the lab looking for signs of trauma to the skeleton, I don't want them to be masked by damage done to the bones while we were moving the body.

Finally, we were ready to try to move the bulk of the now headless cadaver onto the pole stretcher. Pole stretchers used to be just a sheet of canvas suspended from two long, wooden poles, which also served as handles. In that form, they played a big part in past in wars and other types of emergency evacuations. Pole stretchers are a little more evolved now; the poles are aluminum and the sheet is nylon and there are cross bars underneath the nylon so the sheet doesn't sag.

Brandon and I both squatted to the right of the corpse, Brandon at the chest and I at the legs. We reached over and across the body and very gently lifted its left side while John and Mitch eased the stretcher under the body as far as they could push it, about halfway. Then Mitch joined Brandon and me and we lifted the right side of the body and just sort of slid it the rest of the way onto the stretcher, while John kept the whole thing from skidding over the ground. The body held together remarkably well. But it was still gross and stinky work.

The four men picked up the stretcher and moved it a few feet away. John laid a sheet over the top of it.

Where the body had lain there was a depression, an outline of the corpse in dead leaves and dirt, and a honeycomb of insect tunnels. And a hypodermic needle. Cyd photographed it. I bagged it.

"We'd better get that analyzed," I said to John, needlessly, of course. I said it out loud, though, so that the cops would hear and be assured that it would be done.

I SAT TO ONE SIDE, making notes on my clipboard while John reswept the site with the metal detector. I'd drawn a scale map of the body and of the area around it and I'd been adding to my notes all day.

Cyd came to sit next to me.

"Did you get pictures of where that nest was found?" I asked her.

"Yeah, Brandon showed it to me. That was beard in there?" She gave a little shudder of disgust.

"Looks like it. Not too surprising to find a beard on a guy living out of a tent, like this."

"I never liked beards," she declared. "So many of these Puna guys look like mountain men or prospectors or something. It's hideous."

I laughed. Hideous was a strong word.

"When I was in college," I told her, "I kind of went through a beard phase, but I don't like them much, any more. It seems like a distancing thing, like a man's putting up a barrier to the world."

"They're excluding themselves from the dating pool, is what they're doing," Cyd shot back. "They're saying 'I don't like sex' or," she groused, "anyway, they're not going to get any from me."

"Really," I joked, "if shaving's too much of a daily challenge, how could a man ever manage to give *me* all the attention *I* need, sweetie darling? But you know my friend Stephanie, the one who lives up the block from me? She *likes* beards. They turn her on. She's actually attracted to them."

Cyd was on a roll. "When I see a beard, I think, *Could I kiss that face? No!*" But then she admitted, "Well, at first, I want a clean-shaven man and then, maybe later, a little stubble is sexy. One time, I was kind of interested in this guy who had a beard. When he found out I didn't like them, he shaved it off. I was impressed."

I became aware that John had quit using the metal detector and was standing nearby, headphones off.

"Nothing," he told me. "I'm going to go back to the truck and put this away."

I stood back up and busied myself taking soil samples from where the body had lain. Poison or drugs from the stomach or other organs could have leeched into the soil when the body decomposed. You never know. I was almost ready to leave and I hoped the gurney would arrive soon so John and I could head back to town.

While I was labeling the soil samples, Mitch approached me. "The Captain just called. He asked me to tell you that Devin Kitagawa is alive and well. He reported his wallet missing about a month ago. He thinks he left it in the men's room when he was down here at Pohoiki."

"So, that explains that," I replied. "I'm just about ready to finish up here. As soon as they show up with the gurney, I think we can take the body back to the lab and leave the rest of the scene to you."

"Sounds good to me." Looking past me towards the path, he added, "I think I might see them coming now."

139

11 BED AND BATH

TRAFFIC LEAVING HILO WAS HEAVY and, even though we were going against it, it was slowing us down. The rain had started again, too. We'd just passed the usual bottleneck in *Kea'au* when the appointment reminder on my cell phone chimed. I'd completely forgotten that I was supposed to have dinner with Rob, my friend who had just moved to Hilo.

"Uh-oh," I said to John, "do you mind if I make a call?"

"Nope."

I quickly dialed Rob.

"Hi," I greeted him, "I've been out of town today, working on a case. I'm just on my way back to the ME's office now. I'm tired and I'll have to go home and change clothes and shower. Could we do dinner another night?"

"Of course we *could*," he reassured me, "but why don't you go on home and have a nice bubble bath or something and I'll bring dinner to you? I can just whip up some pasta. Do you have some wine?"

"I've got to admit, that sounds nice. I do have wine. Are you sure that's not too much trouble?"

"No problem at all. I'll just let myself in if you're in the bath. Do you have some nice bath salts?"

"Yes," I laughed, "I think I have some jasmine bubble bath."

"Well, I'll see you in about a couple of hours, then. Will that work for you?"

"Absolutely. Thanks so much. See you then." I disconnected the phone.

John looked at me with one eyebrow raised.

"He's gay," I told him. "He just moved here but his husband, Alex, has had to stay in L.A. until their animals are ready to be brought over. We were supposed to have dinner together...."

"It's not that," John interrupted me. "It's – you got jasmine bubble bath? Really?"

"I can be girly when I feel like it."

"Mimi," he turned and looked me straight in the eyes, "I've got no doubt you're a girl. A woman." He shifted his gaze. "I just think lavender might be more your scent."

"Makes me sneeze," I told him. "What do you use? I don't suppose they make bubble bath with Old Spice scent."

"I wouldn't know, I'm a manly man. I only use flea and tick soap." After a pause he said, "I guess you won't be coming in to work tonight, then."

"God, no. I just want to go home and get out of these clothes."

John raised his eyebrow again.

I opted to change the subject. "Have you heard anything more about Lehua? I've been thinking about her all day." I knew John was staying plugged in to any progress on finding her.

"Not much. They've been doing some interviewing but it doesn't seem to be leading anywhere. That Kuali'i guy's family apparently doesn't hear from him very much and none of them has gone to visit him in prison, on the mainland. Some of his family knows some of Lehua's and Walter's families, but not well.

"I heard Walter says pretty much the same thing. He only knows Kuali'i by reputation from when they were teenagers. The guy was considered bad ass. Walter didn't even know he

141

was in prison, but he wasn't surprised to hear it.

"The FBI interviewed Kuali'i in Arizona yesterday. He said he remembers Eskil Bentson, of course, and that Bentson used to want to hear about the Big Island all the time. He thinks Bentson got used by the Mexican car-theft ring because he looked so haole and could fit in better in neighborhoods where they were targeting their high-end thefts."

"So, nothing very useful then," I noted.

"Nothing really stands out to me."

"There's something I want to run by you."

No response.

"Something my friend, Stephanie, asked me. I don't think she's right, but it's been bugging me ever since she said it."

"Yeah, and?"

"She asked me whether Lehua might be having an affair and, well, I don't know, tried to cover it up with this abduction...or something. I don't know. What do you think? Do you think that could be true?"

"You never know what goes on in people's private lives. But, no, it doesn't seem right to me. Walter's the person Lehua runs *to* when she's got problems, not the person she runs from. You saw her when he showed up after she got mugged." He paused for a moment then asked, "You know what the name means, right?"

"What, *lehua*? It's a flower. The flower on the *ohi'a* tree."

"Yeah, but do you know the story?"

"Uh, no, I guess not."

"Well, once upon a time, there was a warrior named Ohi'a and he fell in love with a woman named Lehua. They got married and were living happily until, one day, *Pele* saw him and wanted him for herself. She flew into a rage when Ohi'a refused her propositions and she turned him into a tree. You know how the ohi'a is kind of gnarled looking? Twisted? Well, when Lehua saw her husband like that she asked some gods

142

to undo Pele's work. They couldn't do that so, instead, they turned Lehua into the blossom of the tree so that she and Ohi`a would always be together."

I was *very* surprised that John was telling me such an overtly romantic story. He took his eyes off the road for a moment and looked at me. "If somebody picks a lehua blossom, it rains. It's supposed to be tears shed when the flower is separated from the tree." He looked forward again. "You know how the ohi`a is the first tree to grow on new lava? Strong, tough. Remind you of Walter and Lehua?"

"Yeah, I think it does." So much for Stephanie's idea; I liked John's much better.

JOHN WAS DRIVING THE LONG WAY back to the ME's office. We stayed on Highway 11 all the way to its end and then turned left, onto Highway 19, to drive along the Hilo Bayfront. The two highways go pretty much in a circle around the whole island. Highway 19 makes the northern half of the circle and Highway 11 makes the southern half. At the intersection of the two highways in Hilo, mile marker zero for both, sits Ken's House of Pancakes, a local institution. I realized, as we passed Ken's, that I was feeling hungry again. Good thing Rob was bringing dinner. But what was up with my appetite? It seemed like I was hungry all the time.

My cell phone rang again. "Okay with you?" I asked John.

He shrugged yes.

"Hi, Honey, what are you doing?" Emma greeted me.

"Riding in an ambulance with John...."

"Oooh, do you both want to come over and have a drink? It's kind of rainy but we can sit inside."

"Rob's bringing me dinner. But I'll ask John if he wants to come."

John could hear me, of course, and he was already shaking his head no.

"Nope, he's gonna pass, too. Maybe tomorrow afternoon. I'll probably be working at the lab most of the day."

"It was a long shot," she told me. "I knew you guys were working at Pohoiki because Mick just got home and he told me. Mick was in Orchidland, where Eddie Paiva went after he left you at Pohoiki."

The coconut wireless is fast.

"Yeah, we're both tired, like I said, but maybe tomorrow," I repeated.

"Okay, Sweetie, get some rest. I'll talk to you then. Hugs to John," she said, and rang off.

The rain was a steady drizzle as we reached the HMSE and the clouds made the dusk seem even darker. HoneyGirl was one of a very few cars left in the parking lot.

"Can you just drop me off next to my car? There's no need for me to go inside, is there?"

"Yep, and nope," John replied. "I'll just wait here until you lock your doors."

Cops' work exposes them to the worst of human nature so they can get a little paranoid. I really appreciated his concern but I wasn't going to lock my doors. It's Hilo, for heaven's sake.

"Thanks, John. See you tomorrow." I gathered my raincoat and canvas bag and climbed out of the vehicle.

As I pushed closed the heavy ambulance door, I heard, "Drive safe, Mims."

I put my damp and dirty things in the back of the car, on the rubber cargo mat. I slipped off my boots, too, and exchanged them for my rubber slippers. John waited patiently for me, Pua's large, idling motor vibrating my whole body. When I started up HoneyGirl and switched on her lights, he gave a little toot of the horn and pulled forward, into the open bay of the ME's building.

MY GARBAGE CAN WAS STILL by the road, collecting water in its upturned lid. It seemed like a long time since I'd left the house that morning. After I parked, I walked back down to the street, in the rain, to collect the mail and bring in the can. I didn't care that I was getting wet, my clothes were going right into the washing machine, anyway.

Inside the house, I dropped the mail on the kitchen island and walked straight to the laundry room and stripped. My clothes and my raincoat got tossed into the washer along with my wet PJs from that morning and I started it up. On my way to the bedroom, I ducked into the office to do a quick check of the answering machine. One of the state's senators had left a prerecorded message to remind me that the primary election was coming up soon and I should maybe vote for him. There I was, naked and listening to his recording, and I didn't even like the guy. A second call was from Stephanie, from a couple of hours earlier when it had still been light out, asking if I wanted to go for a walk. I erased both messages. I was beginning to enjoy the chill on my bare skin because I knew how much nicer that warm bath was going to feel.

It turned out I didn't have any jasmine bubble bath, after all. But I had something better: Magic Dust my friend Erika had sent for my birthday. When I sprinkled it on top of the water, it fizzled and turned violet and released a light floral scent. I pinned my hair up to keep it out of the bathwater and, remembering that Rob might come while I was still in the tub, I laid my big terrycloth robe on the counter, in easy reach. Jay gave me that robe and I love to wrap myself up in it. I also decided to really pamper myself by lighting a candle and putting on some soft Hawaiian music. I got out my special towel, too - extra big and soft and monogrammed. And then I turned off the light and eased myself into the luxurious warmth of the water.

ROB WAS GENTLY CALLING MY NAME from the bedroom doorway. The bathwater was still warm, but just barely.

"I'll be right out!" I called. "I must have fallen asleep."

"I know, I tried to wake you before. Dinner's ready. I hope there's enough."

I knew Rob - there would be leftovers. I was so hungry, I didn't even turn on the lights as I dried off quickly and wrapped the big white robe around me. I blew out the candle and padded on bare feet to the kitchen.

Rob had set the table with my good china, crystal and silver. The lights were dimmed. It was gorgeous. I looked at him in amazement.

"What?" he asked. "If something's worth doing, it's worth doing beautifully."

"This is so wonderful! I haven't used this china in ages. It's been such a long day and this just balances the mud and the..." I almost said *death* but that was too grim "other parts of the day."

Rob pulled my chair out for me, a nice touch. I made up my mind to not talk about work; I just wanted to enjoy the dinner. Rob had made some fusilli pasta with sautéed onions, garlic, spinach and cherry tomatoes; it was drizzled with olive oil and topped with toasted pine nuts and goat cheese.

I raised my glass to take a sip of wine but Rob intercepted me by raising his glass and saying "Cheers". We clinked our goblets together with the lovely light *ting* that good crystal makes, and then I took a large sip of wine.

I inhaled the aroma of the food. "Oh, boy, this really smells good. I can't thank you enough for coming over like this. Next time, I'll make dinner for you. And pretty soon, Alex will be here, too. Has he made his reservations yet?"

"He got tickets for early May. I'm so excited but it's going

146

to be a ridiculous amount of work."

I knew what he meant; I'd gone through it with my dog, Fred. Hawaii doesn't have, nor understandably does it want to have, rabies, so before a pet can be brought into the state it has to be microchipped and inoculated. Then a blood sample has to be sent to Kansas State University - I don't know why there. One hundred and twenty days after the blood sample is cleared by KSU, then the animal may be imported to Hawaii. That's a pretty long wait but it beats the old days when the animals had to be put into caged quarantine here, in Hawaii, for that long.

At the moment of arrival, animals are taken directly to the quarantine facility where they're inspected and their microchips are scanned. *If* the paperwork is all in order and *if* the quarantine officer passes the animal, *then* it's released to its exhausted owner. And, to top it all off, Hilo's airport doesn't have a quarantine facility so pets have to fly into the Kona airport, a two hour drive from Hilo.

Alex, bless his heart, was going to be flying from Los Angeles to Kona with all three of their pets - two dogs and a cat. Rob was going to drive over in a rented van to pick them all up and then drive back to Hilo.

"I'm not really worried about Orion," Rob said, referring to their small dog, "he's used to being in a carrier and he'll be in the cabin with Alex. And Fluffy is a tough cat - he'll be okay. But Max...." I could see worry written on Rob's face. "Max is getting old. He's such a big sweetie but he's not used to being in a crate at all. I'm worried about him in the cargo hold. I know my sister in L.A. loves him and she'd keep him if I asked her to. He'd be happy with her but I just can't. I can't. They're our children. We can't leave one of them behind."

"I know. I was frantic when I brought Fred over here," I told him. "But, honestly, he didn't seem to mind. I was the one who was a wreck. It's just going to be one long, long day for

147

everybody. What time do they get in?"

"Four o'clock. It'll be dark by the time we get back to this side of the island."

"Well, you know I'll help you out in any way I can. Just let me know what you need."

"Thanks," he replied. "I'm so lonely without them."

At least he was going to see them soon. Jay and Fred were gone forever. Our problems are all relative. My mind flashed for a moment on Walter and the kids.

As we were cleaning up the dishes, my phone rang. "Go, go," Rob said to me, "I'll finish up here."

THE CALLER ID SAID David Chung. Just as long as it wasn't Matt Ortiz again.

"Hi, David."

"Oh, hi, Mimi. Sorry to bother you at home but Sam called me a while ago and said you recovered a skeleton from Pohoiki today and he wants me to look at the teeth. He asked me to coordinate with you. Can I come by sometime tomorrow?"

"Fine with me. I'll try to start work around nine. There's no reason why you and I can't work on it at the same time. It shouldn't be too hard to get an ID – if, you know, somebody filed a missing persons report."

That's always the big *if.* There are plenty of Jane and John Does who have dental work and all sorts of other identifying features but nobody ever reports them missing. Of course, sometimes the people who should report them missing are the people who killed them, so they just keep mum. After a certain point, the bodies are used for medical research and/or buried in a pauper's grave.

"I thought there was some ID with it."

"Yes, but it was the wrong person's."

Wrong ID is such a common occurrence that David didn't

even register surprise. "Okay, I'll see you tomorrow morning, then. Bye-bye."

"Bye."

I went back into the kitchen where Rob was wiping off the countertop.

"That was just work," I told him. "I've got to spend tomorrow at the ME's. But I'm going to Emma's for drinks after, if you want to come. The weather's supposed to be clearing up."

Rob told me he had other plans and couldn't come to Emma's. So, after thanking him once again, I walked him to the door and watched him drive away. I was still in my robe.

I locked up the house and brushed my teeth, and then I collapsed into bed. I usually sleep easily and I was really tired, but my mind was racing. I turned on the lamp and tried reading until I was drowsy. As soon as I turned off the lamp, I was awake again. Sometime around two thirty, I finally fell into a deep sleep.

MY EYES WOULDN'T FOCUS but it looked like the clock said 4:20. It was definitely still dark out. I walked groggily to the office to pick up the damned ringing phone. The caller ID was a blur.

"Hello."

"Hi! I hope I'm not calling too early," the chirpy voice on the other end said. It was a woman.

"Who is this?" Manners go out the window at that hour.

"What time is it there? Oh, no, I can't believe I did this to you! What time is it?"

By now, I was recognizing the voice of a friend in Texas.

"I don't know. It's before dawn."

"I can't believe I did this. I always get confused - are you ahead of us or behind us?"

"Behind. It's earlier here. It's a four hour difference, right

149

now," I reminded her. "We don't do Daylight Saving Time, either, so it'll be five hours in the summer."

"I am just so, so sorry," she repeated. "You go back to sleep. I'll call you later. Go back to sleep. I'm so sorry."

"Okay, talk to you later," I said, and hung up. That happens kind of a lot in Hawaii. I can't be too judgmental about it; I've done the same thing myself, only in the other direction.

I trudged back to bed and fell into another deep sleep.

It was eight fifteen when I awoke again. Both David and Eddie were going to meet me at work so I dressed quickly and hurried to fetch the newspaper while the teakettle was heating.

I ate a fast bowl of cereal at the kitchen island while I checked the newspaper's front page. Nothing about Lehua.

I grabbed a sweatshirt for the chill in the morgue, and some slippers for later at Emma's, and hurried out of the house. On the drive, I noticed with wonder, for the millionth time, how many colors of green there are; the night's raindrops had set all the leaves sparkling in the morning's sunshine.

12 DORSAL DEFECT OF THE PATELLA

OZZIE POPPED OPEN THE HMSE DOOR to greet me. I was a little late and I hoped David wasn't already there, waiting for me.

"Hi, Oz," I said, "how you doing?"

"Okay, I guess, but I can't stop thinking about Lehua. It's been three days, already."

I knew it was three days, on one level, but hearing him say it still hit me hard. Three days. That's a chillingly long time. Was she terrified, or in pain? Was she alive?

"*Nothing* new?" I asked.

"No, not that nobody's told me."

"Damn. I...." Well, there was nothing I could think of to say.

Ozzie knew why I was there so he volunteered, "Dr. Morris and them's at a scene. John, too. I'll go get your guy."

His eyes dropped to my white pants. "You going to change?"

"Yeah, see you in a minute."

We parted ways and I headed to the women's locker room.

Less than five minutes later, I entered my work room, wearing my underwear and a sweatshirt and swathed in an oversized pair of green cotton, surgical pants and a gown so big that I wrapped it around myself twice. I slipped some protective "footies" over my shoes.

Ozzie had already parked the body in my room. The black,

plastic, zip-up body bag laid on top of the gurney with the brown paper bags containing the skull, hands and feet perched on top.

There was a time in the past when we'd had so many John Does in a row that, to avoid confusion, we had to find another way to name them. We'd started using names that described where they'd been found - names like River Doe, Dump Doe and, the worst of all, Refrigerator Doe. Unplugged Refrigerator Doe would have been more descriptive, but we weren't giving middle names at the time. I'd already decided to call this one Pohoiki Doe.

I stuck my head out of the door and looked up the hall. Ozzie was at the work station. I pulled my hair back into a ponytail while I called out to him, "Ozzie, would you please come help me for a while?"

Ozzie left what he was doing and came to join me.

"Before I get started, I want to get everything x-rayed. Would you do that, please?"

"I already did it, already." He pointed to an oversized manila envelope on the counter.

I felt a little embarrassed for asking – for assuming that he hadn't already done it. Already.

I busied myself filling in forms while Ozzie began to affix the x-rays to the wall-mounted reader. He flipped on the switch to illuminate them and stood back a little for me to see, too.

"There's stuff in the pockets," he observed. "There might be a little bottle."

I wondered what that was going to be about.

I pulled on some latex gloves. "Let's put a sheet on the autopsy table and transfer the body over."

Ozzie locked the wheels of the gurney to keep it from rolling. Then he called in another diener to help us lift the bulk of the corpse out of the body bag and onto the autopsy

152

table. We deposited it there with a soft thud.

There was a lot of leaf debris, dirt and bugs left behind in the body bag. I inspected it to make sure I hadn't overlooked anything and then I zipped the bag back up to keep the homeless bugs from travelling.

I opened the bags marked *Left Hand*, *Right Hand*, *Left Foot* and *Right Foot* and reunited the bones with the rest of the cadaver. Then I took a towel, rolled it lengthwise and coiled it into a doughnut shape. I placed the cranium on top of the towel ring. It's important to put the cranium on something soft and supportive so it doesn't get damaged by rolling around. It also protects the upper teeth from getting banged on the hard, table surface. I set the mandible next to the cranium.

When everything was laid out, I climbed a little ladder and photographed the entire length of the corpse, from above.

I was itching to see what was in the pockets and I could tell Ozzie was, too. He handed me a pair of blunt nose scissors and watched with curiosity as I cut open the fabric. And Ozzie was right, in the left pocket there was a small bottle - a partially full vial of insulin - and a broken green crayon. In the right pocket, there was a house key, a quarter and two pennies, a pocket comb, some lint and a loose lens from a pair of prescription glasses. The insulin might explain the hypodermic needle we'd found under the body. Or it might not.

Next, I cut the left leg of the shorts from the hem to the waist band. I did the same thing to the right leg. Ozzie helped me lift the body a little, while we pulled the shorts free. A few startled bugs burrowed deeper, away from the room lights, into the darkness of the body's decomposing tissues. Ozzie laid a couple of green hospital towels onto the stainless steel countertop and I laid the shorts on top of them. When I cut open the back pockets, I discovered nothing in the right pocket but, in the left, I found a Hawaii driver license.

The license had expired several years earlier. It was the old, rainbow license, issued before the time of multiple holograms and dual pictures now required by the federal government. It belonged to William Thomas Taylor. The information on the license listed him as six feet tall, one hundred and seventy five pounds, with blue eyes and brown hair, and with a birth date of 9 September 1966. The picture showed a gentle face, with just the hint of a shy smile. He was clean-shaven and his brown hair was short but tousled. He wore a pair of gold, wire-rimmed glasses that the license said was a requirement for the operation of vehicles. The license also listed him an organ donor. His face looked Caucasian to me. Of course, it wasn't necessarily the driver license of *this* guy, but it certainly was a good match for the skeletal characteristics I could see.

Ozzie wrote down the information on the license to check against hospital records; maybe there were some x-rays, or something, on file. Just as he was walking out the door, I called to him, "While you're at it, would you give Captain Paiva a call and tell him what we've found?"

"DID SOMEBODY SAY MY NAME?" asked a voice from the doorway. Speak of the devil.

"Oh, hi, Eddie. We just found an ID on the guy. This one's a pretty good match."

Eddie took some gloves from the countertop and picked up the license, holding it carefully, by the edges.

"Oh, no! Not this guy," he said. "His family's been looking for him. They've been calling practically every day."

"If it's him," I reminded Eddie.

Ozzie and I had laid out all the pockets' contents on a clean towel on the counter. Eddie looked at the insulin vial.

"You found that on him?" he asked me.

"Yep, in his pocket."

"Well, that fits. Billy was a diabetic but he drank too much and couldn't regulate his insulin levels, especially when he was drunk. His family tried everything to help him out but I think he had other mental problems, too. They tried to get him to live at home but he just kept going back to his tent. This is a shame. They really cared about him."

"Don't forget we already found one wrong ID with this guy. Ozzie's checking the hospital records to see whether we can find some old x-rays or scans that we could use for a positive."

"Yeah, well, we already asked for records from Billy's family, when they reported him missing," Eddie told me. "But they said he didn't have a dentist."

Ozzie poked his head into the doorway. "William Thomas Taylor had knee surgery in 2002. And his appendix out in 1996. They sending over the x-rays."

STANDARDS FOR POSITIVE IDENTIFICATION are strict. There have to be specific identifying features that match known records of a person, or identifying DNA. Dental x-rays showing fillings and tooth shapes are commonly used. But sometimes evidence is only good enough to *exclude* someone as a match, not good enough to positively identify. For instance, if you find type O blood associated with a crime but your suspect has type B blood, then that means you can exclude your suspect as the "donor". But even if your suspect does have type O blood, that doesn't mean you've found a match because there are billions of other people with type O blood, too - your suspect isn't necessarily the person who left it behind. Likewise, just because the body on the table was the right height, sex, race and age to match the driver license, that didn't mean we had a positive identification. How many six foot tall, middle-aged, Caucasian males are out there? Lots. How many are around Pohoiki? Still lots.

There are actually insurance fraud cases where people find

a lookalike substitute for themselves and then fake their own deaths; their widows or widowers collect the insurance and meet them in some tropical paradise...like Hawaii. There are cases where dentists have even gone to the added lengths of doing dental work on a corpse so that it matches their own. They plant the body, rig a fiery crash, for instance, and disappear. If a dentist was supposed to have been in a fiery crash, that's always a red flag to me.

BY THE TIME DAVID ARRIVED, Eddie was gone again and I was in the process of measuring the skull.

"You going to play golf this afternoon?" I asked him.

He looked down at his dark green polo shirt and khaki pants. "Thought I'd play a little hooky after I'm done here. I've got one of those one month passes at the Muni but it's been raining every time I've had a chance to go."

"Sorry, somebody should have called you this morning. There isn't any work on the teeth and the probable family says there are no known dental records. So there isn't much for you to do. I already charted the dentition but you're welcome to take a look, too."

"Stinky in here. How long you think he's been out there?" he asked.

"I guess a couple of weeks. Less than a month."

"You mind if I look at your chart?" he asked me, as he gloved up.

I handed him my clipboard and he scanned it. "It's different from the one I use," he said, "but I guess you're looking for different things, huh?"

"Yeah."

He joined me at the autopsy table. I'd put the loose mandibular teeth back in their alveoli, and I'd tried to do the same thing with the upper, or maxillary, teeth but they just kept falling out again. Gravity. I'd given up and left them on

156

the table top while I was measuring the skull. I paused in my measurements to let David have access to the teeth.

David turned the cranium over and reinserted the teeth in their alveoli while he inspected the dentition. "I'd say male, thirty to fifty years of age," he mumbled.

"Fits with what I'm thinking."

"What does the ID say?" he asked. He could see the driver license on the counter top.

"William Thomas Taylor."

"William Taylor. Are you kidding? Billy Taylor?" He had a worried look on his face. He walked to the counter and bent to peer at the driver license. "Oh, man, that's a shame."

"That's the same thing Eddie said."

"Yeah, well, I went to school with his younger brother. Billy was a really cool guy until he got to be around twenty. He joined the Army right after high school, but they kicked him out after a few years. Schizophrenia, or something. Jimmy, my friend, he and his family tried to find Billy help but he just kept getting worse and worse. Plus, he started drinking. A couple of times they kind of captured him and got him sobered up, and on medication, but he didn't like it, said it made him feel dull. So he'd quit it and take off again. He'd come around to his parents' house, though, to see his mother every couple of months. She died about a year ago and Jimmy's been really worried about him since. He was diabetic, too, but other homeless people kept stealing his needles for drugs."

That reminded me of something, and I joined David at the counter. I used a paper towel to pick up the vial. Even if Billy had remembered to take his insulin, it wouldn't have been doing much good. It had expired eight months earlier.

"It's probably him," I said. "There are some old hospital x-rays coming over. Maybe something will match up."

"Poor Billy," he said. "Poor Jimmy."

I returned to the autopsy table and resumed measuring the skull.

"Are you busy?" I asked David. "Do you want to help me?"

"Yeah, might as well. I scheduled a couple of hours for this and I'm not meeting my golf buddy 'til after lunch. What do you want me to do?"

"Would you write down the numbers, on those forms there," I gestured to a clipboard nearby, "while I do the measurements? It always goes faster with somebody to help. When we're done, we can plug the data into the computer and see what it says."

With David's help, I finished measuring the skull within an hour, and also some of the long bones of the arms and legs.

"Have you ever seen FORDISC work before?" I asked him.

"No, but I've heard about it. Have you been using it long?"

"Yeah, I started using it when it first came out. That was a long time ago, now. I used to go to some yearly meetings in Tennessee with the guys who started it. We'll just put the measurements into the program and then it'll show us which sex and racial group this skeleton is most typical of. It can calculate height, too."

I took off my gloves and turned on my laptop. "If you just read me the measurements from that form, I'll enter them into the program."

"Does it do age, too?"

"No, age is tricky. It's pretty easy to estimate age in kids but around age thirty, or so, it gets harder. Growth slows and arthritis begins. It's all downhill after that."

"Hey!" he complained, "I thought I had a few more good years left."

"Even the height estimation has to be adjusted for the shrinkage of age, if the person's over thirty."

"I'm shrinking? Why are my feet getting bigger?"

"Well, I should say the *settlement* of age. Your feet are

158

splaying out."

"You're depressing me."

"Aging beats the alternative," I said, nodding at the bones on the table.

"Yeah," he replied softly.

David read me the measurements he'd recorded and I entered them into FORDISC. I pressed a few buttons and the program almost instantly responded with a set of charts and graphs that revealed that the measurements from Pohoiki Doe were most similar to the white males in the databank. I showed David how to read the graphs. Then I entered the lengths of the left femur and tibia, the thigh and shin bones. The estimated height of the individual was 179.5 centimeters. There are 2.54 centimeters to the inch, so that worked out to 70.669 inches. The margin of error was 2.99 centimeters, so that meant Pohoiki Doe was probably between five feet, nine and a half inches and six feet tall. It fit Billy.

I looked at the wall clock. "It's after one. When's your golf date?"

"Oh, damn, I lost track of time! I better go now; I'm supposed to be there at one-thirty."

"It's a good time to stop, anyway. I'm gonna to go get some lunch." I looked down at my oversized gown. "I have to go change first, though. Too bad the cafeteria doesn't deliver."

"I can go get you something," David volunteered.

"No, you'll be late. Maybe I'll ask Ozzie if he can help me out. Where is he, anyway? Those x-rays from the hospital were supposed to be here a long time ago."

I suppressed an irrational twist of fear that Ozzie had gone missing, too. Sam and John weren't back, either.

THE HALLWAY WAS DESERTED as I walked with David towards the dieners' workstation and the exit door. If you're going to have an irrational fear, an empty hallway in a morgue isn't probably the place you want to be.

Finally, I began to hear the murmur of voices from around the corner, in Sam's office.

David noticed my relief, "You weren't thinking they'd all gone missing were you?"

I gave a little shrug.

"So was I," he confessed. "That's not paranoia. Something bad really did happen here, just a few days ago, and none of us knows why. I'm going to go get you a sandwich," he shook his finger *no* to me so that I wouldn't object, "and I don't want to hear any arguments. I'll be right back."

He pushed quickly through the exit door before I could stop him.

I stood in the empty hallway and turned towards the voices. The door to Sam's office was ajar and I could see Ozzie standing behind John, who was seated in front of Sam's desk. Ozzie was holding an oversized manila envelope, probably the x-rays I was waiting for.

Ozzie turned his head and met my eyes, and Sam must have noticed that. I heard him say to Ozzie, "Who is it? Who's out there?"

Ozzie told him it was me.

"Mimi?" Sam raised his voice, "Come in and join us."

I moved forward and pushed open the door. Agent Wagner, the senior FBI guy, was in the office, too. He was seated in Sam's other guest chair.

"Good, God!" Sam exclaimed when he saw me, "we've got to order you some scrubs in your own size. Those look like they'd fit John." Then, noticing that both chairs were taken, he asked Ozzie to grab another.

Agent Wagner rose, looking at his cell phone, and said, "If you'll excuse me, while you're doing that, I have a call I need to answer. I'll just step outside for a moment; I don't seem to have very good reception in this building."

I thought he probably just didn't want us to overhear his conversation. Wagner walked out of the room and Ozzie put the x-rays on Sam's desk and followed him out.

John rose, too, saying to me, "Here, take my chair."

Ozzie wheeled a rolling desk chair to the doorway and John pulled it into the room and sat on it, next to me. Ozzie sat down on another rolling stool, out in the hallway, and then scooted himself and it into the room, crowding in behind John and me.

Sam scowled and told me, "Agent Wagner was just bringing us up to date on Lehua. So far, I haven't heard much that encourages me."

My heart sank but John quickly reassured me, "It's nothing that you and I don't already know."

We all sat in somber silence for about a minute until Agent Wagner rejoined us. He stood in the doorway and didn't enter the room. He reached forward, though, and handed me an egg salad sandwich and a can of soda. "Dr. Chung asked me to give this to you," he said.

I was hungry, and I wanted to eat, but it didn't seem like the time or place so I just settled the food on my lap. The soda can was too cold for my lap, though, so I shifted it to the floor by my feet.

Sam handed me some cheap, fastfood napkins from a collection of surplus ones in his desk drawer. "Mimi, for heaven's sakes, eat your lunch."

I spread out the napkins, to completely cover my lap, and self-consciously opened the wrapping around the sandwich. The room filled with the slightly sulfurous smell of hardboiled eggs. I took a big bite. The sandwich was made with soft, brown bread and it was pretty darned good.

Agent Wagner was looking at his watch. He seemed to have changed demeanor since his trip outside. "I'm going to have to leave soon," he announced. "Another letter has been received at the Ka'awa house. Walter found it stuck inside the screen door again. It was from Lehua. The gist of it is that she's fine and she doesn't want her family to worry about her. And she has the dog and puppies with her."

"What?" we all exclaimed, sort of in unison.

"She seemed to want to reassure her children that the dogs were safe and she reiterated that she will be home in a couple of weeks and to please not look for her. I'm going to have to get on out to their house now. I'll try to stay in touch and, if any of you can think of anything to add to our investigation, please contact me."

To add to *that?* We were all too stunned to respond with more than mumbles. He nodded goodbye to Sam, and then he left.

"What the hell?" Ozzie said, speaking for us all.

I leaned back in my chair and closed my eyes. "This is too much to process. I guess, at least, we know she's alive."

Sam looked bewildered. "I've got to get back to work, I can't think about this right now." He reached for the manila envelope Ozzie had put on his desk and asked, "What are these?"

"The hospital sent 'em over for the Pohoiki case," Ozzie said. "Mimi found some ID on the guy. The hospital got records for the name, so we checking if anything match."

Sam stood up at his desk and pulled an x-ray out of the envelope. He tried to hold it up to the light but I knew he couldn't see it very well that way; he was just using up nervous energy. "Come on," he said to me, "let's go take a look at these."

Ozzie scooted his stool backwards, out the door, to clear a path and John followed Sam and me down the hall to my room. On the way, I ate one more bite of sandwich and tossed the rest of it into a trash can.

"I NAMED HIM POHOIKI DOE," I told Sam, as we entered my room. "David's seen him but there's no dental work present. He says it looks male and somewhere between thirty and fifty years old."

"Can't you do better than that?" Sam asked me.

"Yeah, probably. So far, I'm going with a Caucasian male, between five nine and a half and six feet tall, no obvious signs of perimortem trauma. I haven't done age yet but he's clearly an adult. I'll probably be able to narrow the estimate a bit more than David did."

"Well," Sam said, removing the postmortem x-rays from the reader on the wall and attaching one of the ones Ozzie had gotten from the hospital, "let's see what we've got here. This one's supposed to be of the left knee, from a surgery in 2002."

He paused for a moment, concentrating on the film, and then said, "John, would you ask Ozzie to print out the records from this surgery?"

Wordlessly, John left to go find Ozzie.

"See this, here?" Sam asked me, pointing to a light spot on the x-ray. "What's this?"

"A patella," I joked. It *was* a patella, better known as a knee cap, but Sam was referring to a little, irregular spot on it.

Sam looked at me over the top of his glasses. "Okay, wise guy, but have you ever seen anything like this spot before? Maybe it's why he had surgery. Is it a sarcoma of some sort?"

"Don't know," I said truthfully. "Maybe it's just a defect. Of the patella. A DDP: Dorsal Defect of the Patella. It's a thing."

"Let's check the bone."

We both left the light box and turned back to the autopsy table. Sam passed me some gloves.

I had already freed the patella and cleaned the ends of the left femur and tibia, so that I could measure them. The patella is held in place, in front of the femur, by ligaments and tendons. If you straighten your leg out in front of you but relax it, you can move your patella a little bit; it has some give. In Pohoiki Doe's case, the ligaments and tendons of attachment had mostly decomposed away already, so it had been easy to free it.

I flipped the patella over so that we both could see the posterior surface.

"There it is," Sam said. "That's the spot on the x-ray."

He was pointing to an irregularly shaped dent on the normally smooth, bone surface. It wasn't very big, about the size of my pinkie fingernail. He picked up the bone and held it closer to his eyes, waggling it to try to catch the light. He exhaled deeply, sort of a sigh, and then walked to the switch by the door, using his elbow to turn on the stronger, overhead, surgical lights.

"Is this condition common?" he asked me.

"No. I've only seen it once before. It's not a pathology, as far as I know. It's just random. The case I know about was in Alabama and the defect was allowed in court for a positive ID. Each defect has a unique shape, sort of like sinuses."

"Really?" he asked me. "Well, let's document this. We can still do DNA but this'll be faster for an ID."

There was a breeze, or something, and I looked up to see John in the hall, just outside the doorway, with a small stack of papers in his hand.

"The surgery records," he announced.

Sam removed his gloves and beckoned John into the room. He held out his hand and John, wordlessly of course, passed him the report. Sam leafed through it, quickly at first, but slowing to concentrate over one section.

"Bingo," he pronounced. "Here it is. This'll do for a positive. Mimi, measure that defect carefully, get some pictures, and x-ray the patella again, in the same position as the hospital x-ray. How much longer do you think you'll need?"

164

"A couple of hours, I guess." It was two-fifteen. By five I'd definitely be ready for drinks with Emma.

"Call Captain Paiva," Sam said to John, "and let him know what we've found."

Sam headed for the door. "Good job," he said. He wasn't talking to me or to John, he was making a general comment on everyone's efforts.

But he'd left without ever uttering a word about the new note from Lehua. I just stared at John, waiting for him to say something. He stared back at me and, after what seemed like a long time, he slowly shook his head, then turned and left.

I FINISHED UP MY WORK but I didn't find anything else of significance; no signs of disease or trauma. When I was finished, my estimation of Pohoiki Doe's age was slightly narrower than David's, between forty and fifty years of age.

So, it seemed, we had ourselves an identification: William "Billy" Taylor grew up in Hilo, had friends and a family who loved him, joined the service, had a mental illness in a society that doesn't have much more help available than jail, tried to cope, died. Another blue-eyed boy, Mr. Death.

By four-thirty, I was ready to leave. The office was quiet. Sam and John had already left and Ozzie had been replaced by one of the night crew. I showered and changed back into my own clothes.

When I settled on to HoneyGirl's comfortable seat, I realized how tired my feet were. I changed into my slippers and I put down all the windows and turned on my favorite Hawaiian radio station.

"God, what a day," I exhaled. "Let's go to Emma's and refresh ourselves. You can park by the water and watch the waves and I'll have some wine." The fact that I was talking to my car, because I had no human being to confide in, did not boost my mood.

13 PUTTING ON THE SIRENS

HILO BAY GLISTENED IN THE SUNLIGHT. In the distance I could see a huge cruise ship moored at the docks. It dwarfed the nearby hotels. Tourism is crucial to the islands' economy and, honestly, it's great to live somewhere that people come to visit just for the purpose of enjoying themselves.

At the bay front, I turned left onto the highway for the short drive up the coast to Honoliʻi Beach. When I exited the main road, I had to slow to a snail's pace to cruise along a narrow lane, past all the surfers' cars and trucks crowding the road's margin. Through the parked cars and past the dented guard rail, I could see over the side of the cliff to a panoramic view of the surf. The waves looked smallish but there were people out anyway, a mix of surfers, standup paddle boarders and boogie boarders. I thought I saw a whale spout, out past the surfers, but I wasn't sure. It was early April and the humpbacks were starting to leave, to go back to Alaska for the summer.

The road curved back, away from the beach, and I followed it to Emma's house. As I drove down the driveway Mick's giant dog, Barney, loped towards the car playfully shaking an unhusked coconut in his mouth. I counted the vehicles parked by the house. Six. I recognized Emma's little hatchback, Mick's muscle cop car, Kelly's Ford pickup truck with two surfboards in the back, Katie's black SUV with the hospital parking sticker in the window, Cyd's little white SUV and, to my surprise, John's old, red pickup. Emma had invited him the day before, when we were driving back from Pohoiki, but I hadn't really expected him to come.

I parked HoneyGirl under a *hala* tree, in a spot with a good view. When I opened my door, Barney rushed forward, loosing the coconut towards my feet so that he would be unencumbered to give me a thorough sniffing. Shower, or not, I *had* been in a morgue all day. I hopped out of the path of the coconut.

"Barney!" I heard Mick's voice, "Get away from her!" Mick trotted out of the house and took Barney's collar in hand. "Sorry," he said, but he was laughing.

"I took a shower and *everything*," I protested. "Did he do this to John, too?"

"No, he keeps a respectful distance from John. Can I get you a beer or something? Everybody's out back."

"Thanks, I'll get myself some wine. Looks like there's a crowd here today."

"Not really, just the usual group. Except John."

When we entered the house, I stopped at the counter and poured myself a nice, big glassful of pinot noir and then cruised on out to the patio. I exchanged hugs with Emma, Cyd, and Katie. I just gave John a tap on the shoulder.

"Where's Kelly?" I asked.

In unison, the women answered, "In the water."

"Come sit here by me," Emma said. She was sitting at the end of the picnic table and had her laptop computer opened in front of her. "I want to show you something."

John scooted over and I sat down between the two of them. Cyd was across the table from me.

Emma was tapping buttons and then she swiveled the computer so that I could see the screen. It was me at Pohoiki the day before.

167

"What's this?" I asked her.

"YouTube. It was posted last night. You guys are all in it."

I looked up at Cyd and then turned to John. "How did this happen? Who took this?"

"I don't know," John answered. "Must have been somebody watching us. They don't show the body, though."

"Crap. I hate it when this happens," I said.

From the first case I ever worked on, I learned an important lesson: be as anonymous as possible. On that case, I was feeling a little unappreciated when the newspaper didn't give me credit for helping to expose a murder. But then the killer escaped. Twice. That's when I realized I don't want my name in the paper and I don't want my face on TV. Or on YouTube.

"The area should have been secured better," John said.

"It was probably just somebody with a cell phone," Cyd commented. "We're pretty dull viewing, though."

The video was just a blurry, long-distance view of Eddie and me arriving at the scene. It was raining and we were standing under a tarp and Eddie was introducing the guys to me. Suddenly the video jerked and quit.

"Well, I guess there's nothing we can do about it now," I observed. I felt vulnerable, though.

"I wouldn't worry about it," John said. He took a long drink from his beer bottle, reached past me and shut the lid on Emma's laptop. She raised her eyebrows at him, but she let him do it.

"Mimi," Cyd said to me, "would you come help me with something?"

"Sure." I could tell the wine was going to my head really quickly and I bumped against John as I tried to extricate myself from the picnic bench. He gently took my arm and steadied me.

I suddenly felt a rush of gratitude for his quiet strength

and I gently put my hand on his shoulder.

Cyd gave me such a stare that I quickly lifted my hand and followed her.

AS WE WALKED AWAY from the lanai, Cyd grabbed my arm. "Oh, my God, did you see John?" she asked me.

"Yeah, he was sitting right next to me."

"No, did you *see* him?" she repeated.

"Huh?"

We were walking down towards the river. It is just so impossibly beautiful there.

"Mimi! Pay attention. Did you see his face?" She had urgency in her voice.

"What are you talking about?" I asked her with exasperation.

She halted and took a stance in front of me, face to face. "He shaved his beard off!"

"What? His beard?" My mind was a little foggy from the wine. "Why would he do that?"

Something was tugging at my memory and suddenly it pounced on my consciousness. "His beard? Cyd, he shaved his beard? Did he hear us yesterday? Oh, no!"

Cyd looked scandalized. "He was right by us. He must have heard us. He shaved his beard off because of what we said! Because of what *you* said," she pressed on me. "He did it for you."

"This is crazy," I told her, needlessly. "That can't be right. Why would he shave his beard for me?"

My head was spinning. How could I go back to the table and face John? Beardless John? Crap. What was he *thinking*?

I took a breath. "Okay, here's my plan. I'm not going to do anything. Except go get something to eat. That's my plan. I think I'm a little drunk."

She gave me a smile. "Good plan. Come on, let's go raid the

refrigerator; Emma won't mind."

We walked, arm in arm, back to the house. There was actually a plate of cheese and crackers out on the counter and Mick was snacking from it. I got a glass down from the cabinet and filled it to the brim with water and started drinking.

Emma walked into the kitchen. "What's up?" she asked us all.

"The wine went to my head," I told her. "I need something to eat. And water."

"Okay, Baby," she answered. "I just came in to get more pupus. Why don't we all carry them back to the table?"

I filled some bowls with pistachios and Emma handed Cyd a platter of sliced 'ahi.

"Mick, put some more cheese and crackers on that plate and come join us," Emma instructed him.

Emma gathered chopsticks, a tube of wasabi and a bottle of shoyu, and then herded us all outside.

Just as we walked out the door, Emma softly asked me, "Did you notice John's beard?"

"Oh, look!" Cyd interrupted. Her voice was excessively boisterous; she was trying to hush Emma. "There's Kelly. He's back. Hi Kelly! How was the surf? Hey, did you ever realize you have the same name as Kelly Slater?"

"Yeah, I think I might've noticed that," he patiently answered her. For a surfer, sharing the same name as the eleven-time World Champion is a noticeable thing.

There were more hugs all around and I was spared answering Emma's question. Cyd and I traded seats at the table so that she was sitting next to John. Bless her heart.

I couldn't make eye contact with him.

"So, anything new with Lehua?" Katie asked. "I heard there was a second letter."

Man, news travels fast around here. Agent Wagner had

170

only told us that a couple of hours before.

"I don't know anything about it," Mick said, looking from me to John. "What happened?"

John responded. "We heard Walter found another letter from Lehua today, at their house. It didn't say much. She said she's okay. I guess she thought the kids might be upset about their dogs, too, so she said they're with her."

The way he phrased that caught my attention. "Wait, John. Are you thinking she doesn't really have Sweetie and the puppies with her? She's just saying that to calm the kids?"

"It crossed my mind. There might be something else going on."

"Like what?"

"Like maybe somebody's telling her to write that stuff."

"What if," Kelly spoke up, "she's leaving Walter and the kids but taking Sweetie? She'd have to take the puppies, too, until they're weaned. How long do puppies nurse?"

I knew Kelly was just spitballing but what he was suggesting disturbed me. Lehua would never do that. I was pretty sure. I was almost pretty sure.

"Let's see," Emma replied, as she opened her laptop again.

"I had a dog once," Katie remembered, "who nursed her puppies for, like, eight weeks. She was so tired of them towards the end, she just wanted to be left alone." She smiled at the memory.

"Here it is," Emma told us. "There are a whole bunch of answers but it looks like dogs nurse for around five to eight weeks."

"But Lehua said she's coming back in a couple of weeks," I pointed out. I hoped I wasn't being naive. I knew that John, with his long, dark trail of experiences might think so. I was glad I couldn't imagine all the scenarios he could.

"What kind of dog does she have?" Emma asked, still engaged with her computer screen. "It looks like different breeds nurse for slightly different times."

"Sweetie's mostly Chihuahua, but the father's an unknown quantity," I told her. "Lehua says he's a mutant."

Emma laughed, "What does she mean by that?"

"He has extra toes. The puppies do, too. But, like all puppies ever, in the history of the universe, they're adorable."

"So, she saw the father?" Emma asked.

"Yeah, she said he was just a poi dog, but he had extra toes. When the dog handlers were in the office, before they started their search, they saw a picture of the puppies on Lehua's screensaver and the woman said there's some new AKC breed of dog that has extra toes, too. The handler's name is Piggy. Not Peggy, Piggy. Can you believe that?"

"Piggy Spencer," Emma said. "That's who did the search? I know her from the club. Never thought she had much sense."

"She said the toes on the new breed aren't like just dew claws, they actually function and the dogs can climb things. Apparently, they're hard to have in the house because they can get up into the cabinets."

"What? You're kidding," Cyd protested.

"It's what she said," I shrugged.

Emma was still engrossed with her laptop. "Here it is. The AKC approved six new breeds. I can't pronounce most of them. Hold on, here that one is. Oh, it's kind of cute. It looks bigger than a Chihuahua, though. Its face looks a little bit like a small husky."

She turned the screen so we all could see the picture.

"Are there any pictures of its paws?" Katie asked.

"Yeah, hold on," Emma told her, turning the screen back to herself. In a moment she mused, "Well, there it is. It does have six toes."

She turned the screen back for us to see again.

"What's it called?" Kelly asked her.

"The Norwegian Lundehund."

"Norwegian?" I blurted.

I looked at John, trying not to stare at his non-beard. "Another Norwegian thing? That's a lot of coincidences."

"You know what they say," Mick observed, "there are no coincidences."

"Don't start talking like that," Katie grumbled at him. "It's crappy science. What if I thought that everybody who came into the ER with a broken arm and a cold, for example, needed to be worked up as though the two were connected? I'd waste a huge amount of time. Of course there are coincidences. That's why the word coincidence exists. Two things *can* happen at the same time and not be connected. It happens all the time."

"But," I said, "this is, like, *four* things. The guy who mugged Lehua was from Norway, too. I know not everything's connected but a *Norwegian* Lundewhatever?"

"Wait," Cyd interjected, "how could somebody leave that letter at their house and not be seen? Isn't it being watched?"

"Probably watching it *now*," John said under his breath.

Cyd continued, "I mean, if people can sneak videos of us at Pohoiki, how hard would it be for the police to rig a camera at Walter and Lehua's?"

"Hey, John," Katie changed the topic again, and my head started spinning even more. "Whatever happened to that guy's body? The Norwegian guy? Did anybody claim it?"

"Somebody from the Norwegian consulate...."

"Norway has a consulate *here*?" Katie interrupted him.

"In Honolulu - I think it's probably because of their cruise line. They have an honorary consul there. They contacted us, on behalf of the brother in Norway. Nothing's happened yet. We're still holding the body."

"I say we should go plant a camera at Walter and Lehua's," Cyd asserted as she pointed at Mick, "and *you* should drive me there."

173

Perhaps I was not the only tipsy person at the table.

"Me? Why me?" Mick protested.

"Because I want to ride in your car," she explained, "and put on the siren."

"Sound logic," Kelly commented.

"No, absolutely not," Mick replied.

MY THOUGHTS WERE TRYING TO RACE but they kept stumbling over each other. The food and water weren't really helping much yet. There was a vague but pressing question forming in my mind. I wanted to call Walter and ask him about it, but I didn't want to bother him or get his hopes up. And worse, the FBI was probably listening in on his phone line and they'd know I wasn't going through proper channels. They might get pissed off, especially if I was wrong. But the answer might matter.

I rose from the table and tried to walk nonchalantly back into the house, like I was going to use the bathroom. I felt John's eyes tracking me until I was out of his field of vision.

Once I was inside, I got my purse, which I'd left on a table near the front door, and fished out my cell phone. I found Rob's number and dialed him as I walked out onto the broad, front lawn that faces the ocean. I didn't want anyone to overhear me.

"Aloha," Rob answered. He was picking up local ways already.

"Hi, it's me." I hurried into my question, "Hey, do you have the phone number for that vet in Kona who's going to do the quarantine thing for your pets next month?"

"Yes, I have it in my phone. She's being so nice about everything. She just said, 'Don't you worry, I'll meet you at the airport even if the plane's....'"

"Rob," I interrupted him, "sorry to cut you off but it's kind of an emergency. Can you give me the number? Right now?"

"Oh," he sounded a little wounded, as he should have, by my rudeness. "Okay. It's area code 808, of course, 555-9273. Her name's Marcia Blackard. Anything else?"

"No. Sorry to be so rushed. I'll explain later. Gotta go. Thanks."

I disconnected before he could even say goodbye and quickly punched in the vet's number.

"Marcia Blackard," she answered.

"Hi, my name is Miriam Charles," I told her. "I work with the Medical Examiner's Office, over in Hilo. I wonder if you could answer a question for me. It's related to a case we're working on."

What I was saying was technically true but I didn't have any business calling her like that.

"In the last couple of months," I asked her, "did you clear a dog through Kona quarantine that had six toes on each foot? Like that new AKC breed, the Norwegian Lundehund?"

"You mean a Puffin Dog?" she asked me. "Yeah, I sure did. It's the first one I've ever seen. Those toes are crazy. I wanted to ask more about it but the owner wasn't very chatty."

"Do you happen to know where...wait, was the owner alone? Was it a man or a woman?"

"It was a man. I don't know if he was travelling alone but he's the only one I saw with the dog," she answered.

"Do you remember when you saw the dog?"

"Mmm...let me think. Oh! It was my son's birthday and I was in kind of a hurry to pick up his cake before the store closed. I ordered him the cutest little train cake. He loves trains, even though we don't have any in the islands any more. He's seen them in his story books. His birthday's January seventeenth. So I guess that's what day it was."

"January seventeenth," I repeated. "And do you happen to know, are there any records about where he took the dog? Or if he left the state, again, with it?"

175

"Well, he would've had to put a Hawaiian address on his importation form and that would be on record with the Department of Agriculture. I have that information on my computer at work, but I'm at home right now and I'm not planning to go in until tomorrow around noon, to meet a flight from San Francisco. But, you know, we wouldn't know if he took a dog back out of state. It's not part of our mandate to keep track of that."

"Okay," I told her, "I'll call you back if I need more information. You've been very helpful. I really appreciate it."

"Well, if it's really important, I could drive over to the office..." her voice trailed off.

"No. Thank you. This is enough for now. I really appreciate it," I repeated. "Thank you so much. Bye-bye." I clicked off.

"What was that about?" John's voice startled me. I spun around and he was standing close enough to touch. Certainly close enough to have heard everything I'd said, for as long as he'd been standing there.

"I think I know where Lehua is," I told him. "I just want to check one more thing."

I pressed more buttons on my cell phone and I looked straight into John's eyes as I spoke. "Hi, Walter, this is Mimi from Lehua's work. Um, Walter, I hope I'm not bothering you but I was just wondering, did you ever see that dog that got Sweetie pregnant?"

I listened to his answers and nodded my head, yes, so John could follow the conversation.

"Uh-huh. Okay. Do you have a computer in the house?" I began shaking my head, no, as Walter explained that Lehua's computer had been taken by the FBI.

I listened to him for a couple of moments and then I said, "Listen, Walter, I have a hunch about something. Do you think you can take the kids over to your sister's house, or somewhere like that, for the evening? I want to come down

176

there to see you and show you something. I'm probably going to call a couple of more people to join me there, too. Will that be okay with you?"

I listened some more. "Yeah, I know it's hard not to get your hopes up but will you try to stay calm until I get there? This might be nothing, so I don't want to make a big fuss about it. I should be there in about forty minutes, okay?"

John was giving me quite a look. Not necessarily a good one.

I hung up and stared out at the ocean.

John moved to my side. "Mimi, this doesn't sound like a good idea. You can't just go off on your own. It's dangerous and...."

"What's up guys?" Mick asked us. He was standing about two feet behind us.

Really? No wonder news travels fast around here.

"I think I might know what's happened to Lehua," I told him.

He didn't respond at all; he just stared at me, and then flicked his eyes to John's.

John held his gaze for a moment. "Mims, why don't you explain to us what you're thinking?"

"I will, but I need to get to Walter's. I told him I'd be there and I don't want to leave him hanging. I also don't want to make a big deal about this, in case I'm wrong. And, you know what? I need to talk to Eddie. Mick, can you get Captain Paiva on the phone for me?"

"Maybe...." He looked at John for confirmation.

"You heard the lady," John told him.

Maybe there are still some vestiges of that macho attitude around, after all, but it just wasn't the time to get into it.

While Mick tried to get ahold of Eddie, I said to John, "I need Emma to print out a picture of a Lundehund for me so I can take it to Walter's. Will you drive out to his house with me? I don't want to get everybody all stirred up if I'm wrong, but I think the dog that got Sweetie pregnant might have belonged to Anders and Anna Bentson, that banker and his wife. I could wait and explain this to everybody but it would be faster if I just show Walter the picture myself and then, if he recognizes it, I'll pass it on to Eddie. I'm not going to get involved in anything more. I don't want to put Lehua in danger. Or myself."

"So all you want to do is show Walter a dog picture?" he verified.

"Yes, but I've got to go get it from Emma, first," I reminded him as I began walking back to the house.

EMMA WAS IN THE KITCHEN, adding a mix of brown and white rice to the cooker. "What are you guys so busy with out there?" she asked.

I ignored her question. "Can you print out a picture of one of those Lundehunds for me? It's kind of important."

"Sure," she said, "just give me a couple of minutes to do the rice."

"I need it right now," I explained to her.

She raised her eyebrows and opened her mouth to respond but I think she heard the urgency in my voice. And she didn't have a chance to speak, anyway, because Mick walked up and handed me his phone.

"Captain Paiva," he said.

When Emma heard that and saw the looks on all of our faces, she left the kitchen and went outside to retrieve her laptop. While I spoke to Eddie, I saw Emma walk back past me again and go upstairs to her printer.

Katie wandered into the kitchen but halted, silent, when she noticed the mood of the room.

"Eddie, hi, it's Mimi," I said needlessly.

"Mick says you think you know something about Lehua."

"Well, yeah, I have a hunch about the connection between the dead guy and her. I was wondering if you could meet me at Walter's house."

Cyd crowded in next to Katie. Crap. I started walking out of the house to get away from all the ears but they, and the people attached to them, followed me.

"I want to show Walter a picture of a certain kind of dog," I told Eddie. "It's a little complicated but I think the dog that got Lehua's dog pregnant belongs to Anders Bentson, Eskil's missing brother."

"Wait. Say that again?"

I turned left around the corner of the house and the group followed me, now joined by Emma carrying the Lundehund picture in her hand. I repeated my idea to Eddie.

"Yeah, I'll meet you at Walter's," he told me. "Put Daniels back on the phone."

"Okay." I handed the phone back to Mick and kept walking until I'd circled the house and was again at the backyard picnic table.

Kelly, alone at the table, looked up at our little flock. "What's going on?" he asked.

"Mimi's going to go show Walter a picture of that dog from the computer," Katie informed him. "She thinks she knows where Lehua is. And I'm going with her."

"What? No!" I protested.

Mick joined us and said to me, "Captain Paiva said for me to drive you, and to get you there fast."

"I'll follow in my truck," John added.

We all laughed.

"You're the slowest driver I know!" Katie said to him. "I'll take you in my car."

"Wait!" I exclaimed. "Katie, why are you coming?"

"Because it's a forty minute drive to the nearest hospital when you're down there in Puna. Somebody might get hurt."

179

"No! Nobody's going to get hurt. I'm just going to show a picture to Walter."

"Well, we're all coming with you," Emma declared.

"Nobody can ride with me but Mimi," Mick said. "Captain just said to bring her."

"I'll drive everybody else, then!" Katie cried.

"I think I'll just stay here and hold down the fort," Kelly told her. "You guys go ahead without me. Too much excitement."

Katie paused a moment and cocked her head, then stooped to give him a quick peck on the cheek. Straightening again, she said with relish, "Okay, then, let's move!"

MICK'S ENGINE AWOKE with an impressive growl and he whooped the siren as we tore up the driveway. I fastened my seatbelt. When I looked in the side, rearview mirror, I could see Katie at the wheel of her SUV - John in the front and Cyd and Emma in the back - following closely behind us. At first, we drove slowly and silently past the string of cars parked overlooking the beach but, at the top of the road, Mick turned on the siren and lights and accelerated onto the highway.

My cell phone rang. "Okay, explain to me what you're thinking," John said.

I glanced into the mirror and saw him in Katie's car, with the phone to his ear, waiting for my response.

"Well, it's a little disorganized," I told him, as our two-car convoy raced down the highway. "Basically, I'm thinking that when Anders and Anna Bentson went missing with all that money last year, they came to Hawaii. I think they're the people living in that big, fenced property, way back off the road, next to Walter and Lehua's.

"You told me that, back in Norway, Lars took over all the family property, including the family house *and the dog*. So, remember that trip Lars made to Kona in January? I just

180

talked to the vet who does the Kona quarantine and she remembers a Norwegian Lundehund, she called it a Puffin Dog, being brought to the island around that time. I'm pretty sure that was Lars bringing Anders and Anna their dog."

John wasn't responding, in any way, but I could see he was still listening so I plunged ahead. "We already know the dog that got Sweetie pregnant belonged to Lehua's neighbors. And we also know that the puppies have six toes, just like a Lundehund does. So, if I'm right, a couple of days after Lars brought the dog to Anders and Anna, it got loose. From what I know about Lundehunds, I think it could have climbed over the fence.

"When the puppies were born with all those toes, and Anna Bentson saw them, she and Anders might have started worrying that someone would make a connection to them through their dog. It's probably the only Norwegian Lundehund in Hawaii. I'm guessing it wasn't a big worry for them - I mean, how many people would put that together? - until Eskil died here. Maybe they decided to try to take the puppies, or get rid of them, and somehow Lehua got in the way. The whole Eskil thing is a little unclear. I still have no idea how he fits in.

"So, I was just thinking that if I show Walter a picture of a Lundehund and it looks to him like the dog from next door, then maybe I'm on the right track. Of course, their dog might *not* look like a Lundehund at all. Plus, we don't even know whether the dog the Bentsons had in Norway was a Lundehund, because if it was a Doberman or something, I could just be dreaming all this up and Lehua's totally innocent neighbors might just own a mutant dog."

"That's quite an imagination you've got there," John said. "Why don't we put in a real quiet call to Eddie and ask if he can find out what kind of dog the Bentsons had in Norway?"

"Do you want to call him, or should I?"

181

"I'll do it," he said, and he hung up.

We were moving so fast that we were at the intersection of Highways 11 and 19 already. We flew past Ken's House of Pancakes as we rounded the corner, Katie right on our tail. I wasn't sure that what she was doing was completely legal, or even a little legal. Probably tailing a police car is considered a bad idea, but what was Mick going to do? Stop, get out and arrest her? His primary job was to get me to Walter's, fast, and he was certainly doing that. I tightened my seatbelt a little bit more. Actually, it was sort of fun blasting down the road; Mick was being cautious and, except for a near miss with an overloaded pickup truck full of papayas, I felt pretty safe. Where was that guy going with all those papayas at dusk, anyway? The sun was quickly setting behind the volcanoes.

About halfway to our turnoff near Kea'au, Mick asked, "Who was that on the phone?"

"John." I thought he would have guessed.

I saw Mick's eyes cut to the rearview mirror for a moment. Then, refocusing on the road, his hand rose to the steering column and switched on the car's headlights. A few seconds later, the beams from Katie's headlights came on, too, and illuminated the backs of our heads.

"You heard what I said to John. What do you think?" I asked Mick.

"Me? I don't know. I'm kind of trying to figure out how the dead guy fits into everything."

"Yeah." I paused for a moment to think. "If I keep going with the idea that Anders and Anna Bentson are living here now, probably with all that bank money, then it makes sense that Lars brought the dog over for them. He's probably happy to have them gone and wants to keep it that way. The reason Eskil came here might have been something to do with the money, too."

"Follow the money," Mick said.

I didn't answer. We were coming up to the junction with Highway 130, the same road John and I had travelled the day before, on our way to Pohoiki. At the intersection, two lanes continue straight, towards Volcano National Park, and two lanes split off to turn left at a traffic light. We were going to turn left but both of those turn lanes had about six cars apiece stopped for a red light and the drivers couldn't really pull over, although a few tried. Mick stayed on the main highway and passed them all on the right, then made a sharp left in front of them at the light, cutting in front of oncoming traffic that had stopped for us. All the drivers were doing the best they could to comply with the urgent siren. Katie was sticking close behind us.

In a couple of miles, the road was going to collapse down to a single lane and that, plus the dark, was going to make driving conditions more precarious. A light drizzle began to fall.

My cell phone rang again and I checked the caller ID.

"Hi, John."

"Just talked to Eddie, he's already at the house. But Walter isn't there."

"I asked him to take the kids to his sister's. Maybe he's still doing that."

"I'll call you back," he said and then, of course, the line went dead.

"That was John again," I explained to Mick. "He says Captain Paiva's already at the house but Walter's not there."

"Uh-oh."

"Yeah. It shouldn't have taken Walter this long to get the kids to his sister's; she only lives about a mile away."

I could see a wall of rain on the road ahead. Mick slowed slightly and we drove into it like passing into a car wash. The windshield wipers were on their highest setting but they weren't really making much difference. We drove like that for

183

about ninety seconds and then we passed right out the other side of the cloud burst and, aside from some glistening puddles on the road, it was as if it had never happened.

My phone rang again.

"Hi, John."

"He left his sister's more than half an hour ago. Also, his car's parked at his house."

"I bet he's gone to the neighbor's house on his own."

"Yeah, Eddie's on that. Only he doesn't want to go barging over there and endanger Walter or get into who knows what with the owners, especially if they're Anders and Anna. So he's calling in the SWAT team."

"What! Isn't that a bit much? What if I'm wrong?"

"He doesn't want to take any chances."

The line went dead. I held the phone in front of me and just stared at it. It rang again.

"Sorry, dropped call," John said to me.

And then the line went dead again. The Big Island has a lot of dead spots for cell phone reception. But, then again, it was John, so maybe he had just hung up.

"*Unbelievable,*" I said to Mick. "Captain Paiva is calling in the SWAT team because he thinks Walter might have gone to the neighbors' on his own to try to find Lehua."

"Yeah, I've been hearing something about that," he said. I realized Mick's radio was crackling with activity but it was on sort of low and I hadn't been paying much attention to it, not that I could've understood it anyway. Whatever else happened, we were going to get there long before the Special Weapons And Tactics team.

"Hold on," Mick warned me, as he slammed on the brakes to avoid someone slowly turning left onto the highway in front of us.

As we passed the driver, I could see it was a very tiny, elderly woman, propped up with pillows so that she could just

184

see over the steering wheel. She didn't seem to even notice us. Katie, behind us, must have managed to control her car, too, because we didn't get rear-ended.

As we passed *Pahoa* Village, we were joined by another police car that pulled in behind Katie, lights and sirens on. At the next intersection, Mick slowed a bit and the cop car shot past us and led us into the turn and onto Highway 132, going towards *Kapoho*. We were on a very rural road then, overgrown on both sides.

Within a mile or so, all of our cars slowed and Mick and the other cop turned off their emergency lights and sirens. We cautiously turned onto the dirt lane where the Ka`awa family lives.

There were no street lights or any other kind of lights, for that matter, for about half a mile, as we crept along the rutted lane. As we neared Walter and Lehua's house on the right, I could just make out the long, crushed lava-rock drive leading to the neighbors' house. It disappeared into their densely wooded lot. There was no sign of their house visible from the road and the heavy, driveway gates were wide open.

Walter and Lehua's house is familiar to me. It's a simple, one-storey, wooden house, painted a light tan color with white trim. Although the house sits on a half-acre parcel, most of the lot is overgrown with ohi`a and strawberry guava and albizia trees. The house, itself, is in a cleared area close to the road and surrounded by a small, grass lawn and crushed red cinder. A large catchment tank sits behind the garage.

All the house's windows and doors were closed and, although there was only a single light on inside the house, eave-mounted spotlights illuminated the yard and three cars. One car was Walter's, in the driveway, and one was Eddie's black SUV, parked right behind Walter's. Another SUV, dark blue and with the familiar blue light mounted on top, sat next to Eddie's.

We all parked along the wooded, left side of the dirt road, opposite the house. Mick and John and I got out of the cars, along with the other cop, but Katie, Emma and Cyd stayed seated.

14 URINATING IN AND ON NATURE

AS JOHN AND I APPROACHED the house, I recognized the owner of the other cop car. It was Mitch Kaupu, who had been working with us at Pohoiki.

Eddie studied Katie's SUV, parked on the other side of the dirt lane. "Who's in the car?"

I didn't know how to answer him, but I didn't have to because John said, "Backup."

Eddie gave a wry smile and repeated, "Who's in there?"

I gathered my wits and spoke. "Katie from the ER and Cyd, the new crime scene photographer, and another friend." That sounded sort of reasonable. Then I added, sheepishly, "We were all together when I talked to you and they just wound up tagging along."

Eddie looked at Mick and softly said, "Keep them out of the way."

"Yes, sir," Mick answered, and he began to walk towards Katie's car.

"Daniels," Eddie called him back, "stick around for a minute. They're not in the way yet. I want you to hear what's going to happen."

"Sir!" Mick responded. He pivoted and stood in that stance that the military calls "at ease".

Mitch had been talking on his cell phone but he clicked off and pocketed it.

Eddie raised his eyebrows at Mitch, with a questioning look, and Mitch responded with a silent nod towards Walter's car.

Eddie let out a sigh. "Well, here's the story. I just live in Paradise Park, so I got here pretty quick after you called, Mimi. Walter wasn't here but John told me you'd suggested to Walter that it would be a good idea to take his kids to his sister's house, so I figured he just wasn't back from that yet. I saw his car in the driveway but, you know, I thought maybe he had another one to use, too."

"Right," I said. "Well, to be perfectly factual, I asked him if he could take the kids over to his sister's, or somewhere like that. I don't know if his sister's is actually where he went with them."

"He took them to his sister, Ruth's," Eddie confirmed. "And he did it pretty soon after you talked to him. Then he came back here. When you arrived, Mitch was just calling Ruth to confirm which car Walter had used." He reached out and tapped the hood of Walter's white SUV for emphasis, "And it was this one."

A mosquito whined in my ear and I tried to swat it away. I was glad I had on long pants.

Eddie swatted at a mosquito, too. "I've got some people doing a search right now for the name and telephone number of the neighbors back there and we're going to try to make contact with them, if we can get that information. The SWAT team is still a good forty minutes out."

"Show him the picture," John prompted me.

"Oh, yeah." I fished in my purse for the Lundehund print and handed it over.

Eddie took a long look at the picture and then passed it to Mitch. The other cop, the one who'd led us to the house, joined our group.

"Do you know Sergeant Nakamura?" Eddie asked me, by way of an introduction.

"Uh, no." I held out my hand to the sergeant and he took it

in a surprisingly gentle grasp.

I noticed, from his name tag, that his first name was Glen. I gave the sergeant a quick, slight smile but then returned my attention to Eddie.

"At this point, we're in kind of a holding pattern," Eddie said.

There wasn't much to say to that. We all just sort of shifted feet and stared at each other. Shrill coqui chirps filled the roadside forest, the vocal equivalent of fireflies flashing on and off.

I realized that the wine and all the water I'd drunk earlier were now at the end of their trip through my body. I needed to pee. I looked around. I couldn't go into the house for about a million reasons so I thought the best plan would be to just walk down the road a little way, until I was out of range of the flood lights, and sort of crouch in the woods behind Katie's SUV.

"Excuse me," I said, "I'll be right back."

Nobody paid very much attention.

THE WINDOWS IN KATIE'S CAR were all up, probably to keep the mosquitoes out, but as I approached, the front passenger's window slid down.

I peeked inside the dark interior. "Walter's not here," I told them, "but his car is. Eddie's worried he might have gone to the neighbors' on his own."

"We know," Katie said, "we could hear when John was on the phone in the car."

"Oh, yeah. Well, I've got to pee. I'm going behind these cars."

"Me, too," Emma said from the back seat.

"I'm going, too," Cyd added.

"This is funny," Katie commented, as all three of their doors popped open.

As a group, we began to head off into the darkness. I looked back over my shoulder and saw that, unfortunately, Mick was walking our way. I backtracked a few paces.

"We're just going to go pee in the bushes. You don't need to follow us," I said to him.

The look on his face was somewhere between amused and embarrassed, but he came to a stop in the middle of the road and stayed there.

I turned and joined the other women. "Mick's supposed to be keeping an eye on you guys," I told them, as we squatted down in the darkness.

"Poor Mick," Emma laughed.

"Does anybody have any toilet paper?" Cyd asked.

"I've got Kleenex," I said, as I pulled a few out of my purse.

"You know," Emma said, standing up. "I've been here before. I sold that big house, next door, a couple of years ago."

I stood, too. "That one, over there?" I pointed to the neighbors' driveway.

"Yes," she said, conversationally. "I sold it to a couple about three years ago. It's a really nice house. They paid cash for it. I haven't seen them since, though."

"Emma, those are the people who I think took Lehua! Come tell Eddie this; it sounds important."

"Well, nobody told me you were interested in *this* house," she said defensively. "Are they the ones who have the dog?"

"EDDIE!" I CALLED OUT. We all began walking quickly back across the road towards the house. "There's something you need to hear."

Mick, still standing in the middle of the road, looked confused. He was supposed to keep Emma and the others *out* of the way. On the other hand, I was bringing them right *into* the way. Common sense ruled and he stepped aside to let us pass, and then fell in behind us.

190

"Eddie!" I started talking while we were still walking towards him, "Emma's a real estate agent and she sold that house over there to the neighbors. Three years ago. That was *before* Anders and Anna disappeared with the bank money. That means these people have been around for longer than I thought. Emma knows what they look like, too. Do you have a picture of Anders and Anna?"

Eddie turned to her, "Emma?" he asked, to confirm her name. "Would you mind going over all of this again for me?"

I heard a cell phone ringing over by Katie's car, where we had just been, but nobody was standing over there. Then I realized it was my phone. Crap. It must have fallen out of my purse when I was squatting by the roadside. Good thing it was ringing or I wouldn't have known I'd lost it. Emma was answering a string of questions for Eddie, so I slipped away to go get my phone. John followed me.

"Where are you going, Mims?"

"Do you hear that cell phone over there? It's mine. It must've dropped out of my purse when I was over behind the cars. I'm just going to go find it."

He fell into step with me.

By the time I got to where I thought I'd lost it, the phone had stopped ringing and I couldn't see it anywhere.

"Hey, would you call me on your phone so I can hear mine when it rings?"

John gave a little laugh, and shook his head. He peered at his cell phone and pushed a single button. A few feet away in the roadside grass, I heard my phone ring and saw the green light from its screen illuminate a small area. I walked over and stooped down to retrieve it but as I rose and turned towards John, a movement on the other side of the road caught my eye.

John saw my reaction and turned in the same direction. In the distance, on the neighbors' long, dark driveway, something was stirring. We began to hear a low moan.

I dropped my purse and cell phone in the dirt and stood motionless next to John. We were both trying to understand what we were seeing. I could make out a large mass, larger than a human being, moving in an erratic pattern. The noises were getting stranger, too. A moaning, choking sound.

"John," I whispered.

I saw his hand slip back to his hip, towards his gun. Then I finally heard something I recognized. I heard Lehua's name come from the figure. It was getting clearer now. It was Walter, and he was carrying Lehua. I stepped forward and Walter saw me. John hadn't realized who or what it was yet and he grabbed my arm to hold me back.

But Walter knew it was me now and he began to cry out, "Help! Help me! Help Lehua!" and he broke into a lumbering run. At the same time, I began to drag John forward.

Walter lurched towards us and I could see Lehua's limp body flopping around in his arms.

"Katie!" I shouted. "Katie! Help!"

Everyone at the house turned and responded immediately. I could see that Mitch and Eddie and Glen were running towards us with their hands on their holsters.

"It's Walter and Lehua," I called out as they drew nearer. "They need help."

John shouted at Mick, "Turn your light on them."

Mick unfastened the heavy, black flashlight from his belt and shined it on Walter.

Katie pushed through the group and quickly assessed Lehua, still in Walter's arms.

"Take her to the back of my car," she told him. She led him forward and opened up the tailgate of her large SUV.

Walter placed Lehua's small body gently on the floor of the cargo area. The interior lights illuminated her face.

"Is she dead?" Walter whispered, tears streaming down his

cheeks.

Katie climbed half in, half out, of the vehicle. She bent her head down close to Lehua's face and made a gesture for silence. We were all immediately quiet, except for Walter's soft, low crying. Katie held a finger to Lehua's neck to check for a pulse. She raised Lehua's eyelid. And then she slowly lowered it.

Katie knelt, very quietly and almost motionless for a moment, composing herself. Then she turned and sat on the edge of the bumper, and looked into Walter's immensely sad eyes.

"She's asleep," she said. "I think she's been drugged, but her pulse and breathing are fine."

"Asleep?" Walter asked, as though Katie were speaking another language. Then he tipped forward and collapsed on top of both Katie and Lehua.

"Mmmph," Katie exhaled. She struggled to push Walter's bulk off of her and to protect Lehua.

Walter's legs began to buckle and he started slipping. Eddie and Mitch moved forward to grab him before he hit the ground hard. On his downward slump, Walter's sheer body-weight began to drag Katie along with him. She reached up and grabbed the top of the door frame to stop her slide.

Eddie and Mitch manhandled Walter's unconscious bulk and brought him to rest on the dirt road. Mick ran forward to aid them but there was no room for him to do much good. Katie was left dangling by her hands, her pants pulled down around her knees by Walter's passage over her body.

"Wait until we tell Kelly about *this*," Emma said softly.

For a moment Katie glared at her with a scowl but it quickly changed to a smile and then she began to laugh. She hopped out of the SUV and pulled her pants back up. Then she went back into doctor mode again and set about checking Walter, only to determine what we all knew, he'd just fainted.

"Call the EMS for them both," Eddie ordered Mick.

Mick stepped away from the group and followed Eddie's orders.

I was standing, dumb struck, at the edge of the activity. Sort of on autopilot, I turned to, once again, try to retrieve my purse and cell phone. I could feel John's eyes following me. I paused for a moment to stare down the neighbors' long, dark driveway, trying to reconstruct what had just happened. To my amazement, I once again saw movement there.

"John!" I exclaimed as I pointed in the direction of the driveway.

Everyone, except of course Katie and her patients, again rushed to my side.

"What...?" Emma asked in wonderment. The driveway seemed alive with scurrying little creatures.

"It's Sweetie and the puppies!" I said.

Then I saw another form, standing bravely quiet in the road in advance of the wriggling little group of puppies, like a centurion. It was the Lundehund.

"Sweetie!" I called. I knelt and opened my arms.

WHEN SHE HEARD HER NAME, despite the lights and crowd of people, Sweetie came running forward. The Lundehund didn't know what to do. The puppies tried to follow their mother and they mobbed around his feet and sort of urged him forward. He was clearly wary of us but Sweetie, true to her name, didn't hesitate to come towards affection.

Sweetie danced around, licking my cheeks, but only for a moment, until she saw Walter on the ground. She immediately turned her full attention to him and rushed over to begin CPR. The little herd of puppies caught up to her and they began to wobble up and over Walter's massive form, licking and chewing on him. The Lundehund stood at a distance and watched.

Walter's hand came up to brush away a nose from his ear. His eyes opened and he saw Sweetie standing squarely on his chest looking him straight in the eye. A broad smile covered Walter's face, as though he were just waking from a long nap in a comfortable bed to find her there. Slowly, though, he began to register where he was and what had happened. He gently began to remove Sweetie and the puppies from his body. The Lundehund gave a low, protective growl from his spot a few feet away.

Walter looked over at him quizzically. Then he gently said, "I not going hurt your family, little man."

Eddie saw that Walter was going to try to sit up, so he knelt amongst the puppies. "Lehua's fine," he reminded him. "She's just asleep and the doctor's taking care of her. If you want to get up, do it slowly, okay?"

Walter grunted his accord and rose up onto one elbow.

Eddie, still kneeling, looked up at Mitch and John and said, "As soon as we can, let's move everybody over to the house. I want to clear this area before the SWAT team arrives."

I'd forgotten about the SWAT team.

Eddie spoke to Katie and said, "Is it okay to move Lehua? Can you drive your car over to the house so we can take her inside, to her bed? I want to get away from the neighbors' driveway, and out of the road. Will that be safe?"

"I think so," Katie answered him. Then she turned to Mick and said, "Hop in the back with her. I'm not going to close the tailgate. Just make sure she doesn't roll around or anything."

Mick looked at Eddie who made a small gesture with his hand to tell him to comply with Katie's request.

Katie gently moved Lehua's legs a little to the side to make room for Mick to crouch next to her in the back of the SUV. Then she walked quickly to the driver's seat and drove the car the short distance to the house.

Walter rose heavily to his feet with some help from Mitch.

He reached down and somehow managed to scoop up Sweetie and all the puppies into his arms.

The Lundehund was trying frantically to be macho but was losing his battle. He began to whine and follow Walter as we all walked slowly behind the SUV.

LEHUA WAS GENTLY TRANSFERRED to her bed and Walter was coaxed into sitting down on a chair, next to her. Katie stayed in the bedroom with them.

Eddie posted Mick outside the house to keep a watch on the neighbor's driveway but the rest of us sort of milled around in the living room and kitchen. Sweetie and the puppies joined us but the Lundehund stood in the doorway, unwilling to come inside. Because Eddie wanted to shut the door and secure the house, though, we finally made a successful effort to lure the little guy into the living room with an offer of some lunch meat from the refrigerator.

John was standing in the kitchen when I joined him there. "I'm going to call Sam," I told him. "I want him to know Lehua's been found and she's okay."

"Good idea."

I stared at his face for a moment. I could see a five o'clock shadow appearing on his jaw. I wanted to apologize to him but I wasn't sure for what. Beards are not usually my thing but they look good on some men and I actually kind of liked John's. Cyd and I had just been playing around when he overheard us the day before. But now I felt sorry for being so...what? So glib? I wanted to reach up and touch his face. I remembered that things could have turned out differently with Lehua; she could have been harmed. Life is short, as the cliché goes, and I don't want to pass up the opportunity to connect with those I care about. So, for whatever reason, I reached up and touched his face.

John held eye contact but stayed completely still and didn't speak.

I turned and walked to one of the children's bedrooms, to a quiet place, to call Sam.

15 BREAKING THE NEWS TO SAM

"I'VE BEEN MEANING TO CALL YOU!" Becky cheerily answered the phone. "What's up?"

"Hi. Hey, is Sam home?" I knew my voice didn't sound equally cheery.

"Yes," she replied warily.

"Would you mind putting him on the phone? But stay on yourself, too."

I really didn't mean to frighten her, but I didn't want to have to explain everything twice. I heard her urgently call out to Sam.

"Mimi," Sam spoke into a second phone.

"Mimi's got something to tell us both," Becky's voice explained to him.

"Well," I told them, "it's not bad news. I'm out at Walter and Lehua's and they're both here. They're both okay. Lehua's asleep. Katie Reed's here, too, and she's examined Lehua. She said she thinks Lehua's been drugged, but she also thinks she's just sleeping and is going to be fine. EMS is on the way. John's here, too. But the SWAT team is also coming."

"What the hell?" Sam said.

"Mimi," Becky asked with alarm, "what are you doing there? Are you in danger? Why's the SWAT team coming?"

I didn't know where to start.

There was a knock at the door and Eddie poked his head in the room.

"Hold on," I said to Sam and Becky.

"Who are you talking to?" Eddie asked.

"Doctor Morris."

"Oh, okay. The EMS is already here and they'll be taking Lehua back to the hospital. I'm sending Walter, too, just to cover my ass. I want you all to go back into town with them. Mitch is calling Walter's sister and asking her to keep the kids. I need to clear this area before SWAT gets here.

"I don't know what we're going to encounter in that house. Walter said it seemed empty. He looked in the window and only saw Lehua, lying on a couch, and he just smashed the door and went in after her. He didn't see anybody else and nobody came when he made all that noise. So, maybe he's right and there's nobody there, but I can't take any chances."

"Okay, I'll be right out."

I hadn't bothered to cover the phone while I was talking to Eddie and I didn't know how much Sam and Becky had heard. "We're leaving now," I told them. "We're headed for the hospital. Eddie wants us all to clear out before the SWAT team gets here."

"I'll meet you at the hospital," Sam said. "You can explain everything to me there. Did you say John's with you?"

"Yeah."

"Well, I'm glad for that. See you soon."

Sam hung up but I could tell that Becky was still on the line.

"Are you safe?" she asked me.

"Yeah, I'm safe. A little shaky, though. This has been quite an adrenalin rush."

"Well, be careful," she reminded me.

"Yeah, I will. Are you coming to the hospital, too?"

"Probably not, but if you want to come over afterwards, no matter how late it is, you know I'll be here."

"Thanks. If not tonight, then maybe tomorrow. I gotta go

199

now. Love you."

"I love you, too," she said.

When I walked out into the living room, everyone was standing. Through an open door, I could see the EMS folks strapping Lehua onto a stretcher. Walter was refusing to allow the same thing to be done to himself, however.

It was finally decided that Walter would ride, seated, alongside his wife. The second EMS van that had answered the call would stay put to wait for the arrival of the SWAT team and whatever eventualities that might bring.

I knew Mick was silently praying that he wouldn't have to leave all the action and drive me back into town. So, I took pity on him and told Eddie I'd crowd into Katie's car, between Cyd and Emma; John still had shotgun.

WE WERE ALL SEATED in Katie's car when Emma said, "Wait! What's going to happen to the dogs? We can't leave them in the house alone. We have to go get them. I'll take them home with me."

She had a good point. I wasn't at all sure how Barney would take to the Lundehund, and vice versa, but Emma seemed confident it would all work out.

Even though it took some convincing to get the little guy into the car, we actually left before the EMS van carrying Lehua and Walter did. Nobody talked much on the drive back. We made a few comments when the ambulance passed us on its way into town, and again when we saw the SWAT team blazing towards the scene. Stupid comments really, just small talk.

Once, Cyd nudged me and quietly said, "You know that thing we were saying yesterday? About fainting?"

I knew she meant fainting into Mitch's arms, but she was being purposely vague so that John wouldn't understand.

"Yeah, I remember."

"It's kind of funny that Walter was the one to do it."

That brought a smile to my lips. And on the other side of me, Emma said, "Yes, well, he beat me to it. Because, *whoo baby!*"

John didn't give any indication that he was listening.

Cyd reached over, into the back, and brought the four, wriggling little puppies up to sit on our laps. Sweetie seemed happy to have babysitters and the puppies soon dozed off.

It was about ten o'clock when Katie delivered us all to Emma's house. I left right away for the hospital to meet Sam, leaving the others behind.

THE GLARING WHITE-BLUE LIGHTS and the chill of the hospital's air conditioning assaulted my senses. I turned to go back to the car, to retrieve my sweatshirt, but the receptionist stood and knocked on her window.

"Are you Miriam Charles?" she mouthed at me.

I nodded yes.

The large, double doors next to her desk slid open.

I hugged my arms around me for warmth. I could see Sam, standing at the end of the long beige hallway. When he spotted me, he walked to join me.

"Everything okay?" I asked him.

"Yeah, Lehua's still asleep and Walter's fine. Let's go to the cafeteria and get some coffee."

That was the last thing I wanted to do but I followed him anyway, through the authorized-entry-only doors, down the low-lit back hallways of the hospital.

There was no one in the cafeteria but a night guard and a cashier. I found a plastic bottle of orange juice in the refrigerated bin next to the checkout. I unscrewed the blue plastic top and took a swig while we stood at the register. What do they do to oranges to make them taste so bitter and un-orangey in those bottles?

We settled at a table. "You look like you've had a long day," Sam commented.

Really, did he think? Suddenly I felt tears brimming in my eyes. Sam was clearly uncomfortable. He reached over and clapped a hand on my shoulder. It was the best he could do.

When he let go, I took a deep breath and shrugged my shoulders up to my ears to relieve the tension in them. I started to tell him the story about the Lundehund and the way I'd made the connection between the Bentsons and Lehua's abduction. About halfway through my explanation, though, Sam got paged.

He stood up and reached for a hospital house phone, attached to a pillar near the table. He had a short conversation, apparently with someone in the ER and, when it was over, he sat back down across from me and pushed his coffee away.

"It looks like Lehua was given a fairly powerful sedative. She's going to be okay but they've decided to just let her sleep it off, rather than introduce more drugs into her body. They've got her hooked up to a saline drip, just to keep her hydrated, and they've got heart and breathing monitors on her, but nothing else. They're expecting her to recover by midmorning."

Sam and I sat at the table for about ten more minutes as I finished recounting the day.

"So, when you left, the SWAT team wasn't there yet?"

"Nope. According to Eddie Paiva, when Walter saw Lehua inside the house - well, you know Walter - he didn't stop to think about the consequences, he just smashed the door open and went in and got her. He picked up Lehua and left the house with her, so he didn't look around at all. Eddie didn't know what to expect going back into the house."

"I suppose the good news is," Sam said, "the ER reports no incoming from the area and I haven't received a report of anybody being brought into the morgue, either."

Well, yeah, I guess that was a form of good news.

Sam told me he was going back to the hospital, just for a moment, to let Walter know he was available if he needed him. He said he'd keep me posted if there was any news.

"Okay." I stifled a yawn. "Tell Becky I'll talk to her tomorrow."

"Well, she's probably asleep, anyway."

Of course she was. It was after midnight. We all should have been asleep.

In the hallway, outside the cafeteria, Sam gave me another pat on the shoulder and I put my hand on top of his. Then we parted ways and I walked out into the dark, starlit night. I found HoneyGirl and headed straight home.

16 LURKING IN THE POTTED PALMS

THE BIRDS HAD ALREADY SETTLED into their daytime routine when I awoke. I'd heard it raining hard during the night but there was only a trace of dampness left on the leaves and grass, and some minor puddles on the courtyard pavement. Rain water doesn't collect here; it just filters right down through the porous lava. As a result, we have only two small lakes on the island. One of them, *Lake Waiau*, is inside an ancient cinder cone, close to the top of Mauna Kea; it was formed by a glacier during the Ice Ages. It's hard to believe that even Hawaii had glaciers back then.

I wrapped on a sarong and went to collect the newspaper. After I'd scanned the front page, I walked slowly towards the backyard, savoring the morning. I picked up a few fallen avocados and cradled them in my arms while I walked back into the house.

I sat down with a cup of tea to finish reading the paper. It was Friday, April the sixth, and the newspaper was filled with excitement about the upcoming *Merrie Monarch* Festival, a showcase of the best of the best of hula - there's really nothing else like it in the world.

I felt a sense of gratitude for being able to live in Hawaii. Lehua was safe, the sun was shining and the birds were singing. I rose and put the dirty dishes in the sink, and went to my office to do a quick check of emails before I got dressed. As I booted up the computer, I was surprised to notice the message light on my phone was blinking. Fourteen messages. I didn't even know my phone could handle that many. I'd forgotten to check for them when I'd come home the night before.

I pressed the playback button and began to listen. There were a couple of hang-ups, a message from my friend in Texas who was still apologizing for awakening me, a message from Eddie asking me to call him back about Pohoiki Doe, and ten messages from Matt Ortiz, Channel Six News.

This guy was getting on my nerves. I thought Sam had handled him but maybe he hadn't gotten around to it - a lot had been happening. I began to develop a script in my mind in which I called him and articulately brought him to his knees with shame. Or I could just tattle on him to Sam again. Or I could ignore him. The temptation was behind Door Number One but my adult self knew my imaginary script, much as I was savoring it, probably wouldn't unfold the way I thought. From what I knew about Ortiz, trying to ignore him wouldn't work, either.

I sat at the desk, considering my options, while I absent-mindedly skimmed through my Facebook messages. I absolutely froze when I saw a friend request from Ortiz. Oh, this guy had balls. Hairy, greasy balls, covered with flies, dragging in the mud. I indignantly rejected his request. He required more thought than I chose to devote to him at that moment, but I'd get back to him later.

I picked up the phone and called Becky. "Hey," I said when she answered. "Quite a day, yesterday."

"Well, yeah, I guess," she said. "Sam didn't get home until one o'clock and he had to leave again at seven this morning, poor guy."

"I need a day off - a mental health day. Do you want to get some lunch? Or we could go get pedicures."

"Let's do both."

205

"That's the spirit! How about Ocean Sushi?"

Hilo has sprouted a whole bunch of new restaurants lately but I don't want to forget the old, reliable favorites.

"Perfect," she said. "Is noon okay? I'll call and make reservations for the pedicures, too."

"This is going to be great. I'll see you then."

I got dressed in a colorful sundress and fancy slippers, with beads and crystals on them. New toenail polish requires a proper presentation, just like fine art needs the right frame.

AS I DROVE, I COULD SEE the sun shining over downtown, where I was going to meet Becky. On my way, though, I was dropping in, really fast, to see Lehua at the hospital. I didn't want to even get close to the ME's office; I was taking a day off from all of that. Pohoiki Doe would have to wait. His family had been notified of his identification, so there was no rush now. He wasn't going to get any deader.

I walked through the big, open, double doors at the front of the hospital and stopped at the reception desk. There was a large bouquet of anthuriums and heliconia on the counter. Two volunteers, sweet-looking older women, sat at the desk and gently explained to me the HIPAA rules about patients' privacy and all. But they soon directed me to Lehua's floor, anyway.

A crowd of family and friends spilled into the hallway from Lehua's room. Of course there are rules about room capacity, but Lehua was sort of a special case. She was going to get better right away, which is always a cause for celebration amongst everyone at a hospital, patients and staff alike. She was also well known in the community and in the hospital. And *everybody* knew what she had just been through, more or less.

I poked my head around the doorway to her room. At first, I couldn't see through the crowd but then I heard a little voice, "Hi, Auntie Mimi." It was JR, Lehua's six-year-old son.

"Hey, JR, how's your mom?" I asked him.

"Fine," he said as he took my hand and pulled me through the crowd to Lehua's bedside. "Mom," he tried to get her attention. "Mommy. Mommy, it's Auntie."

He tugged at her hospital gown, until Lehua finally looked down at him and saw my hand in his. Her eyes raced up my arm to my face and she blossomed into a surprised smile.

"It's you!" she announced. "Walter, look who's here."

Walter turned from another visitor. "Ho! It's you," he announced.

"Hi," I said, in a muffled voice, as Walter swept me into an embrace.

"This is Mimi," Walter announced to the room.

Then I went through the ritual of hugging, and sometimes kissing, each adult in the room. It was a pleasure. It's always a pleasure to me.

"Sorry," Walter apologized. "Sorry, I no wait for you to bring da picture. I jes' knew what you mean when you said take the kids Ruth's."

He and Lehua locked eyes.

"Yeah," I replied. "Well, I guess everything turned out okay for everybody."

Then I thought about the neighbors. "Did you hear what happened next door after we left? To your neighbors?"

"No," Walter was still looking at Lehua, "nobody told me."

He and Lehua were doing some kind of private messaging with those looks at each other.

Lehua motioned me closer. She said in a voice low enough that the others in the room, who were talking and laughing with each other, couldn't hear, "They gone. They gave me the medicine in the afternoon and then they left. I stayed."

"What? You stayed on purpose?"

I could see she was worried about having said too much.

207

"No tell the police, okay? I want tell you what happen but I don't want them know. You promise?"

"Uh, I think so," I hedged. "I'll try not to tell but, if you're in danger, I might."

She pulled me even closer. "They giving us the house."

"What? What house? *Theirs?*"

"Yeah, but it not theirs. It was the brother one, the one went drown. He want it for Floki."

"Floki?" I was lost.

I knew Floki wasn't a Hawaiian word, because there's no F in Hawaiian, but I thought maybe it was some kind of pidgin term or maybe I just wasn't hearing it right.

"What's Floki?"

"The dog," she whispered back, with a smile on her face. "He mine now. And the house."

I was confused and had about a million questions but Lehua pulled away and looked over my shoulder. Eddie was standing in the doorway.

"Oh, hi, Eddie," I said. The room quietened a bit.

"Hi folks," he said to everyone. He gave a one-armed hug to Walter and to several of the women closest to him, murmuring, "Auntie," to a few of them. A couple of them kissed him on the cheek.

"I'm sorry to interrupt," he announced, "but I need to talk to Lehua and Walter for a little while."

Eddie turned to the oldest person in the room, a seated woman, and said, "Would you mind if the family waits outside in the waiting area? I'm sorry, but I've got to do my job. I need to make sure the family's safe."

"Certainly." The woman nodded and waved her hand in front of her in a sideways fan motion, signifying to the rest of the group that they should move out of the room.

"It won't be long," Eddie apologized to them all.

JR, though, didn't want to go. He tried to crawl onto the bed

208

with his mother, almost tipping over the stand holding her IV drip. Eddie reached out and steadied the stand and Walter scooped JR up in one hand.

"You got go outside," Walter told him.

"No! I want stay!" JR insisted.

Eddie said to Walter, "It's okay with me. He can stay, if you say so."

Walter took JR's little body and tucked it under his left arm, like he was carrying a football, with JR's upturned head in his broad left hand. He looked sternly down at his boy's face but then broke into a gentle smile. "Okay, but no talking. This is quiet time," he told the boy.

He placed his son on the bed with Lehua. JR sat cross-legged, properly solemn and quiet, near his mother's feet.

Eddie turned to me, "You, too, Mimi. Sorry."

"Oh! Of course. I'll talk to you later, Lehua." I gave her and Walter another hug and turned to leave the room.

"I just came by for a quick visit," I explained to Eddie.

As I walked to the door, Lehua said to me, "No forget."

When I walked into the hallway, I saw that the family had gathered in the large, open waiting area, put there just for that purpose. *Ohana*, family, is preeminent in Hawaii so it's customary to have large groups of visitors. However, over in the corner, behind a cluster of potted ti plants, I also saw Matt Ortiz.

ENOUGH WAS ENOUGH WITH THIS GUY. I thought back to something my husband, Jay, once did to a reporter. My husband was the kindest of souls but he could be pushed to his limits, too. One time, he'd been conducting a large study at the hospital where he worked. He was interested in how low birth weight babies progressed in their next few years. Did they catch up to the normal birth weight babies or did they stay behind the weight curve? The small babies' medical records were pulled from the hospital files and invitations were sent out for a free physical examination when each child reached two years old. Because many of the mothers who gave birth at the hospital were very poor, it was a blessing to them to have free healthcare offered to their children and many of them brought their toddlers to join in the study. However, a local reporter had gotten wind of the story and he called Jay to ask if it was true that babies were being *recalled* by the hospital.

At first Jay thought the whole idea of a recall, as though the babies had been installed with faulty steering columns, or something, was funny. He just ignored it. But the reporter was clearly looking for a sensational angle and, when Jay got word that the guy was pestering nurses and others involved in the study, he decided to take action.

"I bored him away," he told me.

He'd invited the reporter to his office and, when he arrived, Jay closed the door and settled himself behind his desk. Then he began to give the reporter every boring, mundane piece of information on infant birth weights that he could think of.

Jay's eyes twinkled when he told me, "I kept him there for almost two hours. He kept saying, 'Well, thanks, but I've got to be going now,' and I would say, 'Oh, but you haven't heard about this important study', and I'd tell him about another obscure paper. By the time he left," Jay laughed, "I knew he'd never come back again."

I miss Jay's gentle heart.

But, now, it was time to deal with Matt Ortiz. I pretended I didn't see him lurking in the corner as I walked up to some of the men in Walter's family. Hawaiian men, descendants of long-distance voyagers and warriors, can easily be double my body size, triple sometimes, so it was easy to stand, sheltered by their bulk, out of Ortiz's view while I explained my plot to them.

210

I asked for their help and, with amusement, they agreed. They pointed out to me two of the senior ladies in their family group. Then, while I walked over to talk to Ortiz, one of the men casually strolled over to the ladies to explain our scheme.

As I approached him, Ortiz tried to burrow farther behind the leaves, but he was cornered.

"Aren't you Matt Ortiz, from Channel Six News? I think you've been trying to call me. I'm Miriam Charles."

He nodded in recognition of my name.

I kept my tone a bit clipped since I didn't want to seem too cordial; he probably remembered the last time we'd spoken, when I'd been less than friendly.

"So, what were you calling for?" I asked him.

"Well, uh," he cautiously emerged from behind the plants, "I was wondering if you'd be willing to talk to me about that body that was found out at Pohoiki on Wednesday. I saw the video on YouTube, so I know you were there."

I didn't answer him but I tried to keep my look neutral.

He began to fidget. "But since you're here now, too, maybe you could tell me about Lehua Ka'awa, instead. Or either. It's your choice."

What a weasel.

"I'm not at liberty to discuss the reason I was at Pohoiki," I told him. "But Lehua is my friend so I guess it might be okay to talk about her."

I looked over my shoulder with, I hope, a well-acted look of concern. "Maybe the family wouldn't want me to talk about her, though. Maybe I should ask one of them to talk to you, instead."

I could see his beady, little eyes light up as he struggled to stay casual. "Oh, sure, I guess that would work. I mean, if you think that's best. Sure. That would work for me. Uh-huh."

"Just a minute," I told him. "I'll go talk to them."

211

I LEFT ORTIZ IN THE CORNER and walked back over to the two, seated ladies. I recognized one of them, *Kukui* Spencer, and I gave her the first hug, taking care not to break any bones in her delicate body. She is a very thin woman.

"Auntie Kukui! I haven't seen you in a while. How are you? And what a beautiful hat!"

She had on an intricately woven *lauhala* hat, a beautiful work of a nearly lost Hawaiian art.

"Oh, this old thing," she gave a dismissive wave of her hand that would make any southern belle envious. "It's nice to see you, too. Do you know my cousin, Sally?"

I bent forward to hug Auntie Sally, a large woman with ginger blossoms arranged in her hair and wearing a spacious, flowered mumu. It was Aloha Friday, after all.

While I hugged her, Auntie Sally whispered in my ear, "This is so much fun!"

Auntie Kukui leaned into the conversation, too, with a conspiratorial giggle and said, "We're going to tell him every story about Lehua we can think of, starting when she was born. We might have to slow down a little bit when we get to her first day in kindergarten because I can't remember the names of all her classmates."

"Oh, yes," Auntie Sally smiled with glee, "and then we can tell him about the time she fell off her bicycle and had to get stitches in her knee."

They were clearly relishing the plan.

"I'll leave it in your hands," I told them with a smile.

ORTIZ HAD RETURNED to his spot in the foliage, so I spoke softly to the shadows amongst the leaves, "I've managed to get some of the elder women to talk to you. You understand, though, that you must show them proper respect."

212

"Oh, yes, yes, of course I will," Ortiz pledged. "Absolutely. No question about it."

"Alright, then, it's those two ladies over there."

I pointed to Aunties Sally and Kukui and they, in turn, waved in his direction, the most saintly smiles on their faces.

Ortiz emerged from his hiding spot and I watched him walk over to the ladies. The large men in the family closed in around them, in a rapt circle, to hear all about Lehua, and to prevent Matt Ortiz from leaving until he was good and bored with the story.

I was ready to depart the hospital but I noticed the women's room nearby and decided to stop in and, you know, freshen up a bit before I left to meet Becky. When I came back into the hallway, a few minutes later, I could hear Auntie Sally saying, "So she gave the third kitten to her best friend. That kitten was named Buttons."

"No, dear, I don't think that's right," interrupted Auntie Kukui. "I think that kitten was named Whiskers. The fourth kitten was Buttons." She looked at the men around her and said, "What do you remember, was it Buttons or Whiskers?"

One of the men said, "I think it might have been Puff."

They all laughed and looked like they were quite genuinely enjoying themselves.

I could see that Ortiz was starting to look restless but Puna, Walter's largest cousin, placed a hand on Ortiz's shoulder that held him firmly in his spot. It could have been interpreted as a friendly gesture. I left the hospital with a smile on my face.

I FOUND A PARKING PLACE on *Keawe* Street, right next to the restaurant. There are a lot of words that could describe old downtown Hilo. Busy, colorful, dilapidated, quirky, funky, quaint and charming, I just know that I am delighted by it. The larger, more substantial buildings mostly seem to have been built in the nineteen twenties and thirties. Tsunamis have repeatedly culled the less robust, wooden structures so that there now are vacant lots forming gaps between the stone and cement buildings. Of the surviving wooden structures, many resemble Main Street buildings from an old western movie, with rickety, weathered wood in the back, fronted by colorfully painted, taller facades. Some businesses have been there for generations but lately there's been a flurry of new restaurants and shops popping up.

I spotted Becky right away when I walked into the crowded, noisy restaurant.

"I already ordered for us," she told me, as I sat down.

"Good plan. What did you get?" I was hoping she had ordered our usual three favorites and she did not disappoint.

"The usual." She leaned in closer, so that our conversation would not be overheard. "Did you hear about the guy who drowned in the river?"

"Bentson? You mean new stuff? I guess not, what do you know?"

"Apparently," she said, putting her forearms on the table and settling into the conversation, "the guy who drowned in the river was the actual owner of the house next to Lehua – not the people who were living there."

"Huh," I said. "I didn't know *that*. Last night, when we were out in Puna, Emma told me she was the agent who sold the house, three years ago. She said she sold it to a Norwegian *couple*."

It was Becky's turn to say, "Huh."

"I've been wondering something. If those people stole money from a bank in Norway, could they have their property in the U. S. confiscated? How does that work?"

"I don't know," Becky answered thoughtfully.

"Of course, if they bought it three years ago like Emma says, that would have been long before they took the money from the bank in Norway, so they wouldn't have actually purchased the house with stolen money. I wonder if the house could still be confiscated. It would be even more complicated if they sold it or transferred it to Eskil."

I thought about what Lehua had told me in the hospital but I couldn't quite put it all together.

Our attention was diverted by the waitress delivering a platter of sushi. After we'd both savored a piece, I made a decision. "You know what? I've had enough of this crime stuff. Lehua's safe. Would you mind if we don't talk about it anymore today?"

"Absolutely," she answered. "I get too much of it at home. Besides, you're right, Lehua's safe and that's all that really matters."

We each popped another piece of sushi into our mouths. When I could talk again, I asked, "What color of polish are you going to get today?"

"I think I'll probably get something in a hot pink. I have some new pink slippers and I want to show them off."

She chose another piece of sushi. "Oh, my God, this is so good!"

We chatted and ate until there were only a few pieces of sushi left on the platter. We couldn't take them to go because they wouldn't last in the warm cars. And we couldn't leave them behind, either, because of, you know, the starving children in Biafra. Not that Biafra still exists, but my guilt over having so much abundance still does. Nope, we had to eat all of the pieces. And we did.

"I'm stuffed," Becky said as we walked outside. "Where'd you park?"

"Right here."

We were standing at the curb next to HoneyGirl. Rock star parking. Or, as Rob calls it, Doris Day parking.

"Where are you?" I asked her.

"In front of The Palace," she nodded in the direction of her

215

car and I spotted it right away.

"Okay," I told her, "See you at the pedicure place."

Becky walked away from me, to cross the intersection, and I opened the door to HoneyGirl to let out the heat that had built up inside. I threw my purse onto the passenger's seat and my cell phone slipped out of it. I noticed that it was blinking. I guess it had been too noisy in the restaurant to hear the little chiming noise of a message being received. Curiosity, of course, beat out my desire for comfort so I dropped down into the hot driver's seat to fetch the phone.

The text message said, *"dont tell eddie what i said ill explain 2 u later"*. It was from Lehua.

Well, she was safe with that wish because I was taking a mental health day and I had no intention of talking to Eddie. I was really curious about what she had to tell me, though.

AFTER WE CHOSE our polish colors, Becky and I settled onto our thrones. The large, leather massage chairs were mounted a step up from the rest of the floor in the room. Our feet were bathed in pink porcelain basins filled with bubbles and warm water. By using handheld controls, we could program our chairs to give our backs a gentle massage or a through working-over. I chose the working over. It felt good but the percussion made it kind of hard for me to talk like a normal person.

It was a lovely, relaxing time. Afterward, I really just wanted to go home and read a novel for a little while and maybe take a nap. I'd been up pretty late the night before.

"Thanks," I told Becky, as we hugged goodbye, "this was just what I needed."

"Me, too," she said. "Let's go to the movies this weekend, and dinner after, okay? I'll see what's playing." She meant that Sam would come, too. When Jay was alive, the four of us used to do that every Sunday afternoon.

"Sounds good to me," I told her, as I stifled a yawn. "See you then. Love you."

I carefully got into HoneyGirl, protecting my newly painted toes, and headed off in a different direction from Becky. I could see a little snow left at the top of Mauna Kea as I drove up the slope to my house.

I FLOPPED ONTO THE living room couch and reached for the mystery novel I was reading. A friend of mine, and a fellow forensic anthropologist, had written it. I like his books but I have trouble reading them when he writes in the voice of female characters; I always hear his voice instead. And I struggle to remove his mustache from their faces. Still, Aaron can weave a good story.

I'd hoped to goof off all afternoon but thoughts of work kept sneaking into my head. Finally, I put the book down and wandered into my office to look at the notes I'd made on Pohoiki Doe.

One thing led to another and I wound up working on my report. There weren't many surprises but I did notice something I hadn't in the lab. Pohoiki Doe was probably a leftie.

It isn't very helpful, in identifying someone, to learn that he or she was right-handed - because most people are right-handed. Only about ten percent of Americans are left-handed, though, so discovering a leftie skeleton helps reduce the field of possible identities for the police to sift through.

Of course, we already had a positive ID on Pohoiki Doe but it would be good to confirm, one way or the other, whether I was reading the handedness signs on his skeleton properly. I sent Eddie an email and asked, if he could do it without disturbing the family, for him to find out whether Billy Taylor had been left-handed.

When the phone rang at about seven thirty, I realized that

it had gotten dark outside. I must have turned the desk lamp on at some point but I couldn't really remember having done it.

"Hello?"

"Hi, it's Eddie. I just got your email."

"Oh, okay. What's up?"

"How could you tell the guy was left-handed? Which he was, by the way."

"Oh, good, I thought so. How much do you want to know?"

"Five minutes worth."

"Okay. Well, it's simple, really. Your bones are alive. When you're young, they grow pretty fast, but they slow down when you're an adult. They don't stop, though. They have to be able to grow enough to heal from breaks and to respond to heavy use. If you start building up muscles, through exercise or whatever, your body also has to build up the bones that anchor them, otherwise the bones could wind up snapping under the strain of use."

"I know a guy who actually did that once," Eddie told me. "He was a weight lifter and he just snapped a bone in his arm. I guess he just built up his muscle too fast."

"Yep, that could happen. And maybe he was using steroids; they can make it worse. So, anyway, a healthy person's bones respond to the muscles' pull by bulking up. When people are right-handed, they're using the muscles of their right hand and arm more often, and maybe for harder work, so the bones on that side of the upper body will often be larger. And vice versa for left-handed people. And because the body has to balance itself for walking, oftentimes a right-handed person will have a slightly larger left leg and foot. So," I told him, "there's your five minutes worth."

"Okay, got it," he said. "Thanks."

"Our guy didn't have a very pronounced difference between his right and left; I didn't really see it with my eyes but I noticed that the measurements I took were just slightly larger for his left, upper body."

"Well, like I said, you got it right," he told me.

Score. I gave myself a little pat on the back. They wouldn't employ me if I got things *wrong*, of course, but I still like to get some positive reinforcement.

"By the way," Eddie said, "did Lehua give you some information at the hospital that I should know about? What were you guys whispering about when I got there? What did she want you not to forget?"

Damn. How did he do that?

"Well," my mind was racing, "she told me the name of the dog. It's Floki."

"Uh-huh...," he said, and then waited for more.

"Oh, come on, Eddie! She asked me not to tell you. Knowing you, you already know anyway. Would it be okay if I just ask you some questions and then, if you already know what she told me, I wouldn't technically be giving away her secrets?"

"Not sure I follow you."

"Okay, let me just try this. Do you know who the neighbor's house belongs to?"

"Yeah."

"Eddie," I said impatiently, "you've got to help me out a little bit here. Cooperate, you know? I already know that you know the house belonged to Eskil Bentson."

"Did Lehua tell you that?"

"Well, yeah, but I heard it from another source, too." I was thinking of Becky. "Putting together what Emma said last night with other stuff, I'm guessing that Anders and Anna Bentson came to Hawaii about three years ago and bought the house but, at some point, transferred it over to the ex-Eskil Bentson."

"Yeah," he said grudgingly, "that seems to be what

happened."

I didn't respond. I waited for him to give *me* more information.

He finally added, "We looked up the property records. They transferred the title to Eskil Bentson about a month after they bought it. He was in prison at the time."

That was probably as much as I was going to get out of him on that subject. "Alright, then, do you know whether Eskil had a will?"

I could sense the wheels turning in Eddie's mind.

"A will? Like he made a will in prison?"

"I hadn't thought of that, but maybe."

"I'll have to check." By the pacing of his words, I could tell that Eddie was writing a note to himself. "Okay, what else?"

"What happened to Anna and Anders Bentson? Did you find them at the house?"

"Nope."

"Cooperation, Eddie," I reminded him.

"They're gone. I don't know where the hell they went."

"Well, what about the note?"

"How do you know about that?" he sounded surprised.

"Dude," I laughed. "I didn't know, I was just fishing." Finally, I had scored one on Eddie.

"Yes, Mimi, they left a note."

"And…?"

"And, they said that they were giving their dog, and any claim to the puppies, to Lehua."

"Wow. Well, I guess an unusual dog like that is worth some money. That was nice of them." The Bentsons probably couldn't have taken Floki with them, anyway, if they'd run off. Lehua would take good care of him and, since he had already fathered those puppies, that kind of made sense.

"They both signed and dated the note, too. I thought that was sort of unusual."

"Hmm." I was checking out my toes. The polish was a pretty color. "That does sound unusual, I guess."

"So, you got anything else to tell me? Or *ask* me?" Eddie sounded impatient.

"Um, well, yes. Is Lehua still in the hospital?"

"No, they discharged her this afternoon. The drugs cleared her body and she's fine. Walter took her home."

"Do you know what kind of drugs she took? I mean, was given?" I hoped Eddie hadn't noticed that slip.

"Apparently it was some mixture of antihistamines and Rohypnol. You know, that's the 'date rape' drug they call a roofie."

"What! You don't mean...." I felt a wave of panic come over me.

"Oh! No, no, no. That didn't happen. She was checked very thoroughly. It seems the only reason she was given Rohypnol was to send her into a deep sleep," he reassured me. "The doc told me that the antihistamines probably just tipped her over the edge without adding much danger. She should be fine." He corrected himself, "She *is* fine, according to the hospital."

"Well, that's a relief."

"You got any more questions for me?" he asked.

"Nope. I don't think so."

"Uh-huh. Any reason you asked what kind of drugs she 'took' before you corrected yourself and said 'was given'?"

"Um, no," I said, trying to sound innocent. "Just a slip of the tongue, I guess."

"Okay." He didn't sound like he believed me. "Well, I guess I've gotten all you're going to give me for now."

I said a silent little *thank you.*

"Great, then," I said cheerily. "Well, I guess I'll talk to you later." I was trying to get off the phone before I gave away every secret in my life.

"Yeah. Oh, hey, Mimi, just one more thing...."

221

I could tell he was playing with me, like some demented cartoon cat with a mouse.

"Did you notice that John shaved his beard?"

"Oooohhh," I moaned. "You bastard, leave me alone! You're just torturing me now, aren't you? How do you know about these things?"

I mean, really? How *did* he know about that conversation Cyd and I had about beards? He wasn't nearby. Who else had been in earshot besides poor John? The young cop, Brandon? Would he have told Eddie, who would then have just filed it away for future use?

I could hear Eddie lightly chuckling.

"I'm hanging up now," I told him, and I put the receiver down quickly.

17 THE WILL OF A CONVICT

BY EARLY SATURDAY AFTERNOON, my report on Pohoiki Doe was finished. It was a sunny, beautiful day in the tropics, so I decided to call Emma.

"Hi, Honey," she answered her phone. "How are you? What are you doing?"

"I'm just hanging around the house. I was wondering if you want to go boogie boarding."

"I was just getting ready to do exactly that. How soon can you be here? I'll wait for you."

"Probably about twenty minutes."

"Well, come for dinner, too. We're just doing barbeque."

"Do you want me to bring anything?"

"No, not this time. Just bring yourself."

"Okay, see you soon."

I always keep my beach gear ready to go, in a satchel in the laundry room. I checked it to make sure I'd put my bathing suit back in after the last time I'd used it. I took off my earrings and put my hair in a tight ponytail. As I locked up the back door, I grabbed my orange boogie board and threw it into the car.

AS I DROVE PAST THE LINE of cars at Honoli'i, I slowed to gaze over the guardrail. The waves looked like a friendly size for me. There were lots of surfers and standup paddlers in the outside break but Emma and I would stay closer to shore where we wouldn't be in their way.

I drove down the steep driveway and parked HoneyGirl in a nice spot, with a view. Emma's two dogs and Barney ran up to greet me as I opened the car door, and they followed me on into the house. Emma was out on the lanai, waiting for me.

"Hey, where are the puppies?" I asked her. "I expected to see a houseful of dogs."

"They're in Kelly's garage."

I must have looked alarmed because she explained, "When we got back Thursday night, I realized I couldn't keep them here because there's no fence. So I took them over to his house."

Kelly only lives at the other end of the street from Emma.

"We tried putting Sweetie and the puppies in Kelly's backyard, because it's fenced. But we knew the Lundehund could climb the fence, so we put him in the garage, by himself. *That* didn't work out. He started barking and howling, and it was late at night. We didn't want to bother the neighbors, so we finally just put all of the dogs in the garage together. Once the Lundehund was back with the puppies, he settled down. The garage isn't a good place for them, though, and I want to take them all back to Lehua's as soon as I can.

"I went over to Kelly's this morning and played with them on the lawn for a while. Their little paws are *so* cute."

Emma had on board shorts and a bathing suit top. I was just wearing my regular old bathing suit, a turquoise bikini with a tropical print. As we spoke, Emma fastened her curly dark hair into a short ponytail.

"The Lundehund's name is Floki," I told her.

"Floki?"

"Yep, I guess it's a Norwegian name."

We both pulled on our rash guards and grabbed our flippers and boards and then we crossed to the edge of the lawn, where a ladder was propped against a stone seawall. We climbed over the edge of the wall and descended the ladder to one of the streambeds that lead towards the broader river and then to the beach. The smooth black rocks in the streambed were slippery and hard to walk on so we both used the edges of our boards, like walking sticks, to stabilize ourselves.

Children were playing on the shore, ahead of us. The beach at Honoli'i doesn't have much sand; it's really mostly made up of varying sizes of river and wave-smoothed stones. Everything is black except for a few pieces of beach glass and a few chunks of sun bleached coral. Even the small crabs along the shore are black. Emma has found small bone fragments there, too, and she always saves them for me. I think she's hoping someday I'll say one's human, but so far she's found mostly pig and goat bones, probably from old barbeques.

MY FACE WAS ACHING from smiling and my right calf was starting to get a little cramp from my new flippers when Emma and I decided to leave the water and head back to the house for tea time. Emma's British background includes a possibly genetic urge to drink tea around four o'clock.

After we rinsed off our gear, we sat in our wet suits at the picnic table, with mugs of tea. I had a towel draped over my shoulders to protect them from the sun.

"Have you recovered from Thursday night yet?" I asked her. "That was a late night."

"I know, and Mick's car woke me up when he came back around three in the morning. I think I made up the sleep last night, though."

"Yeah. Me, too," I said.

"Do you know how Lehua's doing?"

"I went by the hospital and saw her yesterday morning. Eddie told me they released her a little while after that and she's home again. Apparently, the drugs cleared her body and she's fine now."

"Well, that's a relief. More tea?"

"No thanks."

"I'm going to call Kelly. I want to go down to Lehua's tonight to return those dogs. Let's the three of us go."

"What about dinner?" I asked her.

"Oh, that was only going to be you and me, and Mick maybe. He can get his own food. Let's go take the dogs back." As she spoke she used her cell phone to dial Kelly.

"Hey," she said to him. "Mimi's here and she just told me that Lehua's back home again and feeling fine. So let's all go down there and take the puppies back to her. We can get dinner in Kea'au, after."

I couldn't hear his end of the conversation, of course, but Kelly must have said yes because when Emma hung up she told me, "That's settled. He's bringing the dogs over here in a little while."

"Okay. But, before he gets here, I'm kind of interested in hearing more about when you sold the house to Lehua's neighbors. Do you remember much about that?"

"Sure. Eddie asked me the same question but there really isn't that much to remember. I only showed them a few houses. They wanted to buy something secluded, in the Puna area." She turned her mug in her hand. "Of course, I had plenty of properties to show them but they chose the third house they saw. And that was that. It was an easy sale since they paid cash. I had to do a little extra paperwork because they weren't citizens, but they seemed to have all their documents ready ahead of time. I can't remember much about the woman, really. Her English wasn't very good and she stayed in the background. The guy was just sort of average; nothing stood out about him. I thought the house was an odd buy for them but, you know, to each his own. Once we closed on the property, I never saw them again." She took a

226

last sip of tea.

"Apparently," I told her, "pretty soon after they bought the house, they transferred the title to the guy's brother, the one who drowned last week."

"Yes, well, I didn't know anything about that. Eddie told me. He called me yesterday morning because he wanted to see if I still had any old paperwork from the sale. I told him to call the broker." She stood up. "I'm going inside to change before Kelly gets here."

"Yeah, I should do that, too. I'll use the outdoor shower, though."

I love using the outdoor shower. I want one at my house. I quickly rinsed off the salt and detangled my hair. I changed into jeans and a tomato red t-shirt.

KELLY WAS PERCHED on a stool at the kitchen counter, talking to Emma, when I walked inside. The Lundehund sat at attention at his feet.

"Hi. I'd give you a hug but I don't want to get up," Kelly gestured to the Lundehund's leash - its hand loop was secured under one leg of Kelly's stool.

I put one arm around his back and hugged him anyway.

"Emma tells me he's named Floki," Kelly said, looking at the little dog.

"Yeah, I guess it's a Norwegian name."

I looked over to the middle of the living room. Sweetie and the puppies were there. She had jumped up on a couch, out of reach of her progeny, but she was still keeping a mother's eye on them. Mick's dog, Barney, had stretched out his massive bulk in the middle of the Oriental rug and he was good-naturedly letting one of the puppies gnaw on his ear. Occasionally, when it started to hurt, I guess, he'd gently paw the little guy away. Sweetie was paying special attention to that. The puppy would immediately return to Barney for

227

more, though. The other puppies were exploring the room. Emma's two adult dogs were also up on couches, protecting their ears for future use.

"Floki," Kelly mused, "sounds kind of like 'low key'. That's not a good description of him, though. I wouldn't say he's high strung but he's really vigilant. He really watches those puppies."

"I called Lehua and told her we're coming," Emma advised me.

We all watched the puppies for a few minutes. How could anyone not love a roomful of puppies?

"Okay, let's go," Emma finally said.

It took us about fifteen minutes to herd the dogs into Emma's SUV but we were on the road to Puna by five-thirty. Fortunately, it was a weekend so there was no rush hour traffic and we had an easy, uneventful trip, except for one small episode of puppy barf.

"IT CERTAINLY LOOKS DIFFERENT in daylight, doesn't it?" Emma said, as we pulled up to Walter and Lehua's.

"Yeah," Kelly said to me, "Emma tells me you had a pretty exciting night out here on Thursday."

"You could say that," I agreed. "Let's hope this evening isn't a repeat."

At the sound of our car, the two youngest kids, JR and his older brother, eight-year-old Benny, came running to the car to greet us. Well, more like to greet Sweetie and the puppies. Walter and Lehua followed the boys at a slower pace and *Momi*, a blasé thirteen-year-old beauty, hung back by the door. I knew she wanted to join us but it would have just been so uncool to run to the car with her brothers.

"Momi!" Benny called to his sister. "It's Sweetie! You not going come see her?"

That was really all it took to shatter Momi's newly

developed, teenage ennui. She came to join us and helped as we carried the puppies to the yard. Sweetie followed at a leisurely pace. Floki, still a little wary of all the strangers, took up the rear, dragging his leash behind him.

LEHUA OFFERED US cold drinks and we sipped them at her kitchen table while we waited for her to initiate the conversation. I wasn't sure if she was ready to talk about what had happened, or whether she would feel comfortable in front of Emma and Kelly. But after we were all settled she said, "I guess you wondering what happen."

"Yeah," I tried to sound casual.

Lehua looked at Emma. "You the one who help me? Are you the doctor?"

"No," Emma answered her. "That was Katie Reed, the same one you saw at the hospital before. She's Kelly's girlfriend."

Kelly nodded his head.

I could see Lehua trying to work out all the relationships. "Oh, okay. So she help Walter, too, yeah?"

Kelly continued to nod his head and softly said, "Yeah."

"But you wasn't here," Lehua said to Kelly.

"No, I stayed home," he answered her. "Too much excitement."

"You got that right!" Walter laughed.

Lehua said, "I guess everybody want know what happen. Complicated, but." She took a long look at Walter, and then she moved her gaze to Emma and Kelly, "I need you keep one secret. Not all, just a little bit."

"Is it against the law?" Kelly asked her.

"I don't think so," she answered him.

"I think I know what it is," I said to Emma and Kelly, "and I'm pretty sure you'll be okay with it."

"Alright," they both agreed, in unison.

"Where's the kids?" Lehua asked Walter.

"Playing with the dogs," he reassured her. "They fine - cannot hear."

Rather than looking apprehensive, Lehua began to look like she was about to burst with happiness. She wiggled in her seat a little bit, to find just the right spot from which to tell her story. "Okay, so, you not gonna believe this," she started. "You know the guy? The guy in the parking lot who went grab me?"

Walter interjected, "The one you get by the balls!"

"Yeah, that one," Lehua confirmed. "I nevah see him before that day, but he was the guy who own Floki. Anders told me. Anders was our neighbor. And the drowned guy was his brother.

"He told me all kind stuffs about when him and his brothers was kids. The brother, the one went drown, his name was Esco or Exso, or something like that. Anders say Exso was a little mental. He could not control hisself and he would get real angry about little things, this and that, all the time. But he was always real good with animals. He got calm with dogs so the family always made sure they was dogs around.

"Anders say when Exso came America, the family was, you know, kinda relieved he was gone. But they was also worried 'cause he didn't have his dog, Floki, with him. He was going go back for Floki but nobody was real surprise when he got arrested and put in prison.

"Anders was the oldest boy in the family so he got the parents' house when they went die. But Anders say Exso act like *he* the boss of everybody. Even from America, he doing stuff like sending them money so he could be a big man. They didn't really want his money 'cause, for one thing, they didn't know where he got it. But Anders work at a bank so he jus' put the money Exso send in a account there.

"Exso, he was always sending letters home, too. He was talking about his cellmate at the prison, a local boy from Big

Island. Exso say he want come Hawaii someday. That when Anders get one brainstorm. He take Exso money from the bank and come Hawaii with it for buy one house. You know, maybe Exso won't come back live with them in Norway if they tell him they, like, *invested* his money on the Big Island."

I interrupted her to say, "We know a little bit about that because Emma," I nodded at Emma, "is a real estate agent and she's the one who sold them the house."

"Ho!" Walter said, under this breath.

Lehua shifted her gaze to Emma. "Yeah," she said to Emma, "they bought it but they nevah want keep for theirselfs. They was just hoping it would get rid Exso in their lifes. You remember them?"

"Yes, a little bit," Emma replied. "I remember him more than her. I didn't spend very much time with them, though."

"You want another beer?" Walter asked Kelly.

Kelly looked at his empty beer can in surprise. He waggled it to listen for any sounds of liquid but apparently heard none. "Yeah, sure, that would be nice."

"How about you?" Walter asked Emma and me.

We both declined. I'm not a beer drinker. Now, if he'd offered mezcal with some lime and salt....

Walter tipped his chair back until he could reach the refrigerator door. With a one-handed motion he liberated three cans of beer, two for Kelly and himself, and he placed one in front of Lehua, too.

Lehua continued, "Anders idea went bad. The money Exso sending not exactly his *own* money. Some Mexican guy come their Norway house and say he want it back. He say he kill them, or he kill Exso, or he get the money - he don't care - and they got twenty-four hours. Only they already went spend the money on the house over here. So, they run. Nobody know they got this house except them and the other brother, Lars. That's why they was just sort of hiding real quiet here."

"Um," I interrupted, "I think there's maybe more to that story than he told you. Anders took a *lot* of money from the bank when he ran. The FBI guy said 'a shitload'. That's when the police in Norway started to search for him."

"Oh," Lehua said softly. She was quiet for a moment and then her voice came back and she continued, "So, they was doing okay and just living here real quiet and all but Lars, he call say Exso getting out prison in America. So they all think, well, Lars can bring Floki over here and they going tell Exso come straight here, after prison, to his new house. Anders and Anna, they going leave. Everybody just want Exso out of they hair. Nobody knew Exso going get kicked out of America.

"But, Lars, he don't know all the Hawaii laws for bring dogs. He had go make one special trip for bring Floki New York for blood tests and stuff. It took long time but he got everything ready. When he finally came Kona, Anders and Anna went over there get Floki and bring him back Hilo side with them.

"That's why they put that big fence - for Floki. But he escape anyway. And you know where he went go." She nodded her head in the direction of the yard where the kids were playing with the puppies.

Walter said, "Tricky little buggah."

"Excuse me," I sheepishly interrupted again. "I need to use the bathroom. Is it okay if we take a little break?"

"Oh, sure," Lehua said. "Break time."

She and Emma and I all stood and headed towards the two bathrooms. Walter and Kelly cruised outside to find some convenient bushes and, I hoped, no bodies.

LEHUA BROUGHT ANOTHER set of drinks to the table and put out some Maui potato chips, too. I knew those were probably reserved for company because they're expensive, even here in the islands. I realized we hadn't brought

232

anything with us. That was a breach of etiquette but, I hoped, forgivable under the circumstances.

"Okay," I recapped, "Anders and Anna were living quietly next door and Lars had brought Floki to them. But Floki escaped and got Sweetie pregnant. He climbed the fence?"

"Yeah, but they fix it after that so he couldn't do it no more."

"Floki's going to be a handful," I teased Lehua. "How are you going to keep him in your yard?"

She didn't answer me but a big smile spread across her face and I could tell the answer was coming soon.

"When Exso got sent back Norway, Lars tell him, 'Surprise! Anders and Anna bought one house in Hawaii for you with your money and Floki already there.' He tell him about the Mexican, too, so maybe Exso would get some *motivation* to stay gone. So Exso, he took Lars passport and come Big Island.

"When Exso come, Anders and Anna was getting ready leave but one day our kids was out playing in the yard with the puppies and Anna, she was walking by. When she see them, she knew they was Floki's 'cause the toes. She went tell Anders. They was real worried Exso going see the puppies, too. If he saw the toes, he gonna know who's the father.

"Anders say the only thing Exso really care about is Floki. When he in prison, he made a will 'cause he's worried the Mexicans was going kill him. The will was only just so somebody take care Floki, if Exso get killed. Whoever do that, going get everything Exso own.

"You know," she added, "Anders tell me Floki some kind special hunting dog. Can climb mountains and stuff, for catch birds. He not a mutant, after all."

I felt myself smiling. I was liking little Floki more and more, with time. I think Lehua and Walter were, too.

"And then it happen. Exso see the puppies. Only, good thing, he see them one day when Walter and his cousin, Puna, was in the yard. You know Puna?"

"Yeah," I answered her, "I met him at the hospital." Puna was Walter's cousin, the one who had helped me deflect Matt Ortiz's attentions. Big guy.

"I know him, too," Kelly added.

"Well, you know we got that *monster* burglar alarm," Lehua jerked her thumb at Walter, who beamed with pride. "Exso not going get in this house without setting that buggah off. And they was no way he going try take the puppies from our yard when Walter or Puna was around. Anders knew trouble coming - he say every day Exso just getting more crazy about the puppies. But Anders, he didn't guess Exso going try come grab *me*, for bring me here and open the house."

Walter slapped the table top and boomed a laugh, "He picked the wrong *wahine* for that! Everybody know, better not mess with Lehua."

We all smiled and nodded in agreement with that. Unfortunately, the encounter had been lethal for Eskil but that was certainly not Lehua's fault. It did enhance her reputation somewhat, though.

"Next thing, Anders and Anna, they was watching TV. You know that Matt Ortiz guy, on Channel Six? He showing pictures of the river and all and saying somebody went drown. I guess they just freak out when the news say it the same person who try grab me. They knew it Exso. They worry maybe Exso told me something about them. Anders, he a kind man but he was real scared and, so, he came to the parking lot and sort of kidnap me."

"Sort of?" Kelly said.

"Well, yeah. He wasn't rough or nothing. But he kind of pull me in the car with him and say he need me help him. I don't know why, but I wasn't afraid or nothing." She shrugged.

It was hard to believe anybody could "sort of kidnap"

Lehua.

Walter had a glowering look on his face and Lehua saw it but she just smiled at him. Then Walter let out a breath and smiled back.

"When we was coming back here," Lehua went on, "in the car, Anders start telling me everything. He wasn't thinking clear, though. His brother dead and he worried somebody going put things together and the Mexican going come find him and Anna. He keep saying he just want take the puppies his house for hide them. But he also saying he want leave with Anna, for be safe. It wasn't making no sense.

"I ask him, 'where you going go wit' all them when you leave? How you going take them wit' you?' And I was thinking, 'What he going do with *me* after I get them puppies for him?' So, I just keep talking with him all nice and calm. We come get the puppies, and Sweetie so she can nurse them. And, then, Anders say he want me go his house, too. I didn't know what he was going do if I say no. So I went.

"It a real nice house; they got it all fix up. Him and Anna just keep saying they only want leave, be safe, but now they went make one big mistake and got me and things was just more worse. Anna, she start cry and Anders look real miserable. They scared stay, even if I don't tell nobody, because now people going come look for them. I thought they was talking about the Mexicans but now, maybe, I think the bank people might want them, too. Pretty soon, I get a idea.

"This the part you got keep secret. I say, 'Walter and me can take Floki and the puppies and you guys can go. I won't tell nobody.' Floki, you know, got Sweetie hapai, so it kind of make sense that Walter and me sort of had a claim on him. They want Floki stay with his little family and they thought Exso, he woulda like it, too. They was kind of scared of Exso but he was still the brother. Family, you know."

"So, because you're Floki's owner now," Emma asked, the

idea just dawning on her, "do you inherit the house? That's what was in the will, right? But what about the brother in Norway?"

"Lars get the Norway house. Anders say Lars won't make no fuss."

"Well, I don't think you need to keep all this a secret," I told her. "I can see that you were bargaining for your own safety. The fact that you benefitted from the bargain in other ways, too, seems okay."

"Yeah, well, there more," Walter said.

Lehua gave a little shrug again. "I sort of stayed they house for a couple days while they got reservations and stuff to leave."

She looked apologetically at Walter and said, "I sent notes. I knew you was real worried but I also knew we was going get a big boost when they left, if we got they house."

Walter looked halfway convinced. I knew he'd been frantic for days while Lehua was missing.

"When they was ready leave, they give me some medicines. I took them so I could sleep through everything while they left. You know, so I'd have a excuse for not reporting it until they was gone."

"Do you know where they went?" Kelly asked her.

"No," she answered. "They didn't tell me. And I didn't want know."

It was an incredible story, but I believed her. Still, I was pretty sure she should get herself a lawyer, and I told her so.

"Oh, me and Walter's got one already," she told me. "He said it's good the will was written in the United States. He told us we shouldn't sell this house, or nothing, but we should probably move into the big house pretty soon for 'establish our presence'. He going keep on top of it. Besides, Floki need that yard because that fence built for him."

"So, the only part you really want us to keep secret," I

236

reconfirmed, "is that you stayed over there for a couple of days when, maybe, you could have left?"

"Yeah, I guess," she answered. "And maybe I took those drugs on my own."

"Okay," I agreed. "Nobody, including you, could really have known what would have happened if you hadn't cooperated with Anders and Anna. I do think you should tell Captain Paiva what happened, but I also think you should ask your lawyer to be present when you do."

"Who's your lawyer?" Kelly asked her.

"Oh, it Walter sister husband cousin. He doing it for free."

Ah, the Big Island.

"You know, you guys," Kelly said, glancing at his watch, "it's eight thirty and I've got to get up early tomorrow to take my dad to church. I need to leave for home pretty soon."

"Oh, yeah," Lehua said, looking at Walter, "we got put them kids to bed, too, 'cause they going want get up early for church and go Auntie's for the Easter eggs and all."

BY EIGHT FORTY-FIVE, WE WERE ON OUR WAY back to town. Kelly was driving and he put the windows down to let in the cool night air. When we picked up speed on the highway, though, he put the windows up and the AC on, and we could finally hear each other talk.

"Do you think they'll really be able to keep the house?" Kelly wondered.

"You know, as screwy as it all sounds, I can't really find a hole in it," I answered him. "Anders and Anna bought the house legally. After that, they transferred ownership to Eskil. That part seems legitimate. Does it seem okay to you?" I asked Emma.

"As far as I can see, if they did all the paperwork properly and recorded it with the county, it seems okay."

"Eddie says they did. But I was wondering whether the U.S.

or Norwegian government could try to confiscate the property to recover the money Anders and Anna took from the bank. The thing is, if they bought the house before the bank thingy *and* they transferred it to Eskil before that, too, then I think it sounds safe. Don't you?"

"Yes," Emma answered. "Because, you know, if you buy a house from someone who later commits a crime, it doesn't have any impact on whether you own the house. The only difference in this case is that the house was transferred, instead of sold. But that happens all the time."

"So, if that part's solid," I mused, "then the next question would be whether the will Eskil made in prison is legitimate. He probably could have gotten access to one of those boilerplate forms that let you make up your own will. Maybe prisons even offer inmates help to write one up. Who knows?"

"They do it in the movies," Kelly noted. "Like, if you're on death row and they let you make a will."

"It seems like you could make a will in prison," Emma agreed.

"When Eskil died, Anders would have inherited Floki and, then, the last question," Kelly reminded us, "is did Anders and Anna legally gave Floki to Lehua?"

"Eddie told me," I said, "that they left a letter, and they both signed and dated it, giving Floki to Lehua. Maybe that's where the Norwegian government could challenge things. Like, if Floki is the key to the house, then they could try to claim him for reparations. That would be a pretty low thing to do, but governments have done worse. And, of course, the money they bought the house with came from a questionable source but I doubt the Mexican car gang's going to try to step forward."

"No, but Lehua definitely needs a lawyer," Kelly said. "I hope he's good."

"Oh, don't you know who it is?" Emma asked him. "I'm

pretty sure that Walter's sister, Ruth, is Ruth *Kahele*. I think her husband's cousin is...."

"Oh," Kelly and I both said in unison.

Oh, *that* Kahele. Daniel Kahele is a former state senator and major political player in the islands, who has returned to Hilo to practice law.

"Oh, she's in good shape, then," Kelly commented.

"Yeah," I said, "and it sounds like the brother in Norway, Lars, isn't going to try to stick his nose into any of this. He's going to get the house there and he's already on thin ice having given his passport to Eskil. Of course, he says Eskil stole it, but...."

"Yes," Emma added, "and he brought Floki to the U.S. just to give him to Anders and Anna so I don't see how he could lay claim to him now."

"I sure hope it works out for Walter and Lehua," I said. "It would be nice to see them get a break."

Just as we passed downtown Hilo, and crossed the singing bridge over the Wailuku River, we drove into a tropical downpour. Kelly had the windshield wipers on full blast for the last few miles of our trip.

As we eased down Emma's driveway, and passed HoneyGirl parked there, Kelly said, "I'm just going to let you off here, by your car, so you don't get soaked."

I got out my keys to ready myself for the dash to my car. There was no way I could make it even those few feet without getting drenched, but it was a nice gesture on Kelly's part.

"Keep us posted," Emma said to me.

"Yeah, I will. See you guys later."

I quickly hopped out of the car and bolted for HoneyGirl.

18 THE CONSULATE

IT WAS SUNNY WITH HIGH CLOUDS when I woke up around seven-thirty. I shuffled to the kitchen and had a cup of tea and a cinnamon bun for breakfast. I was working on a puzzle in the newspaper when the phone rang.

"Is this Miriam Charles?"

"Yes."

"This is Detective Kealoha."

I paused, waiting for my memory to retrieve information but, blessedly, Detective Kealoha filled in the blanks for me, "We were working on those fetal remains?"

"Oh, right. Bobby. Sorry, I sort of spaced out for a minute. Of course. How are you?"

"Fine. Are you busy right now?"

I hesitated before answering such an open-ended question. "I've got a little while to talk."

"Okay, this won't take long," he reassured me. "I just wanted to let you know, since I heard you say before that sometimes we don't let you know what happens with cases, that the stepdad of that girl, he's been arrested and they're bringing him back next week."

"Oh, wow! Thank you so much for telling me. You're right, sometimes I never know what happens and I really appreciate you calling like this."

"Well, I heard you say that once," he repeated. "They caught up with him in California and he waived extradition. I guess he thought he'd stand a better chance in jail over here."

"Well, thanks," I said again.

"That was it. I just wanted to follow through. Are you going somewhere for Easter?"

"Later on, yeah."

"Well, have a good day. And happy Easter."

"Yeah, you too, and thanks for calling."

Nice guy to call. Also, smart guy to call because now I was going to remember him and, in the interconnected system of island relationships, keeping good will like that is always wise.

I thought about the girl from that case again. I wondered where she was. Foster care, I guessed. And her brothers, where were they? They were probably split up, as a family, for years if not forever. I couldn't imagine that any amount of prison time for the stepfather was ever going to be punishment enough for the chaos he'd introduced into those kid's lives.

I MET BECKY AND SAM for a matinee at the mall theater. After the show was over, we sat until the end of the credits had run, while we reprised our favorite lines from the movie. As usual, we were the last ones to leave the theater. Outside, we picked our way through puddles in the parking lot, to cross to the storefront Chinese restaurant we all liked.

Sam was pretty quiet through dinner and Becky and I carried most of the conversation but, as we were walking out of the restaurant into the warm night air, he said, "They came for that guy's body yesterday."

"Huh? What guy?" I asked.

"The Norwegian guy. Bentson. They came for his body yesterday."

"Who came? His family?"

Becky was getting annoyed, "Sam, why don't you just tell her the whole thing? Why are you making her ask you questions?"

"What do you mean?" Sam said to Becky, with all innocence.

Becky's frustration broke, "Oh, for heaven's sake, just tell her what happened!"

"That's what I was trying to do," he defended himself.

Becky rolled her eyes at me.

"Okay, so, Sam, who came for the body?" I repeated.

"The Norwegian Consulate came. I guess they're shipping him back to Norway to bury him."

"Like *that*?" I asked. "Aren't they going to embalm him first? Or cremate him? Can they ship him like *that*?" I was thinking about the condition of the body after it had spent a few days in the Wailuku River.

"The consulate had the body sent to a mortuary to be prepared for the flight. I don't know what all they have to do but there are all kinds of regulations about flying bodies out of the country, as you can imagine."

"Sam!" Becky said. "Tell her the whole thing."

I looked at Sam with anticipation.

"Well," he continued, "she came into my office to introduce herself and we were just making small talk and that's when she told me she actually knew the guy. She went to school with him."

"Whoa."

"Yeah, she said she'd always been afraid of him, even at school. She didn't even want to see the body. Well, I can't blame her for that, anyway. But she did say something that made my blood run cold. She said, 'I'm glad Mrs. Ka'awa is safe now.' That made me start thinking about how much danger Lehua had been in when he came after her."

"Thank goodness she knew how to defend herself," I said with a smile.

"Yep, you never want to cross Lehua," he agreed. "She may be small but that just gives her easier access to your balls!" He

242

broke out laughing.

"Sam!" Becky admonished him, but she was laughing, too.

Becky and Sam walked me to my car and we said our goodnights. I reminded Sam that the next day I was going to come into the office to drop off my report on Pohoiki Doe. Then I drove home under a bright moon.

19 SHARK TEETH

"WHAT! I CAN'T BELIEVE you're back at work already!" I was dumbfounded that Lehua had buzzed me into the Medical Examiner's Office.

"The kids is back in school and Walter back at work, so I just figure, I might as well come," she said.

"What did you do with Floki?" I asked her.

"Oh, we put all them dogs over in our new yard. Anders and Anna left the keys, so we going start move over there, little bit at a time."

"Well, I hope everything works out for you."

"The only thing is what is we going do with all those puppies? Even in that big place, four of them little buggahs climbing up the walls is gonna be too much."

"What? They can climb, too?"

"Oh, yeah, they takes after they daddy. They already start climb things."

I was glad I hadn't offered to take any of them. "You know, I just remembered that Dr. Chung said he might want one or two puppies. He would give them a good home, you know. But he doesn't know they can climb. It might be worth a call to find out if he's still interested."

"He coming in here today," she told me. "He got to work on the guy from the car crash on Saddle Road."

I'd read about the crash in the morning newspaper. The Saddle Road is my favorite road but it was never meant for

244

regular traffic. It bisects the island by crossing through the high, dry, lava fields in the "saddle" between Mauna Loa and Mauna Kea. It's really just an old jeep track left over from World War II. Over the last few years it's been resurfaced and straightened in a lot of places but it's still a dangerous road to drive, particularly at night, or in bad weather, or drunk. The guy who died reportedly was playing the odds against all three of those challenges.

"Oh, well, if Dr. Chung's coming in today, maybe you can talk to him about the puppies then. I'm just here to turn in my report on Pohoiki Doe. Is Dr. Morris in his office?"

"I think I hear him in there," she said. She walked backwards across the hall a few steps and looked into Sam's office. "Yep, he there," she reported.

"Who are you talking to?" I could hear Sam's voice ask Lehua.

I stepped forward into his view and said, "Me."

"Oh, Mimi, there you are. Just in time."

"In time for what?"

"David Chung's coming in to look at that guy from Saddle Road but I want him to look at another case, too. Only I want you to look at it first."

"What is it?"

"I don't want to prejudice you. I just want you to look at it and see what you think." He stood. "Follow me. Let's go back to the locker."

"Wait a sec'," I told him. "It's too freakin' cold in there for me. I'll go get my sweatshirt from the car."

"No, that's alright. Stay here."

He called out, "Lehua!"

"Yeah?"

"Go get that thing out of the locker and bring it into Mimi's room."

"What thing?" Lehua called back.

"You know, the thing they brought in yesterday afternoon."

"Oh, *that* thing. You tell her about it yet?" Lehua appeared in the doorway.

"No," Sam lowered his voice to conversation level. "Don't say any more, I want her to see it cold."

"It is cold," she reminded him, "it's in the locker." Morgue humor.

"Oh, and Lehua, where's Ortiz? I thought you said he was waiting to see me."

"He was, but when he saw Mimi come in, he ran to the men's room. I think he left. He didn't say nothing to me."

"Huh," Sam exclaimed. "I wonder why he did that."

I tried to look innocent.

Lehua shrugged and left to go get the "thing".

"HAVE A SEAT, MIMI. It'll take Lehua a minute to get it. You got some time?"

"Sure, I guess."

"What are you doing today?"

"Nothing much. I was just going to go to the grocery store and do some small errands. Maybe go to Honoli'i and boogie board."

"Nice day for go beach," Sam said. He'd slipped into pidgin.

I smiled at Sam, and then over at the picture of him and Jay on the wall, too.

"Oh, hey, here's the report on Pohoiki Doe," I said, handing it to him. "Did you know David Chung is friends with the guy's brother?"

"No, but I'm not surprised. David went to Hilo High so he knows a lot of people in town. It's a sad outcome for the family, I know, but at least they're not left wondering. Apparently, they hadn't heard from him in six months."

"I don't think he's been dead that long," I warned him.

"Oh, I know, but they'd been worrying for all that time. It's a sad situation when society can't care for the mentally ill any more. Fucking budget cuts."

Lehua appeared in the doorway. "Ready," she told us.

Sam pushed back from his desk. "Okay, thanks Lehua. Come on, Mimi, let's go put you to the test."

I rose and followed him down the hall. Lehua followed, too. She was holding something behind her back.

"We left it just the way they brought it in," Sam said, referring to whatever it was he was going to show me. He reached through the doorway of my room and flipped on the fluorescent lights. I could see a large, green, glistening blob on the autopsy table.

"LOOKS LIKE A PILE OF SEAWEED," I said to Sam. "And it smells like a pile of seaweed."

"And it is a pile of seaweed," he told me.

"So why do you need me?" I asked as I moved nearer the blob. But then my eyes picked out the answer. "What's that?"

"That's what I want you to tell me."

I leaned forward for a closer look. "Well, okay, there's a bone tangled in there, with a tooth embedded in it. Have you gone through the rest of the seaweed yet? Is there anything else in there?"

"Nope. I was waiting for you," Sam said.

"You know what I'm going to say next, don't you?"

"I'm guessing you're going to ask if we've x-rayed it yet."

"Good guess. Have you?"

"No," he admitted. He turned to Lehua.

"I did it already."

Sam opened his mouth in an exaggerated expression of surprise. "You did it before I even asked you?"

"Well, I knew what she going say," she explained to him in a very slow, deliberate voice, as if he was a small, slightly dim-witted child. "She always want x-rays first."

Then she revealed what she'd been holding behind her back...an x-ray of the blob.

"Good to have you back, Lehua," Sam said.

He took the x-ray and affixed it to the light box over the counter. We all moved forward to have a look.

"Nothing but that bone," Lehua told us.

She'd obviously already had a chance to look at the x-ray. And she was right. Nothing was there but that bone with the tooth embedded in it.

"Right," Sam said. "What can you tell me about the bone, Mimi?"

I reached for the box of gloves on the counter.

"Is it okay to take it out of the seaweed now?" I asked him.

"Your table," he commented.

I lifted the bone free from the seaweed. It was actually pretty well entangled and I could see why it had stayed in place so well. I laid a green hospital towel next to the seaweed and placed the bone on top of it. Actually, it wasn't a whole bone; it was about six inches of the shaft of a long bone. There was no tissue adhering to it and it was bleached white. One end of the bone ended with a clean, sharp, diagonal edge. About two inches away, a tooth was clearly embedded in the shaft. The other end of the bone was crushed and sharply broken.

"Well, it's not human," I told him. That's pretty much all most medical examiners need to hear. They've generally got no reason to investigate nonhuman remains. But not Sam; he likes to know just because he likes to know.

"What else?" he asked me.

I leaned in closer to the bone. "It looks like a mammal bone. I can't tell if it was an adult or not. It appears to have been butchered; that's why that one end is so cleanly cut. A butcher's saw leaves a clean cut like that. The tooth looks like a shark's tooth to me. I'm pretty sure that's what it is, but you could probably ask somebody more knowledgeable than I am, what species it is."

I picked up the bone off the table and turned it over and then put it down again. "It doesn't look like it was a very big shark because I think the mouth width was only as big as the distance between the tooth and the crushed end of the bone. So," I looked around for the tape measure and found that Lehua was already holding it out to me, "let me just measure that distance."

I measured from the tooth to the jagged end of the bone.

"It looks like the shark's mouth width was about 10.4 centimeters, or around 4 inches. I mean, I wouldn't want to get bitten by any shark but this wasn't exactly a Great White. I wonder if somebody was feeding sharks. Where was this found?"

"A fishing boat brought it up in its nets over on the Kona side," Sam said.

"Are they doing any of that shark cage stuff over there? You know, where they put tourists with cameras in cages and then feed the sharks to bring them near? I know they're trying to put a stop to that sort of thing on a couple of other islands."

"I don't know," Sam said. "I thought they used fish for bait when they did that, anyway."

"Well, that I don't know about. It's just a thought. I guess the point is, you've got a butchered, nonhuman, mammal bone, about the size of a small goat or sheep, which appears to have been bitten by a shark whose mouth was about four inches wide. That's probably as much as I can tell you."

"Good enough for me," Sam said.

"Okay, then, that one's on the house."

"No, no, Mimi. Write it up and I'll get you paid."

"Nah, you've been giving me plenty of work lately. You can have this one for free. It would take more time to write up a report than it's worth."

"Hey," we heard from behind us, "what's that?"

We all turned to see David Chung in the doorway, craning to see over our shoulders.

I looked at Sam, "Is this the case you wanted him to see, too?"

"Yeah, I wanted to see if he could identify the tooth," Sam smiled.

"What? I want to see," David said eagerly.

"Come on over, then," Sam invited him. "Mimi's pretty much got it all wrapped up but tell us what you see here."

"Isn't that a shark tooth?" David asked us.

He looked at me with big eyes, "Is that a human bone?"

"No, you're safe to go swimming still," I told him.

"Well, what kind of bone is it?"

"I don't know, some kind of small mammal like a sheep."

"Or a dog?" he asked. "What if a dog fell overboard from a boat?"

"It was butchered. It probably came from a grocery store."

"Know anything about that tooth?" Sam asked him.

"No, but I think I know somebody who might."

"Okay, we're done here," Sam proclaimed. "Lehua, would you please escort this pile of seaweed back to the locker?"

AFTER LEHUA LEFT THE ROOM, I turned to David and said in a low voice, "Do you still want one of Lehua's puppies? There's sort of a new development with them."

"Yeah, I really do," he told me. "What kind of development?"

"I'll let her explain it to you. You're going to love this. Probably."

"Don't tell Becky," Sam warned us. "I don't want any more animals at our house. She'll want one of them, too, if she finds out."

"Okay, you guys," I pronounced firmly, "I'm done here. I've

got grocery shopping and normal-human things to do. See you both later."

They both said goodbye and I walked quickly out of the building, trying to leave before Sam came up with any more cases for me.

HoneyGirl was waiting for me in the lot and we spent the next few hours happily doing marketing and getting a car wash. After I went home and put the groceries away, I called Emma and received her usual generous invitation to come over and spend the rest of the afternoon. I accepted.

20 EARL GREY

I GATEHERED MY BEACH THINGS and drove to Emma's around three o'clock. The sun was shining brightly and, as I cruised along *Kahoa* Street, I could see small and gentle waves at Honoli'i. It seemed like another perfect body boarding day. I drove down Emma's driveway and my arrival was met by the usual tide of dogs surging forward to greet me. Inside the house, I found Emma, who looked like she'd just awakened from a little afternoon nap.

"Hi, honey," she yawned, "want some tea?"

"Sure."

She moved easily around the kitchen, putting the kettle on the stovetop and readying two mugs.

"Mick just called and said he's coming home early. They told him to get some sleep; he's been working overtime lately. And Katie and Kelley are coming over for dinner…and John's dropping by, too."

Really? What was this all about? John's never hung out at Emma's before.

Emma saw the look on my face and broke into a smile. "When he was here the other day," she explained, "he said he'd like to kayak up the river to the waterfall. So I invited him. And I told him you'd be here."

I rubbed my face with my palms and then pressed on my cheeks with my fingertips. Oy.

"John's a nice guy, don't you think?"

"I don't want to talk about it." To change the topic, I asked, "What's for dinner? I could have brought something."

"Oh, I'm going to make some rice and do a salad from the garden. John's bringing some steaks. Don't you think that's nice of him?"

So much for changing the topic. Without answering the question, I picked up the tea mugs and started out to the lanai. Fortunately, I heard the low rumble of Mick's car coming down the driveway and was able to step out of the way before a hundred and thirty-five pounds of Rottweiler, in the form of Barney, exploded through the doorway like a locomotive with a smile on its face. I stood on tiptoe and arched my body out of his way, holding the tea mugs up high, only spilling a couple of tablespoonsful onto my head. Barney stampeded through the house and out the front door to greet his human. A few seconds later, the two other dogs trotted past in Barney's wake.

Emma looked at my hair. "Do you want a towel?"

"Nah, it'll dry. Tea matches the color pretty well, don't you think?"

She assessed my hair. "My mother used to dye curtains with tea. Come on, let's sit down."

WE SETTLED OURSELVES at the picnic table and began a meandering conversation while we enjoyed the calm afternoon weather. The Honoli'i river rolled quietly by us towards the ocean, carrying flower blossoms and leaves on its broad surface. I'd heard Mick enter the house but he hadn't come outside to join us so I figured he'd gone upstairs to his rooms to take a nap. I'd meant to go boogie boarding but I felt so relaxed, sitting at the table, that the thought slipped my mind.

After a while, Mick strolled out onto the lanai to join us. His hair was wet and he'd changed his clothes into jeans and a

253

plain white t-shirt. He was barefoot, as were we, and he carried a beer bottle in his hand. Barney ambled along behind him. Mick rounded the picnic table to give me a small hug and I could smell the soap on his freshly showered skin. He sat next to Emma, straddling the picnic bench.

"What happened to your hair?" he asked me.

"Tea."

He seemed to think about that for a second or two and apparently decided not to follow up with any more questions. "I just saw Captain Paiva," he commented.

"Yeah?"

"He's going to take one of Lehua's puppies."

Emma bubbled, "Well done. I've always liked Eddie."

"That's a little bit of a surprise," I said. But really it wasn't. Every homicide cop I know has a soft spot for animals. I was only surprised, I guess, by the set of circumstances leading up to it all.

"He knows the puppies can climb things - like their dad - right?" I asked Mick.

"They can? I guess he knows. He's a detective. You'd think he'd have noticed that."

Good point.

"I think David Chung's going to take one, or maybe two, of them, too," I told him. "And I wonder whether Lehua might keep one herself. It seems like that would be a nice thing for Sweetie."

We were quiet for a moment but then I thought out loud, "Maybe we'll wind up with a whole new breed of island dogs that can climb coconut trees."

Mick drained his beer and rose to fetch another. "Kelly and Katie're here," he said over his shoulder as he walked back into the house.

"I think it's time to switch to wine," Emma commented. "It's not too early, is it? We've already had tea, after all."

Katie walked onto the lanai and joined us at the table. "Hey, how are you?" Katie asked me. "How's Lehua doing?"

"She was back at work today, already. It looks like there's a possibility that she and Walter are going to wind up getting possession of that house next door to them."

"Yeah, I saw Sam this afternoon and he told me. What's up with you? Any new cases? What's in your hair?"

"Tea. No, nothing much. Sam had me looking at a pile of seaweed this morning. There was a bone with a shark tooth embedded in it, tangled into the seaweed, but it wasn't human."

"Oh, my God, you should have seen what happened last night in the ER! Some guy got cut with a Hawaiian axe, you know the kind with the shark teeth inlaid along the edges? It really sliced into him. I couldn't believe it. You don't see things like that on the mainland."

"What are you guys talking about?" Kelly asked, as he joined us. He popped some wasabi-flavored macadamia nuts into his mouth.

"Shark's teeth," Emma answered.

"By the way," I said, "does anybody want to go with me to the Kuana Torres Kahele concert next Saturday?"

"Well, I'd like to," Kelly answered, "but my cousin, Walsh, is coming from the mainland. He wants to move over here, so he's coming to look at houses. I don't think his wife really wants to come that much. She thinks it would be boring here. She says nothing ever happens in Hilo."

We all laughed at that thought.

Emma rose from the table. "I'm going to go pick the salad." She fetched a plastic basket from next to the back door. "Come carry my basket, honey," she said to me.

I followed Emma to her garden. The tomatoes were still very small plants and not yet producing but the lettuces were lovely and green and tender looking. Emma was bent to pick the leaves and I was looking off up the river when we heard the rain coming. Emma straightened up and we both looked towards the ocean. A wall of gray was heading for us. We both turned and sprinted for the house, arriving just before the first fat drops began to land.

THE OTHERS HAD EVACUATED the wine and pupus from the picnic table and fled indoors. We joined them and stood, looking out of the big picture window in the living room. We could see that the rain wouldn't last long; there was sun shining on the other side of the shower, out on the ocean. The surfers hadn't bothered to come in. When you're wet, you're wet.

As I appreciated the view, I saw John's old, red pickup truck ease down the driveway. He parked next to HoneyGirl and I could see that he was watching the rain and waiting for it to ease up. Finally, he opened his door and grabbed a bag from the front seat. The truck's door gave a rusty groan as he shoved it shut. He walked to the house at his usual, unrushed pace.

When he entered the house, he followed island etiquette, giving Kelly a guy-style handshake and half hug, but only nodding, across the room, at Mick. As he passed Katie, he gave her a brief hug, but for Emma, his hostess, he stopped to give a longer hug and to allow her to stand on tippy toes to give him a little kiss on the cheek. He handed her a white, plastic grocery bag, which I assumed had the steaks in it, and she turned to put them in the refrigerator.

I was apparently going to be last in the chain of greetings. He turned to me and hesitated. Then he leaned in to give me a slight hug with a fairly quick, awkward release. He stopped, though, with a quizzical look on his face and pulled me back to him for a long, deep embrace. To my surprise, I felt his clean shaven face nestle against my forehead and he slowly

256

filled his lungs with air. A slight panic raced through my body and my heart fluttered. When he released me, he had a smile on his face as he looked down at me and murmured, "Earl Grey?"

HAWAIIAN WORDS

Hawaiian Words often have a glottal stop in them, like the stop your voice makes in the word uh-oh. It is signified with a symbol called an okina which looks a little like a backwards apostrophe. It is a very helpful symbol because how else would you know how to pronounce the name of the state fish, the *humuhumunukunukuapua'a*? See how that okina helps?

It's complicated, but the vowels are mostly pronounced like the a in almost, the e in net, the i in pizza, the o in no and the u in cuckoo.

The letters ā, ē, ī, ō, and ū represent stressed vowels.

'ahi The Yellow Fin and the Big Eye tuna, both the fishes

themselves and their meat.

aloha Love, mercy, hello/goodbye, compassion. It also defines

a style of dress – aloha wear.

ānuenue Rainbow

hala The *Pandanus* tree, also called a screw pine, is

indigenous to the South Pacific. It lives along the shoreline

and its leaves are used for weaving mats, hats, etc. Its fruit is

edible.

hale House

haole Today, this refers to Caucasians; in the past it meant a

person with no breath, or soul.

hapa Part; a person of mixed race

hāpai To carry, pregnant

Hawaii The fiftieth state (hence "Hawaii Five-0") of the United States of America, since 1959. It is a chain of eight islands. The origin of the name is unclear. It is spelled Hawai'i in the Hawaiian language but, as a state's name, it is spelled without the okina: Hawaii. Hawaii is also the name of the eastern-most, and largest, island in the state. To avoid confusion, the island of Hawaii is commonly called The Big Island.

Hawi A small town on the northern tip of the island of Hawaii. The w is pronounced like a v.

Hilo A legendary Hawaiian navigator; something that is twisted or braided (such as the rope that Kamehameha used to tie his canoe); the new moon. Hilo is the county seat and the largest city on the island of Hawaii. It is located on the northeast coast of the island.

Hina A Hawaiian goddess, the mother or wife of the god, Maui.

Honoli'i A beach park located just north of Hilo, at the mouth of the Honoli'i River, on the island of Hawaii. It is a popular surfing spot.

Honolulu Sheltered harbor. It is the largest city and the state capital of Hawaii. It is located on the island of Oahu.

Honomu A former sugar plantation camp town. It is about ten miles north of Hilo and is the gateway village to Akaka Falls.

humuhumunukunukuapua'a The *humuhumu* is a trigger fish. A variety of the humuhumu has a snout (*nuku*) like a pig (*pua'a*).

Kahele A Hawaiian family surname. The Hawaiian meaning, according to Kuana Torres Kahele, is to take a *lei* with you when you travel.

kahoa Probably ka hoa. Ka means the, and hoa means friend or partner. Also a family name.

kai Ocean water

kalo Taro (*Colocasia esculenta*), a starchy tuber from which *poi* is made.

Kamehameha, the Great A king of Hawaii who conquered and unified most of the Hawaiian islands, creating the Kingdom of Hawaii in 1810. The first of a dynasty of Hawaiian kings and queens.

kāne Man/men

Kapa'a Solid. A beach park on the western side of the northern tip of the island of Hawaii.

Kapoho A small neighborhood on the eastern tip of the Island of Hawaii, located adjacent to the Kapoho Tide Pools, an area renowned for snorkeling.

Kaua'i One of the Hawaiian Islands, it is the oldest of the main islands and the farthest north.

kea White, clear

Kea'au A small village, south of Hilo, on the Island of Hawaii.

Keawe/keawe Great grandfather of Kamehameha, the Great. It also refers to a string or strand of flowers in a *lei* and may represent the string of ancestors in one's family.

Keoni The name John, respelled in Hawaiian.

Kona The leeward side of Hawaiian islands. The name often refers to two districts (North and South Kona) on the western/leeward side of the island of Hawaii. The town of Kailua-Kona, often called Kona, is the second largest town on the island of Hawaii.

Kuali'i A lineage of Hawaiian leaders, including the King, or Chief, (in the 1700s) of Oahu and *Kauai* islands; a family name.

kukui The Hawaii state tree, also called the candlenut tree because the oil from its nut was burned for light; kukui also means light or guide.

Lake Waiau At over 13,000 feet, one of the highest lakes in the United States. It is a small lake, inside a cinder cone, near the summit of Mauna Kea. The name means swirling water. The lake is associated with multiple Hawaiian deities.

lanai Patio or porch

lauhala Lau means leaf. It is the leaf of the *hala* tree.

lehua The flower of the *ohi'a* tree. It is the official flower of the island of Hawaii (even though the island is also called the Orchid Island). It is usually a red or yellow blossom that resembles a round bottlebrush flower. Lehua is also a female figure in Hawaiian mythology.

lei A strand, usually of flowers, leaves or shells and typically worn on the neck or head

loa Long, to lengthen

lua Pit, toilet

luku Massacre, destroy (also, possibly, fortify)

mai tai A tropical-style, rum based drink. The name, a Polynesian (but not Hawaiian) word, is properly spelled *maita'i* and means *good!*

makai Towards the sea

Māui A Hawaiian god. Also, an island to the northwest of the island of Hawaii.

mauka Inland, towards the mountains

mauna Mountain

Mauna Kea A volcano on the northern half of the island of Hawaii. Its peak is 13,796 feet above sea level. It was last active approximately 4,500 years ago. In English, Mauna Kea means white mountain but that name is derived from the Hawaiian name for the mountain, *Mauna a Wakea* which has another meaning: Mountain of Wakea (Wakea being the Sky Father). It is considered the point at which the earth connects with the sky and is of deep significance to native Hawaiian culture.

Mauna Loa A volcano on the southern half of the island of Hawaii. Its peak is 13,678 feet above sea level, but its bulk and depth stretch to the ocean bottom, making it the largest volcano on earth. It was last active in 1984. In English its name means Long Mountain.

Merrie Monarch The name refers to King David Kalakaua (1836 - 1881), the last reigning king of Hawaii. The name also refers to a week-long hula competition, in his honor, held each year in Hilo, Hawaii.

mimi Urine, to urinate

momi Pearl

mo'o Lizard. In South Pacific Polynesian lore, a snake or dragon. There are no snakes in Hawaii. Nor are there dragons.

ohana Family

ohi'a An evergreen, hardwood tree from the myrtle family, five species of which are found nowhere else in the world but Hawaii. It can prosper in harsh conditions and is one of the first trees to grow on new lava. Depending on conditions, it can be a gnarled bush or a tall tree. Ohi'a is also a male figure in Hawaiian mythology.

'ōkole Buttocks

Pāhoa A small village on the easternmost part of the Island of Hawaii, in the district of Puna.

pakalōlō Crazy weed, marijuana

pau Finished, done

Pauahi (1804 - 1826) A female member of the Hawaiian Royal Family.

pau hana After work is finished

Pele A Hawaiian goddess most associated with volcanic activity. She is said to live in Halema'uma'u crater, inside the larger Kilauea volcano crater. She is also associated with earth building and fire and is considered to have a fiery, volatile, jealous temperament. She shape-shifts into a white dog or an old woman with long, white hair.

Pohoiki A park, boat ramp and surfing area, inside Isaac Hale Beach Park, on Pohoiki Bay. It is in the district of Puna, and is located just south of the easternmost tip of the Island of Hawaii.

poi Cooked, pounded *taro* (*kalo*) root – a Hawaiian dietary staple.

pua Flower

puka A hole, dent or pit (remember puka shell necklaces?)

Puna The easternmost district on the Island of Hawaii and, therefore, the easternmost district in the state, it is an area considered very sacred in native Hawaiian religious beliefs because it is the place in the islands where the sun first comes up every day. In the past, it was a center of a large population of Hawaiians. It is volcanically active currently. Hawaii Volcanoes National Park is located in the Puna District.

pūpū Shells, hors d'oeuvres

taro See *kalo*

tī Also spelled kī. A plant whose leaves and roots are used for many purposes including roof thatching, food, wrappings for food and offerings, rain protection, and hula skirts.

tūtū Grandparent (or someone of the grandparent's generation). Tūtū *wahine* is a grandmother and tūtū *kāne* is a grandfather. The word is also spelled kūkū.

wahine Woman/women

wai (Not sea) water

Waianuenue The name derives from a waterfall that creates a rainbow in its mist. From *wai* (fresh water) and *anuenue* (rainbow).

Wailuku A river on the Island of Hawaii (also a town on the island of Maui). *Wai* means fresh water, in this case it refers to the river, and *luku* means massacre or destroy.

LINKS TO PEOPLE AND PLACES

American Academy of Forensic Sciences
http://www.aafs.org/

Downtown Hilo images
https://www.google.com/search?q=downtown+hilo&tbm=isch&
tbo=u&source=univ&sa=X&ei=CFySU8y5For2oASky4KYBA&
ved=0CCsQsAQ&biw=1536&bih=749

Hawaii County Visitors Bureau
http://www.gohawaii.com/big-island

Hawaii Volcanoes National Park
http://www.nps.gov/havo/index.htm

Hilo International Airport
http://hawaii.gov/ito

Humuhumunukunukuapua`a – Waikiki Aquarium
https://www.waikikiaquarium.org/experience/animal-
guide/fishes/triggerfishes/reef-riggerfish/

Island News – to see the latest stories about Hawaii Island
http://www.bigislandvideonews.com/

Kuana Torres Kahele
https://www.youtube.com/watch?v=CJU7VEbz40I

Lake Waiau, Hawaii
http://www.instanthawaii.com/cgi-bin/hawaii?Hikes.lake

Mauna Kea
http://mkwc.ifa.hawaii.edu/current/cams/index.cgi?mode=multi

Merrie Monarch Festival
http://www.merriemonarch.com/

Norwegian Lundehund Club of America, Inc.
http://www.lundehund.com/

Palace Theatre
http://www.hilopalace.com/

Pohoiki boat ramp
http://www.hawaii247.com/2009/06/27/state-dedicates-pohoiki-boat-launch-ramp/

Rainbow Falls
http://www.gohawaii.com/big-island/regions-neighborhoods/hilo/wailuku-state-park

U. S. Geological Survey, Hawaiian Volcano Observatory
http://hvo.wr.usgs.gov/
includes Webcams with 24/7 views of volcanic activity

Video of Honoli'i Beach
http://www.youtube.com/watch?v=nBWL8qc8Vig

ABOUT THE AUTHOR

Jane Lasswell Hoff is a professional forensic anthropologist, a member of the American Academy of Forensic Sciences and a lecturer in anthropology. As a forensic anthropologist, she has worked for tribal groups, the U. S. government and in the states of Alabama, Florida, Hawaii, Mississippi, Washington and Utah. She attended the University of Hawaii for her undergraduate degree and the University of Oregon for her graduate degree. She lives and works in Hilo, Hawaii.

Made in the USA
San Bernardino, CA
08 January 2019